THE CLIENT LIST
A Cass Leary Legal Thriller

ROBIN JAMES

Copyright © 2024 by Robin James

All Rights Reserved

No part of this book may be reproduced or transmitted in any form or by any means, electronic or mechanical including photocopying, recording, or by any information storage and retrieval system, without the written permission of the author or publisher, except where permitted by law or for the use of brief quotations in a book review.

This is a work of fiction. Names, characters, businesses, places, events, and incidents are either the products of the author's imagination or used in a fictitious manner. Any resemblance to actual persons, living or dead, or actual events is purely coincidental.

Chapter 1

"He looks terrible," I whispered.

"Well, I mean ... he's dead," Eric whispered back. "So, all things considered, I'd say he looks pretty good."

I nudged his elbow as he knelt beside me. I said a quick Hail Mary and made the Sign of the Cross. There were people waiting behind us. A whole line of them. The crowd spilled into the funeral home lobby and snaked around the hallway.

A good showing. That's what everyone would call it. The caravan to the cemetery would probably take close to an hour even though my GPS said it was only a few miles away.

I knew I should get up. We'd been at the kneeler for at least a minute. Certainly long enough to pay my respects and politely move along for the next well-wisher. Something held me in place though. I tilted my head to the side and stared into the stern, now lifeless face that largely contributed to who I was today.

If I closed my eyes, I could hear his gravelly baritone calling my name.

"Leee-ary," he would say, drawing out the first syllable of my last name. I don't know if he'd ever called me by my first name as long as I knew him. I don't know if he'd called any of us by our first names in my first year torts law class all those years ago.

Twenty, I thought to myself. It had been twenty years since I saw the name on my class schedule.

Anderson Rix.

Of course, I'd known who he was back then. If you lived in Michigan and paid attention to the news, you knew. If you were a lawyer anywhere, you knew.

"Cass?" Eric whispered. "You ready?"

"Oh," I said. I turned back and gave a weak smile to the mourners waiting behind me. Eric's knee cracked as we stood up and moved off to the side.

A large arrangement of red roses adorned an easel right next to the casket. The pink ribbon around it read "Professor." The card attached had a gold block M on it. The U of M Law School faculty had probably spent at least five hundred bucks on that one. It was nice. All the flowers were nice. I recognized a few of the names of the larger law firms in Michigan on some of the cards. I found my own contribution, a tasteful vase filled with spring flowers. I hadn't known what to write. I hadn't even been sure whether I should come here at all.

"Ms. Leary?" A female voice drew my attention away from the flowers. The woman looked exactly the same as the last time I saw her. She'd been the one to hand me my Juris Doctor.

The Client List

"Doctor Wallace?" I said.

Rhoda Wallace had been an assistant dean by the time I graduated. She'd also taught family law and I'd been lucky enough to learn from her. Rhoda stood five feet in heels and wore the same professional uniform all these years later. A black wrap dress, triple strand of pearls, and her gray hair tied back in a purple silk scarf.

"Oh, it's so good to see you!" she said. Rhoda stepped forward and took my hands. She beamed at me. "Look at you!"

"Look at you!" I said. "You haven't changed one bit, Professor Wallace."

Tears sprang to her eyes. She let go of me and reached into the pocket of her dress, pulling out a matching purple hanky. She dabbed her eyes.

"I feel just awful," she said. "Anderson and I had lost touch over the years. He retired from teaching. Did you know that?"

"I didn't," I said. Rhoda and Professor Rix had shared an office together. She decorated hers with bright, cheerful paintings of the ocean and pictures of her children and grandchildren. Rix's half of the room had always seemed dark and foreboding by comparison. He preferred the low light of banker's lamps and kept a bust of Justice John Marshall that stared disapprovingly at anyone seated across from his desk.

"I worried this would happen," Rhoda said. "I warned him. Anderson needed to keep busy. He said you'll have to wheel me off that campus on a stretcher some day."

Rhoda's face fell. "Oh dear," she said. "I didn't mean ..."

"It's all right." I smiled. "It's just us. And I know what you mean." Eric came up next to me.

"Is this your husband?" Rhoda's eyes brightened as she looked up. Eric stood more than a foot taller than her. A blush rose into Rhoda's cheeks.

"My partner," I said. "Eric Wray, Rhoda Wallace. She was one of the good ones."

Eric extended a hand. "Pleasure to meet you."

"I'd say Cassiopeia was one of the good ones. Oh, Anderson would be so pleased to know you were here."

I wasn't so sure. But it didn't seem appropriate to say it. Not to her. Maybe not to anyone. What could it matter now?

"It was good to see you," Rhoda said. "I'm sure it means the world to Glenda. So many of Anderson's former students have been here today. Three State Supreme Court justices too. Oh, and Congressman Beatty."

"He deserves every honor he gets," I said. "They don't make them like Anderson Rix anymore."

"They sure don't," Rhoda said.

"I actually haven't seen Glenda yet," I said. "She wasn't up front when we walked in."

"Oh. She's been a wreck off and on. Judy took her to the back room to try to get her to eat something. You remember Judy? Anderson's old secretary?"

I found it hard to believe Judy Nusbaum was still alive. She'd been ancient two decades ago.

"I do," I said.

"Well, you just mingle. I will go and fetch Glenda for you."

"You don't have to …"

"Nonsense," Rhoda cut me off. "I know she'll want to see you."

With that, Professor Rhoda Wallace disappeared into the crowd with a purpose.

"Come on," I said to Eric. "Let's go find a quiet corner. There's a good chance Rhoda's gonna get distracted on the way to the back room. We'll probably never see her again."

"I don't think I've ever seen this many lawyers in one place," Eric said.

"I know. Creepy, right?"

"I was gonna say it's nice. The old man touched a lot of lives. Do you recognize anybody else? From your class maybe?"

"Not really. It's been so long and I didn't stick around after graduation. I started at Thorne the following week."

Eric bristled when I said it. Then he shot me a smile when he caught me noticing.

"He believed in me," I whispered. "Professor Rix was the first person who made me feel like I could really do this, you know? That I was just as good as anyone else in my class. Better, even. He was the first person who didn't look at me like I was … Delphi east lake trash. When I graduated, he said I'd made a deal with the devil. Rix was so angry with me when I took that job. He told me I was ruining my life."

To his credit, Eric didn't jump to agree with a dead man. He could have, though. As an associate with the Thorne Law Group, I'd spent the first fifteen years of my legal career defending mobsters. I'd told myself—and Professor Rix—that it didn't make me one. That everyone deserved due process and we aren't our clients. But then, one horrible night, I nearly lost my life when I tried to walk away.

"You're here now," Eric said. "I bet if he's up there somewhere, he's proud of you. A guy who lived as long as he did would know everyone's gotta forge their own path."

From where we stood, I still had a clear view of Anderson Rix's open coffin. Until we got here, I hadn't realized how much I still craved his approval. The things he'd said to me the last time I saw him still stung a little.

You'll lose your soul for a quick buck, Leary.

I told him he couldn't understand. Liam Thorne had offered me more money than I could fathom at the time. Enough to help my family. Enough to get out from under so many things. I hated Rix that day. I believed he knew it.

And yet ...

"We should go," I said. "I did what I came here to do." All of a sudden, the air felt stifling. Eric gave me a puzzled expression, but knew me well enough not to question me.

"Whatever you say, boss."

"Cass?"

The crowd parted. An impeccably dressed older woman walked through. Glenda Rix looked exactly like I remembered her, too. Bleach blonde hair sprayed so it wouldn't move. She wore a black dress with a ruffled collar. Black hose and sensible shoes. She had a kind face. Round and heavily jowled. Her blue eyes were still red from crying but her mascara hadn't run. A miracle, that. She rushed toward me and pulled me into a crushing hug that drew attention.

It took me a moment to get my arms up. I hugged her back. Glenda felt so slight and frail in my arms. For a moment, I knew I was the thing holding her up. Then, she recovered. She let me go and settled a hand against my cheek.

"Look at you," she said. "My goodness. I'd almost forgotten how pretty you are."

"Thank you," I said, resisting the urge to deflect. To tell her she needed her eyes checked. I quickly introduced her to Eric. I barely got the words out before she pulled him into a hug as well.

"Come on," Glenda said, taking my hand. "Do you have some time? I was so hoping I'd see you today. Anderson would be so happy. Oh honey, he missed you. He talked about you all the time. You were one of his best. That's what he'd always say."

"That's so sweet," I said. Whatever I expected out of coming here, it wasn't this. Glenda Rix held my hand in a vise grip. She led us through the crowd and into a back room where all the food was spread out.

"How are you?" I asked. "I was so shocked when I saw Professor Rix's obituary."

"I found him," she said. "He was sitting at his desk like always. Staring out the window at his garden. Peaceful. He had a law book open in front of him. Can you believe that? Right up until the end, he was working on something. The doctor said he probably didn't feel a thing. I believe that. Because he just looked so peaceful. Just kind of slumped backward in that brown leather chair. Same one he used in his office at the university. I had it reupholstered for him. Wanted to buy him a new one but he wouldn't hear of it. Said they'd bury him in that chair."

Glenda's expression froze. A hand flew to her mouth.

"Oh my," she said. "I'd forgotten all about that until just now. That's what he said. He ..."

Glenda hiccupped past a sob. She reached for me. I put an arm around her.

"Here," Eric said. He pulled a chair away from the table and helped Glenda Rix into it. She pulled herself together.

"I'm sorry," she said. "I've been falling apart all day."

"It's a shock," I said.

"A heart attack," she said. "Anderson's ticker finally gave out. He had a heart attack a few years ago. He promised me he would slow down after that. And he did. He just had a few clients left."

"Can I get you anything?" I asked. "A glass of water?"

Eric was already at the fridge. He opened it and spied a fifth of vodka. He shot me an arched brow. I waved him off.

"No. Oh no," Glenda said. "I'll be all right. I guess I'll have to be."

"Well, it was good to see you," I said. "You know if you need anything, you can call me. Let me write my number down."

Glenda took my wrist. "I'm sorry," she said. "I'm doing a bad job of this."

"I think you're doing just fine. There's no manual for days like this ..."

"Cass, I need you to come to the house. I have something for you."

I squatted in front of Glenda Rix's chair. She held me tight and locked eyes with me.

"For me?" I said.

Glenda nodded. "Anderson was very specific. He wanted you to be the one. He made me promise."

"The one for what?"

Eric came to my side. I stood slowly.

"Just come to the house next week. Anderson left something for you. And I'm afraid it's the kind of thing that can't wait."

Chapter 2

ONE WEEK LATER, I found myself sitting in Anderson and Glenda Rix's circular driveway on a corner lot in Burns Park. A quiet, coveted old neighborhood in the heart of Ann Arbor with century-plus estate-style homes. Many University of Michigan faculty and employees lived here. The Rix home was notable for its three-story turret.

Professor Rix had hosted dinners here and study retreats for his best students. I remembered the first time I came thinking I'd never truly felt poor until I walked in his front door into a different world.

With the first blush of spring, Glenda's cherry blossoms weren't yet in full bloom. But two months from now, they would be something to see. I always felt like they were beckoning me when I came up this walkway in late spring.

I felt a pang in my chest. Though I hadn't been here in seventeen years, I recalled with vivid clarity the way Anderson Rix would fling open his arched front door and bellow my name in greeting.

"Leary!" he would say. "Come on in before the cats do."

The Burns Park neighborhood had its share of feral cats. The bane of Professor Rix's existence as he fought with his Homeowner's Association about what to do with them.

As I stepped out of my car, I saw a blue-eyed tabby dart out from under one of the professor's meticulously shaped bushes. His garden was a frequent stop on the annual Ann Arbor Garden Walk.

I made my way up the walk, still half expecting Professor Rix to swing that front door open for me. He used the front room as his office so he could see everyone approaching from the big leaded glass bay window.

But the house seemed so quiet now. I rang the doorbell. A minute went by, then Glenda opened the door.

She looked tired. A paisley bandana covered her hair. She wore blue jeans and a U of M sweatshirt. More casual than I'd ever seen her, it made her look ten ... no ... twenty years younger than her seventy-plus years.

"I'm so glad you came," she gushed. "I wasn't sure if you would. I was afraid I might have scared you off the other day."

"Of course not," I said as she invited me in. A sense memory hit me. The house, as all houses do, had a particular smell. One I couldn't describe but knew where I was the instant I took a breath. A mixture of old hardwood, books and paper, the faint underlying scent of the pine cleaner Mrs. Rix's cleaning person used.

Professor Rix's house. A safe place. Or so it had been until that last awful day when I told him I'd made up my mind and was heading for Chicago.

"The place is a mess, I know," Glenda said. "Deanna usually comes on Wednesdays but I just couldn't stand to have anyone in the house this week. I'm tired of people, you know? Oh. Does that sound awful of me to say?"

"It doesn't," I said. "Funerals are hard. And you've earned the right to take whatever time you want to do whatever it is you need."

She smiled. "That sounds like something Anderson would have said."

Glenda looped her arm through mine and pulled me down the hall. She made a sharp right. We stopped at the threshold of Professor Rix's office.

He had a full set of Michigan Compiled Laws and Michigan Reports filling his floor-to-ceiling bookshelves. I couldn't see a speck of dust anywhere. Another wall was lined with wooden file cabinets. His giant mahogany desk was the centerpiece of the room. It was scattered with papers. Some had fallen to the floor. His brown leather chair was turned to the side, not flush.

I remembered what Rhoda Wallace had said. Rix had died here. In that chair. It looked like Glenda hadn't touched a thing.

I quickly turned to her. "Are you sure you're okay? This isn't something you have to do right now. I can come back later."

"No." She shook her head. "This is what I want. I'm glad you're here. I know Anderson would want it this way, too."

She slid her arm away from mine and went to one of the couches at the opposite end of the room. She took a seat and patted the cushion next to her. There were bankers boxes stacked to the side of the couch. I crossed the room and sank down beside her.

"I thought he was fine," she said. "He had that health scare three years ago. His first heart attack. That's what finally got him to slow down. He retired from teaching. He took his practice down to the bare minimum. No new clients. Just finishing up the existing ones. We were going to travel more. Go to all the places on our wish list. I marked them on the globe."

She pointed. Professor Rix had a large globe in a wooden frame sitting in the corner. From here, I could see small yellow stickers covering it. Australia. Parts of Europe. An island or two.

"We took one trip," she said. "We went to Belize last year. Anderson hated it. He said it was too touristy."

"I'm sorry," I said, putting a comforting hand on her shoulder.

"I really don't know what I'm going to do. This house? The gardens? Those were Anderson's projects. I've got a black thumb. It's only been two weeks and already, things don't look up to his standards out there."

"Give yourself some time," I said. "Then decide what you want to keep and what you can let fall away."

She gave me a weak smile. "Oh, he loved you, Cass. He talked about you often. I think he knew he didn't have much time. And that's one thing I'm so angry about now. I know it's silly. I know it's ... unseemly, maybe. But I just can't help myself from running all these things he said back in my mind. Looking for clues. Signs. I should have known. He should have told me!"

"Glenda, you just can't beat yourself up over it. He wouldn't want you to do that. I know you know that."

"It was just us," she said. "He had you. I mean ... he had his students. They were like children to him in a way. A legacy, at least. I don't have any of that. I never cared that I wasn't a mother. That it just wasn't in the cards. I had Anderson. I had our life. Now that he's gone ... it's so awful of me to say but I'm finding myself jealous of him. Isn't that terrible? All those people who showed up for him at the funeral. He built that. Not me. When I go, who will come? Oh, I shouldn't say that. I can't imagine what you must think."

"I think you're allowed to feel however you need to feel. There's no wrong answer."

She patted my knee. "I've missed you too. I know we weren't close. But I liked it when you would come around. When you were a student. You challenged Anderson. Made him think. Kept him on his toes. Though he never would have admitted that to you. But I think he learned as much from you as you did from him."

A pang of guilt stabbed through me. "I didn't know that," I said. "Thank you for telling me."

"It hurt him when you left."

My mouth felt dry. She must have seen something in my face.

"Oh!" she said. "I'm sorry. Oh. No. I didn't mean to blame you for anything. That's not what I meant. I just meant ..."

"He was angry with me," I said. "I understand why. He was trying to protect me. He worried I'd lose something of myself if I went to work for the people I worked for. And I did. He was right about that."

"Well, he shouldn't have been so hard on you. It wasn't his place to judge. I told him that. You weren't really his daughter. You have your own father."

"He was a good man," I said. "And Professor Rix was more proud of me than my actual father was. At least at one time. I'm going to miss him."

She grew quiet for a moment, staring at Anderson Rix's empty desk. I wondered if she'd leave things like this. He was still so present in this room.

"Cass," she said. "He wanted you here. He wanted it to be you. I have paperwork. His estate plan. It's all official. I could have just let the lawyers call you. But I wanted to see you myself. I wanted to tell you here. In this room. Where it almost feels like he's going to walk in any second, you know?"

"Tell me what? Glenda, I'm sorry. I'm at a loss here. You said Professor Rix wanted me to have something?"

"These," she said, placing her hand on the top bankers box beside her. Then she made a sweeping gesture with her hand toward the file cabinets along the wall. "His client files. He told me. He was adamant. He said it six months ago. He said a lot of things. Ever since that first heart attack. He was trying to prepare me, the bastard."

"His client files?" I said.

"Yes. He wanted you to take over what's left of his practice. He said it had to be you."

"I'm confused. Professor Rix handled asbestos litigation. That's a specialized field. That's not what I do. Surely it would make more sense to hand these over to another practice that handles those types of cases."

Glenda rose. She had a mysterious smile on her face. "Please say you'll do it. I know you're not legally required or anything. But it's what Anderson wanted. Everything is in these boxes. He made sure I knew. These boxes have all the files on his last active case."

I didn't know what to say. I felt a mixture of pride, sorrow, and gratitude. Me. After all these years, the great Anderson Rix wanted to entrust me with his client list.

"I'll give you some time," she said. "I was just going to put a pot of tea on. You can look through the boxes."

"But I ..."

She turned and walked out of the room, shutting the door behind her.

I took a moment before lifting the lid on the top box. "What were you up to, old man?" I whispered to a ghost. Then I pulled out the first manila folder. A single case name was typed on the flap. Glenda said it was Rix's last active case.

"People vs. Farrah Sibley."

"A criminal case?" I said. What the hell was Anderson Rix doing handling a criminal case?

I thumbed through the rest of the file in the box. One by one, the same name popped up.

Farrah Sibley. I slid the top box to the floor and opened the second. It was one massive discovery file. Crime scene photos. Witness statements. Cell phone logs.

Professor Anderson Rix had left me his client list. But there was only one active case on it.

Farrah Sibley. And she was charged with murder.

Chapter 3

Two days later, I found myself seated at the last stall of a non-contact booth at the Washtenaw County Jail. Every cell in me told me this was a mistake. A rabbit hole I probably didn't need to go down. But I couldn't get Glenda Rix's pleading eyes out of my mind, or the last thing she said to me as I packed up Professor Rix's bankers boxes into the back seat of my Jeep.

"He said you were the only one he trusted with his client list. He taught thousands of students over the thirty years he had with U of M, Cass. But it's you he told me to call."

A buzzer went off, indicating the door to the inmate entrance was about to open. A moment later, Farrah Sibley appeared in front of me behind the thick, bulletproof glass.

I don't know what I was expecting. I'd given Rix's files only the most cursory read-through. That, too, was unusual for me. It was just ... I knew I couldn't consider anything about this case until I saw the mysterious Farrah Sibley with my own eyes.

She was beautiful. Even in her jailhouse jumpsuit, she seemed regal somehow. Tall, fine features with luminous green eyes.

Long, straight blonde hair she tied back from her face. She wore an unreadable expression as she slowly took her seat across from me and waited until the corrections officer walked back out of view.

"Do you know who I am?" I asked.

No change in her expression. Only the slightest lift to her chin. She didn't even blink.

"My name is Cass Leary," I said.

"I'm Farrah," she said, though she had to know I already knew it.

"You've heard what's happened to Anderson Rix?"

Finally, her eyes flickered. A tremor went through her entire body. She recovered quickly, but it was the one and only time I would see Farrah Sibley visibly react to anything I said.

"He's dead," she answered. "They told me he's dead."

"Yes. A heart attack. It was sudden. I was ... I was a former student of his. Like you."

Farrah Sibley, twenty-eight years old, graduated at the top of her class from U of M Law School just three years ago. Since then, she'd been employed as an associate at the prestigious Ann Arbor law firm of Harriman Dowd. They specialized in employment litigation. Workers' comp claims mainly. And that was the extent of my knowledge from the brief internet search I'd done since leaving Glenda Rix's home.

"He helped me," she said. "I didn't know if I was going to make it that first year. I thought for sure he was going to fail me. But he ..."

The Client List

Her voice trailed off. She stared at a point on the wall above my head.

"He challenged you," I said.

"No. I mean, yes. But it was more that he believed in me."

He believed in me.

I'd said the exact same thing to Eric at the funeral home the other day. Anderson Rix had been the first person who made me understand I belonged at that school. Like he'd done for so many other students before and after me.

"He had that way about him," I said.

"You're a lawyer too?"

"I am. I'm here because ... to be honest, I haven't completely figured that part out. I just know Professor Rix wanted me to meet with you. In case something happened to him. He wanted me to look into your case."

Her eyes went blank. A defense mechanism, for sure.

"Let me be blunt," I continued. "Professor Rix left a letter. He wanted me to take over his client list. I'm a criminal defense attorney."

"He wanted you to help me?" she asked, perking up.

"Yes. But first I wanted to meet you. You understand. I'm not a public defender anymore. You can consider this an initial consultation if you want. Anything you say to me today is protected by attorney-client privilege."

"I don't need you to explain privilege to me," she said.

"I suppose I don't."

"Do you want this? How much do you know about me? About what they're saying I did?"

"Only a little. I wanted to talk to you. To meet with you first."

"So you could figure out if I'm likable."

"Partly. Yes. Do you want to keep talking?"

"Do you?"

I folded my hands on the table in front of me. "For the moment? Yes. I think I owe at least that much to Anderson Rix."

"I owe him everything." Her words came out in a rush. "No one wanted to talk to me. I went through every top defense lawyer in the state practically. But Terrence Dowd's reach and influence is long."

"Well, that explains why Rix got involved in a criminal matter. To my knowledge, he'd never tried a criminal case, much less a murder."

"He told me that. We talked about it at length. But there was no one else. You said you haven't looked through his files very deeply. But you at least know …"

"They're saying you killed Terrence Dowd. Your boss."

She nodded. "That's what they're saying, yes. That's what I've been charged with."

I didn't ask the question. I probably never would. But certainly not here. Though she knew I was thinking it. It's human nature even for defense lawyers. You try to look in their eyes. Read something about their demeanor. Listen for something in what they say or the tone of their voice. But you rarely ask the one question on everyone's mind.

The Client List

Are you guilty? Did you kill this man?

I brought one piece of Anderson Rix's file with me. The summary police report. It listed the barest facts used to form probable cause to arrest Farrah Sibley for the murder of Terrence Dowd.

"What was your relationship with Dowd?" I asked.

"He was my boss. Professor Rix helped me get the placement. A summer clerk after second year. Then they hired me right out of law school. Paid for my bar review course. I never wanted to disappoint him. That's been one of the worst things about this. And I know how strange it sounds for me to say that. I'm accused of shooting Terrence while he sat in his car. But it's Anderson Rix's approval I'm telling you about. I know how that sounds. I know how all of this sounds. How it looks."

"You were sleeping with Dowd," I said.

"Yes," she answered. Matter-of-fact. Emotionless. It was as if she were daring me to judge her for it.

"It ended badly?"

"It ended," she said. "I loved him."

I skimmed the summary report. I'd read it at least a dozen times already. I knew the bullet points. Cold, damning facts. But I came here for one reason. I wanted to hear it all from her.

"I know what that says," she said, pointing to the report.

"I'm sure you do." I flipped it over and sat back. "But tell me what happened anyway."

"I loved him," she repeated. "I know every awful thing that's printed in that report. And I know if this thing goes to trial, I can't take the stand in my own defense. Professor Rix told me that. He said lawyers make the worst clients and that if he were going to get involved, I had to promise to do everything he said, even if I didn't agree with him. Would you make me promise that, too?"

"Yes."

"It says I stalked him," she said, jabbing her index finger into the table. "It says I left threatening voicemails and texts in the weeks before the shooting. It says I was there in the building the night he was murdered. That my keycard swipe and surveillance tape proves it. There was nobody else. Just me. Everyone had already left for the day but I stayed after hours to catch up on some work. It says I owned a gun. The same kind used to shoot Terry in the chest at point blank range. And it says everyone in that office thinks they know what really happened. That they were worried about Terrence. That they were suspicious of me."

"Yes. It says all of that." It was a skillful narrative. She'd admitted to nothing. But neither had she denied anything.

"And I know how bad all of this looks. I know how easy it will be for them to paint a picture of me as some black widow. Rabbit boiling, *Fatal Attraction*. But I'm entitled to a defense. And everything they have against me is circumstantial."

"People get convicted on circumstantial evidence all the time, Farrah."

"I know that. But these people? Detective Eklund? He's incompetent. Arrogant. He made up his mind the second he saw me. He's not interested in the truth. He's only interested in closing this case by doing the least amount of work."

"What did you say to him?" I asked.

"Nothing. I never talked to anyone. They came to my house to question me. I asked for a lawyer immediately. I told them I knew my rights. They brought me in anyway. There's a tape somewhere of it in that file. You'll see. I gave them nothing. I never answered a single question. Because I knew what they were trying to do."

"It's good that you declined to answer questions."

"I'm not who Detective Eklund thinks I am. I'm not who you probably think I am, either."

"I haven't decided what I think of you yet. And I haven't decided what I think of this case."

"But you're here anyway. Because Anderson Rix believed in you."

She leaned forward and held my gaze. Of course, she'd been sizing me up as well.

"Yes. Because Anderson Rix believed in me," I said.

"And I told you. He believed in me, too."

"Do you want me to help you? That is ... if I decide I want to be involved? I don't normally practice in Washtenaw County. I'm in Woodbridge County."

"You say that like it's a negative. I don't see it that way. I don't trust anyone here. I told you, everyone knew Terry. He was part of this club. I'm not. And that's what's going to kill me as much as anything else."

"All right."

"All right, you'll take my case?"

"All right, I see your point. As for the rest of it, I'm going to need some time to think it over."

"So do I," she said.

This got an eye raise out of me. "I believe you said no one else would help you. Is there someone I can call for you if you don't want ..."

"No," she said. "There's nobody. I'm on my own. I wasn't lying about that. There's just me. I thought I had Terry. And I had Professor Rix. I hadn't seen him since before all this happened. But when I needed help, he was there for me. He was the only one. And now, he's gone too."

A buzzer went off. In a few more minutes, one of the COs would reappear to take Farrah Sibley back to her cell.

There was something about her. I couldn't put my finger on it. As smart and calculating as she seemed to be, she had a vulnerability to her as well. I believed her when she said she was all alone.

"I'll tell you what," I said. "I'll take a couple of days with this. Let me review your file in earnest. I'll set up a video conference for us with the jail before I leave. You can take the time to look into me, too. Then we'll see if we're a fit."

"That's fair," she said. "And I appreciate you giving me your time today. Since I heard about Professor Rix, I've been kind of numb. He was ... I was ..."

"I understand," I said.

The CO reappeared. Farrah rose. She patiently waited while she was placed back in handcuffs. She cast a stoic glance over her shoulder at me.

I sat there for a moment, watching her walk away. She didn't look defeated or scared. And she didn't look like she belonged here.

None of it meant she was innocent. I had to decide whether that mattered to me.

Anderson Rix believed in her. It was the one truth I could take with me. And I had to decide if it was enough.

Chapter 4

"Did she do it?"

Jeanie Mills never wasted time or words. She had the big office on the first floor with a large sitting area in front of a decorative fireplace. The building was a converted farmhouse. A prime location just a half a mile from downtown Delphi and the courthouse. Five years ago, I'd convinced Jeanie to come out of retirement and partner with me. Today, she sat in a wing-backed chair wearing a blue tracksuit. She'd just come from physical therapy, six months out from a hip replacement.

"Probably," I answered. "But I don't know."

Anderson Rix's file boxes sat on the table between us. Eric walked in carrying two mugs of coffee. He handed one to Jeanie and the other to me then took a seat beside me on the couch.

It was new having him here. After nearly twenty years working as a detective with Delphi P.D., I'd convinced him to retire and work private investigations for me. He had an office down the hall and was just settling in.

Rounding out my team was Tori Stockton. I'd hired her right out of law school and she developed a knack for handling probate and estate matters. She was also one of the best researchers I'd ever met. Six months from now, she would also become my sister-in-law when my younger brother Matty finally put a ring on her finger.

"Eric, do you know anything about the lead detective on this case?" I reached for the summary police report I had sitting next to one of Rix's boxes.

"Lars Eklund," I read off.

"Big Swede," Eric answered. "First generation, I think. I worked a task force with him on human trafficking maybe fifteen years ago. He was with Detroit P.D. then. He didn't say a whole lot. Delivered solid work but wasn't real personable. He left the task force before I did. Then went to violent crimes for the Ann Arbor Police. So he's been doing it for close to a decade."

"Any idea how many homicides he's worked?" I asked.

"I can ask around." Eric frowned. I knew this was uncomfortable territory for him. There was a certain type of cop out there who felt Eric had gone to work for the "other side" when he set up shop here.

"These voicemails are bad, Cass," Tori said. She had her laptop pulled up. I'd put her in charge of listening to the various audio files included with Rix's discovery materials.

Tori hit play. Farrah Sibley's voice filled the room.

"Terry, I know you're screening me. I don't appreciate it. I need you to pick up the phone and deal with me. You're acting like a little baby. I've put up with about as much as I'm going to. You

The Client List

don't get to screw me over like this. Terry? Terry! I'm done playing around. You got that? You will deal with me. I can make things difficult but I don't want to do that."

Tori clicked off the recording. This wasn't the calm, even-toned Farrah Sibley I'd met yesterday. She was out of breath, almost wheezing with rage on that recording. And I knew that was one of the more mild ones.

"The texts are pretty damaging too," Eric said. He pulled another sheet out of Rix's file box. "This one's the week before the murder. She texted him, saying pretty much the same thing as the voicemail. He's clearly not answering her calls or texts this last week. It's just a sea of gray text bubbles on his phone. One after the other after the other. Don't ignore me. I'll make you sorry you ever met me. Then she switches to sexting. Then more threats. She's unhinged."

"We're only seeing one side of it," I said. "I don't know what kind of mind games Terrence Dowd was playing."

"Did you ever cross paths with him?" Eric asked Jeanie.

"Not really," Jeanie answered. "I mean, I knew of Harriman Dowd. They'd be one of the go-to workers' comp law firms in Michigan. That's what I can't figure. Terrence Dowd would have known better than to get involved with a subordinate like Farrah Sibley."

"The heart wants what the heart wants," Tori quipped.

"Not sure Terry Dowd was thinking with his heart," Eric said.

"There's no murder weapon," I said. "No eyewitnesses. No physical evidence tying Farrah to the crime scene."

I pulled out another file from the box. This one had the crime scene photographs. I laid them out side by side.

Terrence Dowd died half in and half out of his Tesla. His legs splayed out on the parking garage floor. His right arm curled around his leather seat. The bullet opened a large hole in his chest. Blood pooled beneath him and ran down to the drain in the cement just a few feet away.

I flipped to a close-up photograph of Dowd's face. White. Waxen. Frozen in shock. He stared skyward, perhaps into the eyes of his killer as he lay dying. Had he or she stayed there and watched him bleed out? Or had his killer shot him once and ran?

"His cell phone's on the charging dock in the center console," Eric said. "Just out of reach."

"It makes you think he knew who approached him," Tori said. "Like maybe they were talking, then bam! You know? Like he never thought to reach for his phone when they approached. He wasn't scared."

"That's all conjecture," I said, already thinking like a trial lawyer. "A jury would never hear it."

"They don't have to hear it," Eric said. "Tori's right. You can see it in these photographs. They tell a story."

"They tell a nightmare," I said. "Still ... this is a winnable case. On the face of it, anyway."

"She had a clear motive," Eric said. "You may not have an eyewitness to the crime, but you've got witnesses to what was going on between these two leading up to it. They were seen together in the office by the secretary. She heard them arguing. She saw Farrah Sibley hit Dowd."

"Hitting isn't killing," I said.

"Do you want this one?" Jeanie asked.

I picked up one of the crime scene photos and stared into the face of Terrence Dowd. He'd been handsome. Tori pulled up the Harriman Dowd law firm website. A different image of Terry Dowd filled the screen. A thick head of dark-brown hair, bright brown eyes, strong jaw, a set of good veneers as he smiled at the screen.

"I want to know why Anderson Rix was willing to go to trial on it," I said. "Glenda said Rix believed in Farrah. Farrah said the same thing. That Rix was the only person who believed in her, both when she first met him, and over this."

"You found her relatable?" Jeanie asked.

"Relatable?"

"You have a few things in common with her, Cass," Jeanie continued. "I don't mean to psych 101 you, but from what you're saying. From what Glenda told you ... Farrah Sibley was one of Rix's favorite students. Like you were. She came from meager beginnings. Like you. She found herself at one of the most prestigious law schools in the country and Anderson Rix took an interest in her education. Like he did for you."

"He saw something in her," I said.

"Like he saw something in you," Jeanie said. "But none of that's a reason to get involved in this mess if you don't want to. You don't owe Rix anything. You certainly don't owe Farrah Sibley anything."

"But why me?" I said. "I hadn't seen or spoken to Professor Rix since ... since I took the job at Thorne. We didn't end on good terms. But all these years later, he tells his wife ... he tells his estate planner ... that he wants me to take over his client list. Glenda said he was adamant about it. Like he worried this case was going to be the death of him. And he specifically put my name in Glenda's mouth. Why? After all these years?"

"Because you're you," Tori said. "I mean, come on. I don't know much about whatever falling-out you had, but you've handled some high-profile murder cases since you came back to Delphi. We're only one county over. You think he wasn't paying attention?"

"I wasn't," I said, almost whispering it. And that was the truth. I hadn't thought about Anderson Rix in years. To be honest, I hadn't even been sure if he was still alive until the news came to me that he had actually died.

"It's different with teachers," Jeanie said. "They never forget good students. And Tori's right. Rix was signed on to take a murder case. He'd never tried one before as far as we know. I'm honestly surprised he didn't reach out to you early on. He could have used your help in life. Now he's dumped this on your lap in death. How do you really feel about that?"

I put Terrence Dowd's picture down. How did I feel about that? I wasn't sure.

"This mattered to him," I said. "So I think it's worth looking into at least. Making a few phone calls."

"What do you need?" Jeanie asked. That was why I loved her. She would question me. Challenge me. Point out every mistake she thought I was making. But when I made up my mind, she'd be my ride or die.

"I want to talk to some of these witnesses. Lionel Harriman, Dowd's partner, told the police Dowd was scared of Farrah. I want to know why. I want to know whether he's just trying to cover his own rear end now. Never mind Dowd being dead. This thing is a PR nightmare for him. And the secretary who found the body and saw Dowd and Farrah together. Did she have a beef against Farrah? She was older. Maybe judgmental."

"He had ex-wives," Eric said. "I already found out that much. Three of them."

"I'd like one of us to talk to them, too. Were they on good terms? Did they know about Dowd's affair with Farrah Sibley? Between that relationship and his marital history, he might have been a serial philanderer. That means there might be another mistress or two out there as well. I can't help thinking Farrah is a convenient suspect. How hard did Detective Eklund look at others?"

"This thing's set for trial in just under three months. That's your first administrative hurdle," Jeanie said. "Rix's death is grounds for a continuance, but unless somebody asks for one, this will stay on Judge McGee's docket."

"Have you tried cases in front of her before?" I asked.

"A couple of divorces that took on lives of their own. But it's been a while. Ten years. Claudia McGee is the most senior member of the Washtenaw County judiciary. She's fair. But she doesn't really like outsiders. We might be one county over, but to her that's a foreign country."

"Is it worth asking for a change of venue?" Tori asked. "Don't you think the bigger question is how many cases Terrence Dowd tried in front of her?"

"Maybe. I need to take a closer look at her pretrial rulings on this one."

"I'll put a memo together," Tori said.

Miranda walked in from the outer office. She held a pink note in her hand.

"Sorry to interrupt," she said. My office administrator, Miranda Sulier, had sonar for ears and probably heard everything we'd been saying. She also had a way of anticipating what I'd need before I asked for it.

"Whatcha got, Miranda?" I said.

"A call from one Jason Bailey. Assistant prosecutor for Washtenaw County. He wants to talk to you about the Sibley case."

"Already?" I said. "How in the hell did word get out that I ..."

"You were at the jail," Eric said. "The prosecutor's office was probably clued in before you even left. Plus, there were a lot of members of the Washtenaw County bar at that funeral home. Glenda talked to a ton of people."

"He wants to know if you'll meet with him first thing tomorrow morning," Miranda said. "He sounded kind of anxious. You want me to put him off?"

"No," I said. "Tell him I'll be in his office by eight. I'll at least hear what he has to say."

"Can she afford you?" Jeanie asked. "I gotta admit. I've got a bad vibe about this case. But if she's a paying client ..."

"She's a paying client," I said. "Or ... she can be ..."

"I'll tell Bailey you'll be there with bells on." Miranda smiled.

"We've got our marching orders," Jeanie said. "However far you wanna go with this."

How far indeed, I thought. For now, I'd take it one meeting at a time and it looked like I was headed back to Ann Arbor.

Chapter 5

Jason Bailey started my day by playing games. He'd asked me to meet him at 9:00 a.m. It was now forty minutes past and he had me waiting outside his office staring at a plastic plant that needed dusting.

I hated this crap. Every county had its quirks and ways to make "outsiders" feel like they were. I mostly got it from court staff. Most of the prosecutors I worked with understood my time was just as valuable as theirs. By the sheepish looks I got from the county prosecutor's support staff, I guessed this kind of delay was on brand for Bailey.

Five minutes later, I gathered my things and was about to walk out. As I made my way to the door, two men walked in. One younger with a thick head of black hair and an expensive suit. The other, taller, older, and in shirt sleeves.

"Mr. Bailey!" the receptionist shouted. "Ms. Leary's here. Your nine o'clock."

The younger man's smile faded. He looked me up and down and patted his companion on the arm.

"Ah," he said. "Thanks for coming down. Though I don't suppose Delphi is too bad of a drive."

Jason Bailey. Good-looking, yes. Crisp collar. He probably kept a half dozen freshly pressed dress shirts in a drawer. The type to demand his legal assistant ferry them to the dry cleaners when he spilled coffee or spaghetti sauce from lunch on them. He gave me a flash of white teeth and the band of his gold Rolex as he extended his hand to shake mine.

I knew guys like this. Cut my teeth on guys like this. He probably considered his stint in the county prosecutor's office part of a necessary stepping stone to higher office. A judgeship perhaps. The State House. Then maybe the federal government.

"I don't have a lot of time," I said.

Finally, Bailey checked that expensive watch of his. I knew he knew exactly what time it was. This was a show. The whole thing. Keeping me waiting. And it was the act of an insecure, entitled jerk.

"My apologies," he said. "Garth? I'll see you down the hall later."

Garth waved to the receptionist, then quietly excused himself.

"This way," Bailey said. "We'll talk in the conference room. I'm sharing office space at the moment. We're in the middle of some much-needed renovation."

I let Jason Bailey lead me down a short hallway and into a sparse conference room. It had the obligatory, outdated law books lining the shelves, an American flag and a Michigan flag in the corner.

I took a seat in the chair closest to the door while Bailey poked his head out and shouted to another staff member to bring him the notepad off his desk along with the file folder underneath it.

"Can I get you a coffee? A water?" he asked. He took his jacket off and hung it on a coat rack near the door.

"I'm fine," I answered. "And I really do have to get on the road again. I'm due in court back in Woodbridge County in an hour."

Bailey took a seat opposite me. He assumed a casual posture, draping one leg over the opposite knee. He tapped his fingers on the table top.

"Cass Leary," he said. "I have to admit, I was surprised to see your name come up in conjunction with Anderson Rix's."

"Come up where?"

"My condolences, by the way. He's a real loss to the legal community. Quite the shock. Rix was a legend. I'll admit I'm disappointed. I won't get the opportunity to step into the arena with him."

"How did my name come up?" I asked him again. "I haven't filed a formal appearance in the Sibley case."

If it was possible to look even smarmier, Bailey achieved it. He gave me a sickeningly sweet smile. The man had first year law student arrogance written all over him. He wasn't that new, of course. A quick check with the Michigan bar directory, and I knew he got his license eight years ago. So not seasoned in the way that I was, but not completely green either.

"Ann Arbor's still a small town. The Sibley case has generated a fair amount of local interest, as you can imagine. Did you know Terrence Dowd?"

"Not personally. I knew of the firm. I never met the man."

"I liked him. A lot, actually. Never had the pleasure of facing off against *him* in the arena, either. He was strictly civil. But he was well respected around the state. If I ever had occasion to sue an employer, Dowd's the man I would have wanted to represent me. He's another real loss to the legal community. This case just has tragedy coming and going."

"It seems that way."

"So you haven't filed a formal appearance. Are you planning to?"

"I wouldn't be wasting your time if I wasn't planning on getting involved."

He waved off my pointed dig at his own tardiness.

"Appearance or not, do you have an engagement letter with Farrah Sibley? Are you here as her formal representative? You understand I'm not really at liberty to discuss specifics to just anyone."

"I'm here as Farrah Sibley's representative," I said. "And may I remind you that you're the one who called me to set up this meeting? So can we cut to the chase? What is it you wanted to talk to me about?"

He dropped his leg to the ground and sat forward, folding his hands on the table.

"You've reviewed the files? You're familiar with the facts?"

"I'm getting there. Do you have some sort of plea deal you've been trying to float?"

"I think this case is pretty cut and dry. Dowd got into a relationship he shouldn't have. It got out of hand. Your client couldn't handle it. Lashed out. If ever there was a textbook case for a crime of passion, this is it."

He was baiting me, probably. Trying to see if I'd lose my cool and tell him how I saw the case. That's what this whole performance was about. Jason Bailey was trying to get under my skin and get some unguarded reaction out of me.

"I'm aware of what's in the charging document, Mr. Bailey."

"Please. Jason. If we're going to be working together, there's no reason to be so formal. You know, I looked into you."

"I'm sure," I said.

"Impressive resume. You handled some pretty high profile RICO cases back in Chicago. Perfect record on that, I might add. You had to have been making a fortune working for the Thorne Law Group. That's a dream job for most people. I would have thought Anderson Rix considered you one of his prize pupils. Probably even took credit for your success."

I didn't answer. Didn't give the satisfaction of any kind of reaction. He could have just been fishing, but I doubted it.

"Well," Bailey continued. "That he handpicked you to take over his cases says a lot about you. I expect you to keep me on my toes."

"Why am I here?" I asked, letting my annoyance out.

"How well do you know Judge McGee?" he asked.

"I don't."

"I think you'll like her. She doesn't suffer fools, that's for sure. But I imagine you'll be asking for a lengthy continuance. There's a lot of discovery materials to sort through. If there's anything my office can do to facilitate that. Though we've responded fully to everything Rix asked for. You understand discovery is closed now. I'd be amenable to opening it back up for a small window for you. I'll sign a stipulation."

"That's kind of you."

"And I'm willing to stipulate to a onetime continuance. Say, thirty days. Do you feel that would be long enough for you to prepare?"

"I think that would be ample, yes."

"Excellent. Excellent. I'll have my office draft a stipulation and send it over. I can pretty much guarantee McGee won't have a problem with that. She took the news of Rix's passing pretty hard. Not to say that they were closely acquainted. But like I said. Losing him was a blow to the legal community as a whole. She's cognizant of that."

"I appreciate that."

"If you talk to the widow ... maybe you could convey that. My sympathies."

"Glenda," I said. "Her name is Glenda."

"Of course."

The smile faded from Bailey's face. He grew oddly quiet for a moment. The silence became uncomfortably odd. Then all of a sudden, he broke it, shrugging off something. He found that empty smile again.

The Client List

"Second degree," he said. "That's the plea I'm offering. She's facing life. I can wiggle on the sentencing. Though McGee has the final say. She works with this office all the time on sentencing. If I recommended say, twenty-five years with the possibility of parole after twenty, could you make that float?"

"Did you offer that deal to Rix?" I asked. To be honest, it wasn't much of one.

"It'll give your client the opportunity to go before a parole board. You know I can't guarantee the outcome of those things. But it means someday, she might actually get out. Otherwise, she's gonna die behind bars."

"She understands the charges and the sentencing guidelines. Ms. Sibley is a lawyer herself, you know."

"Sure. Sure. That's not something that's gonna weigh in her favor in front of the jury though. I'm sure you've probably discussed that with her. Rix would have."

"I'm not at liberty to disclose my discussions with Ms. Sibley, or Mr. Rix's."

"Sure. Sure. I didn't mean that you would. I'm just saying, this is the best deal she's gonna get."

"I'll bring it to her as I'm obligated to."

"She won't take it." He smiled. "I mean, you've met with the woman, haven't you?"

I knew he knew I had. Eric was probably spot on when he said the COs at the jail would have talked.

"Is there anything else?"

He got quiet again. His smile slipped and Jason Bailey narrowed his eyes, looking almost sinister.

"The thing is. Farrah Sibley shot that man. I think you know it. I know Anderson Rix knew it."

"Okay," I said. "We're done here. I appreciate your time. Though I'm not clear why all of this couldn't have been a phone call."

"Sure. Sure," he said. I recognized it now as almost a catch phrase for this guy. I found it weird. Off-putting. As I gathered my things, he didn't even stand up to show me out. Instead, he sat back in his chair and put a foot up on the desk. As I turned to leave, one of his assistants walked in carrying the notepad and the file he'd originally asked for. Whatever was on it, he seemed to no longer need it.

"Give my regards to Ms. Sibley," he said as I left Jason Bailey there, smirking at my back.

I knew I couldn't let emotions form my decisions in this case or any. But as I walked out of that building, I realized how badly I wanted to kick Jason Bailey's ass.

Chapter 6

IT HAD ONLY BEEN two weeks since my first meeting with Farrah Sibley, but this time, a different woman sat down in front of me. Her eyes had a haunted look, with dark circles underneath. Her skin had lost its luster. Her hair hung in stringy waves. She kept a hand in front of her mouth but within a few seconds, she dropped it, revealing a fat lip split down the center.

"What happened?" I asked.

"It was a misunderstanding. It's nothing. I walked into a door."

Her hands shook as she tried to lay them flat on the table.

"Farrah ... what happened? This is the kind of thing you have to tell me. Was this another inmate?"

"It's nothing," she insisted. "I don't want to talk about it."

She was scared. I couldn't blame her. But if she wouldn't tell me what was going on, I couldn't help her.

"Do you have everything you need? I can arrange for some money to be transferred into your account."

"No. I'm okay. I don't want any special treatment."

"I'm not talking about special treatment. I'm talking about your basic needs."

"I'm doing my best," she said, finally meeting my eyes. "But there's a target on my back already."

"There shouldn't be. You're a lawyer. I would think that would make you popular."

"Oh, it's made me plenty popular. If I ever get out of here, I'll have a built-in client base. But being popular has a particular downside. I'd much rather just fly under the radar."

"I understand. And I'm sorry. I can't imagine how difficult this is for you."

"You're here," she said, finding a weak smile. "That means my case hasn't scared you off yet."

"I have more questions. A lot more questions. But I've been thinking about what you said. It bothers me that there's no physical evidence tying you to the crime scene. That doesn't mean a jury won't convict you."

"Again I say. You're still here."

"I met with Jason Bailey."

This earned me an eyebrow raise. Farrah sat back in her chair. "How'd you like him?"

"Not particularly. If he behaves in court the way he did with me, the jury's gonna hate him. That doesn't necessarily translate to them liking you."

The Client List

"Bailey's a prick. Rix couldn't stand him. He was looking forward to wiping the floor with him in court. It's one of the things that convinced him to take my case."

I smiled. I liked that my assessment mirrored Professor Rix's. Then I felt a small pang. A longing. I would have liked to have compared notes with him.

"But he usually plays well in front of juries," she said. "Everything Bailey does is an act. He can come off almost stupid. He's not though. He was playing you. Trying to make you underestimate him."

"Did you ever cross paths with him before all of this?"

Farrah nodded. "We were acquainted. I didn't have the occasion to work with him. I spent most of my time assisting Terry. He rarely went to court. Most of his cases settled. Hell, Terry hadn't stepped inside a courtroom in probably two years before ... before he died. He was amazing to watch when he did. And he was a tough negotiator. A brilliant closer. Anyway, Bailey's a prosecutor. But we're both members of the Young Lawyers Association in Washtenaw County. Bailey chaired it for a while. So yes. We crossed paths. Luncheons here and there. Fundraisers. Ann Arbor's not that big."

"He's certain of your guilt," I said, not sure why I mentioned it.

"I'm sure he is. I'm sure Jason Bailey can't wait to be the guy to make sure I never see the light of day again."

There was something about the way she said it. Her biting tone.

"He hit on you?" I asked. "At one of those luncheons maybe?"

I got a mysterious smile from her. "He wishes. Jason Bailey thinks he's God's gift to women. God's gift to the legal system.

He absolutely loathed guys like Terry."

"Why is that?"

"You can look up Jason Bailey's salary information. Terry made more in a month than Bailey makes all year."

"I didn't get the impression Bailey's in the prosecutor's office for the money. He struck me as someone with higher political ambitions."

"You're spot on. Jason Bailey wants to run for Bernadette Gladstone's seat in the next election."

I whistled. I wasn't as familiar with Ann Arbor politics. But Bernie Gladstone was a fixture on the Hill. The longest-serving female congresswoman, she was an institution.

"Gladstone's unbeatable. If Jason Bailey has half a brain, he already knows that."

"I have it on good authority that Gladstone's not going to run again."

"People have been saying that for at least ten years. I'll believe it when it happens."

"Well, convicting me will be one nice feather in Jason Bailey's cap. Terry was as much of an icon around here as Bernadette Gladstone. Taking me down will fatten Bailey's political resume."

"Makes sense. But none of that helps me build a defense for you. It has nothing to do with your case. It's not worth worrying about."

"You came here to ask me something. So ask me."

Again, Farrah's demeanor changed. She sat straighter in her seat. The shadows under her eyes seemed to fade right in front of me. This chameleon quality could be an asset or a detriment, depending on how well she could control it. As I sat there, it came over me. I'd bet my career that Farrah Sibley could control it very well indeed.

"You know what he's going to make you out to be," I said.

"Crazy. Yes. He's going to make it seem like I was stalking Terry. And Lydia Whitford is going to help him. She'll be his star witness."

I checked my notes. Lydia Whitford was Terrence Dowd's administrative assistant. The woman who'd found his body. Who told the police she overheard both Farrah and Dowd being intimate, and also threats Farrah made to him.

"I can deal with Lydia," I said.

"She's biased against me. She called me a slut to my face when she found out Terry and I were together. She was tight with Terry's most recent ex-wife, Shondra. I wouldn't put it past her to have been spying on Terry for Shondra."

"I thought their divorce was amicable."

"It was. But if Shondra could figure out a way to get more spousal support, she'd do it. I'm just saying ... Lydia stayed friends with her."

I wrote a few notes. "It's not much," I said. "But it could be an angle to exploit."

"She doesn't like me. That's true enough."

"I haven't seen anything about her in Rix's notes. Do you know if he tried talking to her?"

"I don't know. We talked about her. I told him from the beginning if Lydia could figure out a way to screw with me, she'd do it. She'll be sneaky about it. Nothing overt. But she hates my guts. She did even before all of this."

"Do you have anything concrete? A text? An email?"

"You mean other than her calling me a slut? That was just us though. I don't think anyone else heard her so that'll be my word against hers. But she's your basic professional boomer woman. Ready to punch down on the younger generation."

I held my pen poised over my notepad. Farrah's generalization wasn't one I'd experienced myself. Jeanie and Miranda were my most valuable colleagues and friends. But my life experience wasn't Farrah's.

"You're good on cross," Farrah said. "I don't think it's going to be much of a trick to peel back Lydia's bitchy side. You'll see."

"I appreciate the tip. But I'm going to need something concrete. There are a lot of unanswered questions, Farrah."

"Of yours or a potential jury's?"

"Both."

She spread her hands out, palms up. "Fire away. I'm an open book."

I very much doubted that. I had every instinct that Farrah Sibley had secrets that could bury her. I just had to make sure the first shovelful didn't hit me instead.

"The gun," I said bluntly. "You purchased a Glock 19 five years ago. The same type used to kill Terry."

"So do thousands of other people. I know you'll make that point."

"I think you need to let me worry about strategy if we're going to go forward with this. I'm asking you now. No bullshit. Where's your gun, Farrah? The cops never found it. You never gave a satisfactory answer as to what you did with it."

"I gave no answers. So there's nothing they can say I contradicted."

Every time I wanted to believe her, she said something like that. Something snapped inside of me.

"And that's the kind of comment that makes you seem guilty."

Her face changed again. Falling into that vulnerable, wide-eyed stare.

"I'm sorry. It's hard to shut off my lawyer brain."

"I don't need your lawyer brain."

She smiled. "Anderson said the same thing. Repeatedly."

"You still haven't answered my question. I need to know where your gun is, Farrah."

"I don't have it."

"Again, not an answer."

"I left it at home, okay? When I moved to Ann Arbor, there were a lot of things I didn't bring with me. I put things in storage. Including the gun. When I first moved out here, I had a roommate. A classmate. When we graduated from law school, she took a job in Manhattan. I kept the apartment. But a lot of my stuff is in my dad's garage in Mount Pleasant. Including that stupid gun."

"When was the last time you fired it?"

"I haven't even seen it in like two years. I have bins stacked in my dad's pole barn. It's in one of them. In a metal footlocker with some other things I want kept safe. My mother's wedding dress is in there. It's the only thing I have of hers."

"Is it locked? Does your father have the key?"

"There's no key. It's a combination lock. But look, my dad doesn't know any of this. If he finds my mother's dress, he'll burn it. He doesn't have the combo to that locker. He doesn't even know that's where I put the gun. I never told him."

"What's the address?"

She wrote it down along with the combination to her footlocker. "He lives off E. Jordan Road in Mount Pleasant. Not far from the fairgrounds."

"Your father's name?"

"Victor. Victor Sibley. But he's not going to be any help. We're not exactly on the best terms. My dad's not the biggest fan of some of my life choices. I'd appreciate it if you didn't involve him."

"Has he been to see you?"

"Not once. He sent me a letter a few weeks ago. Not long after, I was arrested. He's super religious. He thinks what's happening to me is God's way of punishing me."

"A jury will notice that. They're going to want to know why you don't have family by your side if this goes to trial. What about your mom?"

"Gone. Long gone."

"I'm sorry for your loss."

"Oh, she's not dead. Actually, I have no idea if she's dead or not. She ran out on us when I was a kid. I haven't seen or heard from her in like fifteen years."

"Okay. Well, I'm going to need to talk to your father. Regardless of your differences, he could help."

"You can try. He might like you. Dress conservatively when you meet him."

"Do you know if Professor Rix tried reaching out?"

"I told him not to. Told him it was a lost cause. Which I still believe. But if you think it's worth pursuing, I'll do what you say."

"Thanks for that. And yes. It's worth pursuing. If I'm thinking it, you can be sure Jason Bailey's thinking it. For all we know, he's already paid your father a visit."

A noticeable shudder went through Farrah. She looked terrified. It only made me want to talk to her father that much more.

"Is there anyone else?" I asked. "Siblings? Close friends? Character witnesses?"

"You can't call character witnesses. Judge McGee won't allow it. It won't be admissible."

"There's your lawyer brain again. Listen, I'm playing catch-up here. Bailey's willing to stipulate to a continuance. We can push the trial date back a little while so I have more time to prepare. I know you're antsy to get this under way, but I'm not going to be rushed. I need to know everything about you, Farrah. Your life. Your likes. Your dislikes. Your enemies. Your friends. Jason

Bailey probably knows more about you than I do at the moment."

"You can ask me anything you want. I won't lie to you. I promise. I know how important this is."

"It's not enough. I need to know what the people in your life are going to say about you. Believe me, Bailey will know. So I need to get there first."

"I don't have a lot of friends," she said. "My life was work. You know how it is. Think back to your first few years at the Thorne Law Group. You were ambitious. Hungry. How many friends did you have outside of work?"

It unsettled me more than a little that Farrah knew so much about my background. I knew next to nothing about hers. And she wasn't wrong.

"And that's the thing people don't understand," she said. "Terry was the only man in my life the last couple of years. We worked together every day. Side by side. Sometimes eighteen-hour days. I didn't pursue him. It just happened. I became like his right arm. He depended on me. And I depended on him. What happened between us was completely natural. And when he started to pull away, yes, I was upset. I was devastated. But I loved that man. With my whole heart and soul. That's what you need to know, Cass. I would never hurt him. He was my life."

"Okay. What about past relationships? Other boyfriends. Did you have any other bad breakups? Guys out there who can come out of the woodwork?"

She squirmed a little in her seat. It was a tell.

"Farrah, what? Tell me who I need to talk to. Because you know Bailey already has."

"There was a guy," she said. "My boyfriend just before Terry. We met when we were both at CMU. We dated a while. I thought I loved him. Or more, I thought he loved me. The breakup was a little messy, but it was nothing out of the ordinary."

"His name," I said.

"Kurt Sommerville," she answered.

"Are there any texts or voicemails with him that can come back to haunt you?"

"No. Nothing. We were passionate. He wasn't happy when I decided to move to go to law school. You asked me about other boyfriends. Kurt's the only one before Terry I was serious about. But he was a jerk. He cheated on me. I called him out on it. But you know what? He's very much alive. I don't kill my boyfriends when things don't work out, Cass."

Her voice broke at the end. Red blotches colored her face. "I don't want to talk about this anymore. I swear to God I haven't done anything wrong."

A buzzer went off. In another few moments, a guard would come to take Farrah back to her cell. She was crying now. Full on. Farrah the chameleon. I hoped like hell what she'd shown me was real.

"I'll be in touch," I said. "Tomorrow I'll head out to see your father. I'll let you know how that goes."

She was still crying as they led her away. Shaken. Broken. I watched a little longer than I should have. Was I seeing things? Or was that a smirk I saw on her face as she turned the corner and disappeared out of sight?

Chapter 7

WE ALMOST DIDN'T FIND it. Eric's GPS took us to the northern end of Isabella County. There was nothing out here but fields and Amish farms.

"It's gotta be this one," Eric said after we'd crisscrossed an old county road that led to nowhere.

"That?" I asked. Eric slowed the car and I pointed to a small break in the tree line on the west side of the road. If it hadn't rained the day before, I might not have seen it. But the ground was still soggy and as Eric stopped the car, I saw a two-track trail leading back into the woods. Fresh tire tracks cut into the mud.

"Terrific," Eric muttered. "I just had this thing detailed."

He slowed his truck and made the turn, careful to stay in the ruts of what had to have been a sizable pickup truck.

"Eric," I said as he drove us deeper onto the property. The trees thinned and on the other side of the two-track was a veritable junkyard. Old hubcaps stacked against a stump. A graveyard of rusted-out sedans stripped to bare bones. What was left of a pontoon boat rested at an angle against a large oak tree. Roots had grown up through the wooden platform.

"She said meager beginnings," I whispered.

"Glad I followed my instincts and didn't let you come up here alone," Eric muttered.

I decided to swallow my usual retort about Eric's misguided chivalry. I was glad he was here too.

The house itself looked fairly sturdy. A huge ranch with a wraparound porch. I guessed it was built at least a hundred years ago, probably longer. As cluttered as the surrounding property was, here at the house, things were far neater. Two cane rocking chairs parked cheerily on one end of the porch. Hanging pots filled with bright pink geraniums swung in the breeze.

Eric parked right in front of the house and got out. His hand went instinctively to the heel of his gun holstered as always on his right hip.

"He's not expecting us," Eric said.

"I tried to call," I said. "Farrah told me he won't answer if he doesn't recognize the number."

"I can respect that actually," Eric said. He went ahead of me up the porch. He knocked on the screen door and with a jerk of his chin, told me to stand behind him.

"It's not an ambush," I said.

"I don't know what it is. Until I do ..."

The door swung open. Victor Sibley peered at us from the shadows of his unlit living room. Another thing Farrah

The Client List

mentioned. Her father didn't believe in using electric lighting until after sundown.

"Mr. Sibley?" I said. Eric frowned, but let me step forward.

"I'm sorry for barging in on you like this. I tried to call yesterday evening."

"I was in town," he said. "Who're you?"

"My name is Cass Leary. This is my partner, Eric Wray. I've been hired to represent your daughter, Farrah. You understand the legal issues she's facing. I'm her lawyer."

Victor stepped out onto the porch and into the light. He was quite a bit shorter than Eric. I guessed maybe five foot eight. He had thin, wavy hair and a long, angular face with a bulbous chin. He wore a pair of readers perched on the end of his nose. The glare from them hid his eyes.

"You're not Farrah's lawyer. He's an old man. I met him."

He met him? Farrah told me she'd asked Rix not to reach out to Victor Sibley. I saw nothing in Rix's notes about him. Who was lying? Farrah or her father? I decided not to confront him about it just yet.

"Yes. You met Anderson Rix. I'm afraid he passed away suddenly a few weeks ago. I've taken over Farrah's defense. Do you have a few minutes to talk?"

"Got nothing to say." He reached into the house and pulled a navy-blue windbreaker jacket off a hook. He stabbed his arms into the sleeves and walked right past us off the porch.

"Fine," I said. "But Farrah told me she still keeps a few of her belongings here. Out in one of your pole barns. I need to look for something. It's important to Farrah's case. Would you mind showing me where her things are?"

I could already see one large pole barn about a hundred yards behind the house. A corn field stretched beyond it.

"She hasn't been out here in years," Victor said. "Whatever she's got out there can't be that important she'd just leave it."

"She's your daughter, man," Eric said. "We're trying to help her. How about you help us do that?"

Sibley turned to face him. He'd stepped off the porch and stood in the yard. It made Eric nearly twice his height now. Sibley pointed a finger up at Eric.

"I know what kind of trouble that girl's in. It's the kind she got herself into. I told her nothing good was gonna come from her in that city."

"City," I said. "It's Ann Arbor."

Sibley waved me off. He started walking toward the barn. Eric shot me a look and stepped off the porch. We followed Victor Sibley. He hadn't run us off yet, so I took his actions as acquiescence.

"I'm sure you're worried about her," I said as I hustled to keep up with Sibley's stride. Eric kept at my side.

Sibley had a jangle of keys in his hand. As he walked up to the barn, I was glad I'd thought to wear rain boots instead of heels. My feet sank into the mud. Eric took my arm to steady me.

Sibley took his keys out and stabbed one into the padlock on the service door to the barn. He swung it open and reached in to fiddle with what looked like a car battery. A moment later, overhead lights kicked on.

The Client List

"That's pretty impressive," Eric said, marveling at the solar panels Sibley had hooked up. There was no electricity running to the barn but it was bright enough with the solar lights.

Sibley disappeared into the depths of the barn. Eric looked back and mouthed, "Weirdo."

I brushed past him and followed Sibley into the barn.

"Dammit, Cass," Eric muttered. He charged in after me. Sibley climbed onto a stool near a giant tool bench he had in one corner. The barn itself was huge. Three thousand square feet at least. He had shelving all the way up to the rafters. There were hundreds of bins and boxes lining the walls.

Sibley busied himself with some sort of small engine on his workbench.

"I'm sorry," I said, losing my temper a bit. "Mr. Sibley. I told you who I am. You know that your daughter is in jail facing a murder charge. I'm here to help her. Do you think you could spare a few minutes to talk to me?"

Sibley didn't take his focus off the engine in front of him. He grabbed a screwdriver and began loosening something.

"I haven't seen my daughter in two years," he said. "She comes out here when she wants something. She calls me when she needs something. She hasn't called me, so I guess she doesn't need me."

"She does need you," I said. "In a couple of months, she's going on trial. It would help if you could be there in the courtroom for her."

Sibley kept right on working his screwdriver. "Is that what she wants or what you told her she needs?"

"Does it matter?"

Sibley sighed. He aimed the sharp end of the screwdriver over his left shoulder. "Her shelf's in the corner over there. All those red bins. Her name's on 'em. Take what you want. But don't leave a mess."

Eric was already headed for the corner. Four red plastic tote bins were stacked on a low shelf. As Sibley said, Farrah's name was written on them with a black sharpie.

"Which one is it?" Eric asked.

"She said it's a lockbox," I said. "A metal footlocker."

Eric took a small Maglite out of his pocket. Farrah's bins were covered in dust and cobwebs along with every other box on this particular shelf.

"Well," Eric whispered. "I'd say nothing's been moved over here in months at least." He took his phone out and snapped a few pictures.

"There," I said. "Bottom shelf, shoved way back."

Eric squatted down. He shone his flashlight under the shelf. A rusted army-green footlocker was shoved behind two red bins.

He pulled at one of the bins.

"Mercy," he grunted. "She keep cannonballs in this thing?"

He pulled the bin out of the way and grabbed the handle of the footlocker. As he pulled it out, dust bunnies flew everywhere. There was a rectangular outline in the dust where he'd moved the footlocker. The thing clearly hadn't been moved in a good long time.

"You got the combo?" Eric asked, shining his light on the combination lock securing the footlocker. He pulled a pair of latex gloves out of his pocket and put them on.

I pulled my phone out and pulled up the note I'd made. I leaned down and whispered the combination to Eric. "1, 19, 37." I looked over my shoulder. Victor Sibley hadn't so much as glanced over at us. He kept right on working on his project.

Eric signaled to me. I pulled up my camera and hit record.

Eric snapped the lock open. He held his flashlight between his teeth and opened the footlocker.

I peered inside. Just as Farrah described, I saw a black plastic bag secured with orange zip ties.

"Her mother's wedding dress," I whispered. "She said it's the only thing she's got from her. Look underneath it."

Eric pulled the dress aside. His light shone on a small plastic gun case.

"It's not locked," he said. "There's no lock." He picked the case up and immediately frowned.

"Son of a bitch," he muttered. "I can already tell you it's empty."

He popped open the latch. Just as he said, the case was empty. No gun. No bullets.

"She lied to you," he said, tossing the gun case back into the footlocker.

"Or somebody else took it out," I said.

"Sibley," Eric yelled. He snapped the combo lock back in place and shoved the footlocker under the shelf.

Sibley didn't look up as Eric strode over to him.

"Sibley," he said again, his tone rising. "Who else has access to this barn besides you?"

Victor finally put his screwdriver down and swiveled to face Eric.

"Nobody."

"You do anything with your daughter's things?" Eric asked.

"Does it look like it?"

I dusted my jeans off and went to join Eric. Farrah insisted her father knew nothing about the gun she kept in his own barn. She purposely hid it under her mother's wedding dress because she claimed he'd want nothing to do with any of it. Farrah feared he'd burn the dress if he knew she was holding on to it.

"Will you help her?" I said. "Will you come to court to support your daughter when the time comes? I understand you haven't spoken to her in a long time."

"She hasn't spoken to me!" he snapped. "She stopped returning my calls. She stopped coming around for the holidays. She sends money thinking that it makes up for everything."

Sibley slammed his screwdriver down on the workbench and slid off his stool. Without a word, he stormed out of the barn.

"The hell?" Eric asked.

"You want my help?" Sibley shouted. Shaking our heads, Eric and I followed him out. Sibley had made it all the way to the porch. He flung open the door and motioned us forward.

Eric had his hand on his holstered weapon again.

"Calm down," I said.

"Right."

We headed up the porch. I didn't make it inside before Sibley charged back outside holding a thick white envelope. He shoved it into my hand.

"Take it," he said. "It's the devil's money."

I looked in the envelope. There were stacks of hundred-dollar bills inside. This had to be at least ten thousand dollars.

"She sends it to me every month thinking it'll make up for what she's done. Leaving me. Working for those people. I won't spend a cent of it. So use it if she wants you to. Pay your bill with it."

"Mr. Sibley, your daughter wanted you to have this," I said.

"And I just told you what I want. Take it. There's your help."

The light changed, allowing me to see Victor Sibley's eyes for the first time. They were filled with tears.

"Mr. Sibley," I said, making my voice softer.

"Is she all right?" he asked.

"She's hanging in there," I said. "But if you're willing to show up for her, I think that will mean the world to her."

Sibley's eyes narrowed. He tossed a glance at Eric, then back at me.

Sibley put one hand on the door. His face changed again, darkening to a frown.

"You don't know my daughter as well as you think you do."

Then Victor Sibley slammed his front door in my face.

Chapter 8

"This is a terrible idea," I said.

My sister Vangie perched on a stool holding one end of a plastic sign with blue and silver streamers hanging off of it.

"It'll look better once I get everything hung. I'm just asking you if it's straight."

"It's straight," I answered, sipping my coffee. It was after five o'clock on a Friday afternoon. I didn't normally load up on caffeine this late in the day, but Vangie's machinations required a jolt to the system for me to get on board.

"It's hanging too low in the middle."

Tori came in from the side door. She was using a cane today after a grueling morning of physical therapy. She'd come a long way both mentally and physically from a horrific car crash almost two years ago.

"Matty!" Vangie yelled, sending a spear of adrenaline down me more potent than the caffeine.

"I'm right here!" my brother Matty yelled back. He had my toddler nephew under one arm, a diaper bag in the other arm.

"Give me that boy," I said, reaching for my nephew. Baby Sean gave me a drooling grin. He was teething. He proceeded to let loose a string of unintelligible and yet indignant baby babble punctuated by a fart.

I kissed his cheeks and spirited him off to the spare bedroom to take off his coat.

"How's my little man?" I said. I got another smile for my efforts. Sean was wearing a toddler-sized Detroit Lions jersey and a pair of adorable designer baby jeans Vangie had bought for him. I sniffed his bottom as I pulled off his coat.

"Only fifteen percent ripe," I declared. "You'll do."

"How about me?"

Eric's voice poured over me like fine wine. He was freshly scrubbed and shaved from his shower. He came into the room and tickled Sean's belly, earning a throaty laugh that provided an instant hit of dopamine to my system. Then Eric poked a gentle finger under the waistband of my jeans, hoping to get a similar reaction.

"Mmm," I said, going up on my tiptoes to kiss him. "You smell good. And I like this."

I ran a hand along Eric's now smooth jawline. He'd sported a scruffy beard for the last two weeks. Something he'd been threatening to try out for the last few months since retiring from the Delphi P.D.

"Don't get used to it," he said. "I think I wanna grow it all out again into a proper beard."

"You'll look like a grizzly bear."

Eric bared his teeth and let out a decidedly sexy growl.

"Not in front of the child," I teased.

"Is he here yet?" Eric asked, gesturing toward the front room.

"No. Jeanie texted and said they're about ten minutes out."

Eric took Sean from me and tossed him into the air. Sean's hair stood on end as he came back down. He chortled and flailed his little arms with excitement. "Gan, gan!" Sean demanded, wanting Eric to toss him again.

"You're giving me a workout, buddy," Eric said, then buried his face into the crook of Sean's little neck and pretended to bite him. This earned him another round of deep belly laughs from my nephew.

When I reached for him, Sean flung his arms around Eric's neck.

"Fine." I laughed. "Uncle Eric's always the favorite. I see how it is."

Eric started down the hall. I followed close behind.

"Jeanie say what kind of mood Joe's in?" Eric asked over his shoulder.

"She didn't say. She just texted that the deed is done and they're on their way."

"There!" Vangie shouted. "It's perfect."

Her banner hung across the threshold of my French doors heading out to the lake.

"Happy Independence Day?" Eric read. "It's April."

"Independence, get it?" Vangie said. "Saying happy divorce seemed a little crude."

"Gotcha," I said. "Well, this is far more classy."

Vangie flipped me the bird.

Sean caught sight of his mother and arched his back. Eric quickly caught him before he succeeded in pitching himself airborne.

Tori settled herself on my chaise lounge. Eric brought the baby to her. Sean promptly stuck a thumb in his mouth and got into a cuddle position.

"Is he happy about this?" Matty asked. "When I talked to him yesterday, I could barely get two words out of him."

"Look," Vangie said. "I've had enough negativity out of all you guys. I don't care what Joe's mood is. We're gonna turn today into a celebration, no matter what. There's no point brooding about what happened. Katie's the villain in this, not Joe. She wanted out? She got her wish. I say we make the best of it. Let Joe know his whole family's supporting him. He doesn't need Katie. She's trash. Now, where are the balloons?"

"She may have a point," Eric said. He went to the fridge and pulled out a bottle of beer. "Not the worst idea to keep Joe out of his head today."

A year ago, my now former sister-in-law Katie started an affair with the sports guy from the local news. Things had gotten ugly fast. Joe had refused to let me anywhere near the legal side of his divorce. Thankfully, he'd let my partner, Jeanie, represent him. He was in good hands, but we both felt he'd given Katie more than she deserved considering what she'd done. Joe had made it abundantly clear he didn't want my advice on the matter. I worried about him.

My niece Jessa, Vangie's daughter, came in from the garage. She balanced three two-liter pops in her arms. Eric rushed forward and took two of them from her.

"Set it up on the counter next to the fridge," I said. I grabbed the ice bucket from the cupboard and handed it to Jessa. Just shy of her thirteenth birthday, Jessa adopted a permanent scowl around the family. I elbowed her and made a face at her. She gave me a begrudging smile and worked on filling the ice bucket.

"Is Emma coming?" Jessa asked. My other niece, Joe's daughter, was just about to graduate from college. Jessa idolized her.

"Afraid not," I said. "She's working tonight at the Sand Bar. Eric and I are heading there later."

"Can we go?" Jessa asked hopefully. "I mean, after this thing's over."

"That's up to your mother," I said. I caught Eric's eye over Jessa's turned head. "Do you mind?"

Eric gave me a thumbs up. Then Joe's truck pulled into the drive. I suddenly wished I'd made that five o'clock coffee Irish. I could see my brother's frown from here.

I watched as Joe climbed down from the cab then went to the passenger side to help Jeanie out. She was doing great since her second hip replacement though she too still needed a cane. She'd gotten matching purple ones with a jeweled handle for both her and Tori. Jeanie pointed hers toward my front door. I couldn't hear what she was saying but from the look on my brother's face, I could guess. She'd probably told him to put a smile on his damn face and appreciate his family.

"Surprise!" Vangie shouted as Joe walked in. Joe read the banner and took in the two dozen helium balloons Vangie had distributed throughout the kitchen and living room.

"Surprise," I said, much quieter. I decided I wouldn't give him the chance to be cranky. I went to him and planted a kiss on his cheek.

He hugged me back.

"It was my mom's idea," Jessa said, rolling her eyes. "Whoever thought it was a good idea to throw a party for a divorce? It's weird."

"We *are* weird," Vangie called out. "Get used to it. You're one of us, kiddo."

"Sorry," I said, putting an arm around Jessa. "You can't pick your family."

She shook her head and shrugged as she made her way over to Tori. She picked up little Sean and became a different person. Smiling, laughing, talking baby talk. Sean was absolutely smitten with Jessa.

"Don't ask," Joe said to me.

"I didn't," I protested.

"You were thinking about it."

Eric made a discreet exit from the kitchen, leaving Joe and me as alone as we'd get in a crowd of people.

"I'm fine," Joe snapped.

"Good. But again. Didn't ask. Did she bother showing?"

Joe grumbled by way of an answer then went for the fridge and helped himself to a beer. He went to join Eric and Matty out on the porch.

Jeanie slid onto a kitchen stool. I poured her a glass of wine and joined her.

"Full report," I said.

"Pretty perfunctory until the last five minutes. Katie tried to convince the judge we'd agreed to a higher amount for spousal support. Brought some handwritten note she claimed Joe gave her. I coulda killed him."

"He negotiated with her behind your back?" I said, nearly launching myself off the stool before Jeanie grabbed my shoulder.

"I said she tried. It was nothing. There was a note but a number just got transposed."

"Still. Joe knows better than to be talking to Katie outside your presence."

"It's handled. Divorce judgment is entered. They're done. She gets a lump sum payment as soon as the house is sold. He's free and clear."

"Did she come alone?" I asked, my voice dropping to a low monotone.

Jeanie took a giant sip of wine. "She did not. The boyfriend showed up at the end."

"Oh lord. How'd Joe handle that?"

"Not great. But it didn't come to blows. You ask me, I think it was a good thing. I mean, not good good. But if Joe suffered from any delusions that Katie might have a change of heart, lover boy showing up put that to rest. I don't think he's sad anymore. He's just pissed."

"Can you blame him?"

Jeanie shook her head.

"Thank you," I said. "If it weren't for you ... I know my brother. He was gonna try to handle all of that on his own. She was gonna screw him over and he would have let her out of some misplaced sense of guilt."

"He's family," Jeanie said. "No need for thanks."

We sat in companionable silence for a while. I poured each of us a second glass of wine. Except to Matty, who was firmly on the wagon these days, the alcohol would flow freely for everyone. Joe was already on his way to being good and drunk.

"It's probably safe now," Jeanie said. "Let's head out to the porch."

I took the wine bottle. As I stepped out from the French doors, I saw my brother had made his way down to the water. It was a bit too early to put the dock in yet. The sections were stacked along the shoreline. Beer in hand, Joe climbed on top of the stack.

"Joe!" I called out. He wasn't steady on his feet. One wrong step and he'd topple backwards into the water.

Ignoring me, Joe raised his bottle of beer. "I'm fine!" he called out. "Better'n fine. I want to take this opportunity to thank all of you for being here."

"He's hammered," Jessa whispered. She walked out, still carrying Sean.

"Shh," Vangie cautioned her.

"I'm the luckiest guy in the world," Joe said. "I mean it."

"I wish Emma were here," Jessa said.

"It's okay," I said.

"Here's to the rest of my life as a bachelor. Never thought I'd say that."

"Oh, Joe," Vangie said.

Eric came up beside me and slid a hand around my waist.

"Should you get him down?" I asked him.

Eric shook his head. "He'll be okay. I've seen him drunker."

I reached back and touched Eric's cheek. Joe saw it and pointed the neck of his now empty beer bottle at us.

"You two," he said. "That's the way to do it. You want my advice? Never get married. In fact, Eric? You should make an anti-proposal to my sister right now."

"Joe, stop," Vangie said. She rose from her seat.

"Swear it and you'll both be better off," Joe said. He swayed on his feet.

"Guys?" I said. Eric and Matty moved as a unit toward Joe.

"Don't you do it either, Matty," Joe said. "Learys are cursed."

"Hey, Joe, time to come on down," Eric said.

Joe raised his arms above his head. "Look at the evidence. Matty's already got one divorce under his belt."

"Joe, stop!" Vangie called out. I looked back toward the house. Thank God Tori was inside. She and Matty had set a date for late fall. She wanted a small ceremony at the courthouse and just a family reception here on a day the weather cooperated.

"Don't marry a Leary," Joe proclaimed. "If you wanna be happy. We're a bad lot. Cursed. Grandpa Leary always said it. All four of us. Told me I should have entered the priesthood."

"Right," I said. "That'd work out swell."

I went to join Matty and Eric.

"Take that ring back, Eric," Joe said.

I saw the blood drain from Eric's face. Ring? There was a ring? We talked around the subject. But that was a long time ago. The air left my lungs.

"Okay," Eric said. "That's it."

Eric nodded at Matty. They shared an unspoken signal. Eric reached up and grabbed Joe by the arm. He jerked him down. Matty caught Joe around the waist before my older brother had a chance to fall.

I expected a fight, but Joe came more or less quietly. He laughed and slung one arm around Eric's neck, the other around Matty's.

"Take him up," I said. But Matty and Joe were already headed for the big barn. Joe was currently staying with me in the small apartment I had built on the second floor. He called it the Barndeminium.

"Well, that went about as well as I figured it would," Jessa said, glaring at her mother.

Vangie locked near tears. "I'm just glad Tori didn't hear any of that," she whispered. "Did Grandpa Leary really say that? That we're cursed?"

"Who knows," I said. "Who cares? He's long gone. Don't start ruminating on it."

A moment later, Eric and Matty reappeared. Eric came to me but an awkward silence settled between us. I couldn't yet bring myself to ask him what Joe meant about a ring. He was drunk. He had to just be drunk.

But the odd look on Eric's face did nothing to ease my concerns.

An hour or so later, the "party" broke up. We scrapped our plans to head to the Sand Bar. Eric agreed we shouldn't leave Joe alone if he woke up later. I hoped he'd sleep through until morning.

I had an early day planned. A meeting with Lionel Harriman, Terrence Dowd's law partner. It would be a welcome distraction from the day's events.

Chapter 9

LIONEL HARRIMAN LOOKED EXACTLY like you'd expect. Gentlemanly with a thick head of white hair, strong jaw, tanned face, wearing a black pin-striped three-piece suit. He sat behind his giant desk with no computer in sight. Just an ink blotter with two gold pens in each corner, pointed at the exact same angle in their holders.

"Good morning," I said. Harriman stood as I closed the door to his office and came to his desk. He smiled politely enough, but his eyes settled on my weather-beaten leather messenger bag. I got a lot of looks like that. The thing had character in my eyes. And you'd have to pry it out of my dead hands before I'd give it up for something fancy or expensive.

"Ms. Leary," he said, extending a hand to me across the desk. I shook it, then took my seat.

"Thank you for carving out some time for me."

"I understand you were another of Anderson Rix's protégés. I was very sorry to hear that he passed."

"Thank you. Did you know him well?"

Harriman and Anderson Rix were of the same generation. Surely their paths had crossed many times.

"Not well," he said. "I knew him in professional circles, of course. And by reputation."

"I see. Well, again, thank you for meeting with me. You're one of the few material witnesses in this case willing to do so. And let me also extend my sympathies to you on the loss of your partner."

"It was a tremendous blow," he said, almost cutting me off. "We'll not see the likes of Terrence Dowd in the legal community again. He was like family."

"Like a son to you?" I asked. I resisted the urge to take out a notepad. I wanted Harriman to feel it was a more casual conversation as opposed to an interrogation.

"A younger brother. Terrence was twelve years my junior. Far too young for us to lose him at all, much less like that."

"He was fifty-eight," I said.

"Yes."

"Mr. Harriman, I don't want to waste your time. But you understand what I'm principally interested in speaking to you about."

"You want to know if I might be mistaken about what I told the police?"

"Not mistaken. I just want to make sure I'm clear on what happened as far as your experience."

"Ms. Leary, let *me* be clear about something. I have no intention of discussing the particulars of my statement to the police. It's all there in the report. I signed my statement. I have nothing to add. You'll of course have the opportunity to cross-examine me."

Oh boy. I was beginning to wonder why Harriman even bothered to take this meeting. I smiled and took a different tack.

"How did you meet Terrence Dowd?"

"We formed our partnership twenty-five years ago. We were planning a celebration of that later this year. I was in my forties at the time. My previous firm, Coleman, Sweeney and Harriman, was on the brink of dissolving. Nate Coleman died. Bill Sweeney was looking to retire. I was looking for a more managerial role. Terrence and I had worked a few cases together across the table. Co-plaintiffs on a pair of product liability cases. I liked his work ethic. He was a dynamo in front of a jury. I approached him about a partnership. He was a solo practitioner at the time. It was a bit of a match made in heaven, as they say. I had the financial resources to get the firm off the ground. The initial client base and foothold in the legal community. Terrence was a top litigator. We fit."

"That's a rare thing," I said.

"He wasn't finished, you know? Fellows his age, approaching sixty as he was. A lot of times they begin to slow down. Not Terrence. He was just getting better with age. You should have seen him. A natural-born storyteller. He could convince a jury of anything. A spin master, that's for sure. It was something to see. You know? That's one of the things I'm going to miss most. Just watching Terrence Dowd in the arena. You could have learned something from him, Ms. Leary."

"It sounds like it. I regret that I won't be able to. And again, I appreciate that you're willing to meet with me. I suppose I might seem like the enemy in this."

"Don't be ridiculous. We're not like other people, are we, Ms. Leary?"

"I'm sorry?"

"I know how this game is played."

"Again, I'm sorry," I said. "I'm not sure what you mean by game."

He steepled his fingertips beneath his chin. I braced myself for the volley of mansplaining I felt certain was headed my way.

"No matter what happened, Ms. Sibley is entitled to a vigorous defense. It's how the system works. A system I'm part of. That I swore an oath to uphold before you were even born. I know what I'm doing. And I know what you're doing."

"I see. Well, I'm really just trying to understand the facts as you experienced them."

"That's an interesting choice of words."

"I don't mean it to be. Look, you have me at a disadvantage. I'm really just trying to get to know Terrence Dowd a little more. I want to understand what kind of person he was. Trust me, I haven't lost sight of who the real victim in this was."

"He was a flawed person. An imperfect person. He made choices in his personal life I didn't approve of and I told him so. He ignored me. Respected my opinions, but rarely shared them. But when he stepped foot in this office, Terrence was the consummate professional. Hard-working. A tireless advocate for his clients. A sharp mind. Brilliant legal strategist. His behavior within these four walls was beyond reproach."

"Until it wasn't," I blurted out. The moment I did, I wished I could swallow back my words. It was the kind of thing I needed to save for cross-examination. Had there been any doubt of that, the flash of anger in Harriman's eyes sealed it.

"Don't get smart with me, dear."

"I'm sorry," I said, though we both knew I wasn't. "But you said you didn't approve of Terrence's personal life choices. He came to you regarding his affair with Farrah Sibley. You disapproved of it. You told the police Terrence was afraid of what she might do. That things had gotten out of control."

"His one great weakness. Always a philanderer. But he treated his women well."

I felt my fist ball at the phrase "his women." I kept a meaningless smile on my face to mask my feelings.

"Did Farrah ever come to you asking for advice about Terrence?"

"Most certainly not. Ms. Sibley was Terrence's clerk, not mine. I didn't interact with his support staff. We kept a clear chain of command here. I never wanted Ms. Sibley or any number of the other interns he had helping him to think I was their boss over Terrence."

"But in point of fact you were, weren't you? It's your name at the top of the letterhead. You were the senior partner. You had the controlling interest in the partnership."

"Irrelevant. I told you. I didn't interfere in Terrence's relationships with his staff. There was never any need or desire."

"Until he came to you and asked for your help with Farrah Sibley."

He set his jaw to the side, a clear sign of displeasure.

"As I told you at the top of this conversation, my statement regarding my conversations with Terrence about the subject of Farrah Sibley is with the police file on this case. I won't be expounding on it outside the courtroom."

"Fine," I said. "What about this? Can you think of anyone else who might have harbored ill will against Terrence?"

"No."

"He had three ex-wives."

"Then I invite you to go talk to them yourself."

"Fair enough. But you're in a unique position to discuss the relationships he had with his existing clients."

"In what way?"

"Did he ever come to you with concerns about how a case was going? Did you ever receive any complaints from one of Terrence's clients? Once again, since your name is at the top of the letterhead, it would seem natural that you'd be the person a disgruntled client would go to if they had a problem with the way their case was being handled."

"That never happened."

"They never came to you or the firm never had a disgruntled client?"

The Client List

"I'm not aware of any disgruntled clients of Terrence's. To the contrary. If I asked, I'd have glowing testimonials."

"Well, I'm asking. I'd like to see Terrence Dowd's list of active clients."

"And you know that's not going to happen. Those files are protected by attorney-client privilege."

"I'm not asking to see the files. Just the names."

"That too. You're welcome to head down to the courthouse and get a list of those cases Terrence filed appearances on."

"I already have. Look, I'm trying to get a sense of who Terrence met with in the weeks before he died. That's all."

"I didn't keep his schedule. And Professor Rix subpoenaed that information. Did you lose it?"

"I've reviewed it. But those are just names. I'd like to know more." In the weeks before his death, Terrence Dowd actually took very few client meetings. His call list consisted of other attorneys and law firms. A few expert witnesses on cases he had pending. And he took very few appointments as he was gearing up to try a case in Oakland County that Harriman ended up settling after he passed away.

"Did you ever sit in on the meetings Terrence had with clients?" I asked.

"Not usually. Not recently. He did his thing. I did mine. As I told you, my role has been more managerial. For a lot of years, I was also the rainmaker around here."

"And Terrence handled the litigation side of that if it came to it."

"That's right. Othe last few years, Terrence became more active in client acquisitions. I would say he brought in all new business in the last, say, five to seven years."

"He even had a few referrals from Anderson Rix. Did you know that?" I asked.

"I'm aware Rix farmed out the last active asbestos clients he had before slowing down his practice to the bare minimum, yes. He didn't want to keep a court docket anymore. So some came here. A few went to a firm in Oakland County. And to answer your question. No. Terrence didn't have any disgruntled clients. Nobody else was threatening to do him harm, but Ms. Sibley. I'm sorry I can't be more helpful. I know this has to be difficult for you. It can't be easy representing a client you know is guilty."

"I don't know that she's guilty. That's why I'm here. But I'm interested in learning the truth, no matter where that leads."

There was a soft knock on the door. Harriman's secretary poked her head in.

"I'm sorry," she said, though I was certain this was their prearranged signal to end our meeting. "Your next appointment just arrived."

"Thank you, Georgia," he said. "Just set her up in the conference room. I'll be right in."

Then he turned his attention back to me. "I'm afraid I just don't have anything else I can offer you, Ms. Leary. I know you must be good at what you do and for Ms. Sibley's sake, I'm glad of that. Anderson Rix must have thought very highly of you to entrust this case to you."

He rose from his seat and extended his hand to me. I shook it.

The Client List

"Mr. Harriman, while I'm here. I'd really like your permission to speak to Lydia Whitford, Mr. Dowd's office administrator. She's also a material witness in this case having discovered Mr. Dowd in the parking lot."

"Ms. Whitford has taken a leave of absence. The circumstances surrounding this ... matter ... as you can imagine ... have been very traumatic for her. And even if she were here today, she wouldn't speak to you without a subpoena. She isn't legally required to. Again, you'll have your opportunity to cross-examine her in due course."

"Naturally. Would you mind at least showing me where Ms. Sibley's office was in relation to Mr. Dowd's?"

"Right down the hall," he said. "You'll pass them on the way to the elevators. I'm afraid I can't let you inside. Both offices are empty in any case."

"Where are my client's personal belongings?"

"In a box we had shipped to her permanent address."

"To her father's?" I asked. "In Mount Pleasant?"

"I believe so, yes."

Lionel Harriman then bid me a hasty goodbye. I walked down the hallway. Terrence Dowd's office was at the end of it on the corner. As it happened, the door was wide open. I looked over my shoulder. A young receptionist sat at the desk in front of the elevators but she seemed undisturbed by my nosiness. I poked my head inside Dowd's office.

As Harriman said, the place was cleaned out. The desk was still there, taking up the center of the room. His bookshelves were bare. Any personal items he had were removed. I could see the outline of where his certificates probably hung on the wall by the square patches of faded paint. But Terrence Dowd himself had been wiped clean from this space.

There was an interior door. I stepped back out into the hall. Farrah's old office was right next to Dowd's. The interior door must have led to it.

Easy access, I thought. That second door to Farrah's office was locked. I walked up to the receptionist.

"Excuse me," I said. "Can you tell me, where is Lydia Whitford's office?"

I read the nameplate on the desk. Kelsey Sorbo.

"Mrs. Whitford isn't here."

"I'm aware. I'm just curious where her office is."

Kelsey rose from her chair. "I'll show you."

She stepped around the small wooden partition that made her station into a sort of island. She motioned for me to follow her down the hall. We walked right past Lionel Harriman's office again. His door was closed. I heard no voices coming from the adjacent conference room. It could have been soundproofed, but I took it as evidence my theory was true. Harriman wasn't meeting with another client. He just didn't want to talk to me anymore.

"Right here," Kelsey said. She'd led me to the other end of the hall. Lydia Whitford's name was on a nameplate on the door.

I turned and looked down the length of the hall. The elevators were at the opposite end.

"Is there a common area somewhere? A break room? Coffee station?"

"The firm owns the floor below us as well. That's where the employee lounge is. Mr. Harriman and Mr. Dowd never liked people walking around with food or eating at their desks or the smell of food on this floor."

"I see," I said. "Thank you. That's very helpful."

"No problem."

I made my way back to the elevator and pressed the button for the parking garage level. Kelsey took her seat behind her desk and gave me a pleasant wave as the elevator doors closed.

I looked up. The black dome of a closed-circuit camera blinked at me from the corner.

Farrah Sibley would have known it. She stood in this very elevator countless times. And yet that night, she took the stairs, she said. The one place where there would have been no cameras. I thought about doing the same. But the elevator was already in motion.

I got off on the top floor of the parking garage even though I was parked one floor down. This was where the employees of the building parked. Farrah had told me as much.

I could see Lionel Harriman's BMW from here. His vanity plate read LHMAN. A placard on the cement wall proclaimed it was reserved for Harriman alone. Beside it, my heart flipped.

Another placard read, "Reserved for Terrence Dowd."

Here. It was here. The space was empty. Whatever bloodstains had once been here had long since been sprayed clean.

I stepped into the empty parking space. The air felt colder somehow. I positioned my body as if I were climbing into the driver's side door. Terrence Dowd's last moments, the last thing he would have seen in this life was an ugly green sign with an arrow directing traffic to the upper parking levels or the downward arrow to the exit below.

No cameras here. No parking attendants. Just a key card to record the entry and exit times of every car going through. And I knew that alone might be the very thing that would spell Farrah Sibley's doom.

Chapter 10

THE FOLLOWING WEEK, Glenda Rix asked me to meet her back at her house. I'd asked her to come to my office but she didn't feel up to making the trip. Jeanie and Eric came with me, armed with their own questions.

We found Glenda out in the yard, crying. She knelt in the dirt, surrounded by dying rose bushes. Eric rushed up to her.

"Mrs. Rix, what happened?"

"It's too much," she said. "It's all just too much. I've got a black thumb. I don't know if I'm supposed to trim them or when to trim them. He put bananas and egg shells out here in the soil but I don't think it's working."

Eric took her hands in his. His eyes were kind, his voice calm.

"How long have you been out here?"

"All morning. I'm just making it worse. He tilled the garden. That's all he was able to get to before …"

"Come on," Eric said, gently lifting Glenda to her feet. He put an arm around her.

"You're so tall," she sniffed. "It's good to have a man around. I know that's not very politically correct or whatever of me to say. But I liked letting Anderson handle all of this out here. I don't want to learn. Is it bad that I don't want to learn?"

"Of course not," I said.

"What if I don't even want those stupid rose bushes anymore? They just ... they remind me of Anderson."

"You can do whatever you want," Jeanie said. "Plant some bushes. Or don't. Let the grass grow. It'll be lovely out here no matter what."

She kicked off her gardening boots and gloves at the back door, then led us in through the kitchen.

"Would any of you like tea? Or lemonade. I've got some freshly squeezed."

"Don't put yourself to any trouble."

Her mood lightened considerably once away from her husband's high-maintenance gardens. Glenda washed her hands in the farmhouse sink, dried them on a red-and-white-checkered towel, then led us back into Anderson's study off the living room.

The place looked different since my last visit. Gone were the rows of law books. She had boxes stacked against the wall.

"I couldn't look at any of that either," she said. "Nobody wants it. Anderson spent thousands and thousands of dollars keeping those books up. I thought maybe the law library would want them. They don't. Everything's digital now. So you know what I did? I called the local community theater. Thought maybe they'd want them for props or something."

"That's a great idea," I said.

"They're coming by later in the week. The lady said they're going to take all the pages out and replace them with Styrofoam. So they're not heavy for the actors to pick up. It seems a waste but like I said, nobody wants these. Unless you might."

"No," I said. "Donating them seems right. I'm sure Professor Rix would want that."

"You have to deal with those at some point," she said, pointing to ten other boxes stacked next to Anderson's desk.

I went to the top box and opened it. More client files. She must have cleared out the cabinets along the wall.

"I don't know what needs to be done with any of them," she said. "I think those are all from his big asbestos clients. All settled. But he told me he had to keep them for a period of years. I told him he should hire somebody to digitize them. If you haven't already figured it out, my husband was a bit of a Luddite."

"I remember." I smiled. "As soon as this Sibley case is over, I'll come back and collect them. I know a reputable service. I finally convinced Jeanie to digitize her old files. We'll take care of it."

"I suppose they're all yours now anyway. Since he left his practice to you."

"Right. I'll make sure these all get properly stored. There's nothing you have to worry about."

"What was it you needed from me?" Glenda sat on one of the two couches in the room. Jeanie busied herself looking through the client file boxes. Eric and I went to join Mrs. Rix.

I slipped my bag off my shoulder and took out a fresh notepad and accordion file filled with a few of Anderson's trial prep documents.

"There are a few things in here, some of Professor Rix's shorthand I wanted to ask you about."

"Never mind his shorthand," she said. "Anderson wrote in chicken scratch. I should be able to decipher most of it. What do you have?"

I took out a few loose notes I'd found clipped to various witness statements and handed them to her.

"We've been trying to piece together Terrence Dowd's movements the last few weeks before the murder. It looks like Professor Rix did the same. I just can't make out what he wrote."

Glenda gave me a motherly smile. "Honey. If Anderson were here, I think he'd tell you it's time to be on a first-name basis. He was done being your professor a long time ago. He was just Anderson to me. It's okay if you call him that, too."

"It'll take some getting used to." I laughed. "And I don't care what he said, I'd never have felt comfortable calling him that to his face. But for you? I'll make an exception."

She had a pair of readers on a chain around her neck. She slipped them on and read through the notes I gave her.

"Dowd was gearing up for a trial on a workman's comp claim to take place two weeks after he died."

"Paul Runyon," Glenda said. "I remember. Anderson kept calling him Paul Bunyan. First as a mistake. Then because he thought it was funny. He was corny like that."

"That explains one thing," I said. Rix had written "PB" in his notes.

"Most of the meetings Dowd had were related to that trial," Eric said.

"Mr. Runyon was a sad case. I remember talking to Anderson about it. A machinist of some sort? Lost his arm in some sort of press? I remember Anderson saying he was surprised the company was willing to take it to trial."

"They made a settlement offer," I said. "A million dollars."

"That's what I recall. Anderson said he thought Dowd was a fool not to take it."

"Harriman must have agreed," I said. "After Dowd died, the insurance company renewed their offer and Harriman convinced Runyon to accept it."

"So all these notes in the margin," I said, pointing to the pad she held. "That's Professor ... er ... Anderson noting these meetings were related to the Paul Runyon case? Where it says PB?"

"That would be my guess, yes." Glenda handed the notes back to me.

Dowd met with his client, Paul Runyon. His medical expert, and two eyewitnesses to Runyon's gruesome injury. The rest of his time in the office was made up with mundane trial prep matters in the two weeks before he died.

"Just these three meetings weren't related to Bunyon. I mean Runyon." Eric pointed to the notes. "Going back about ten weeks."

Glenda read over Eric's shoulder. "Tracy Talbot. Jerome Peters. Amelia Connolly," Glenda rattled off, reading Rix's indecipherable shorthand.

"You should have notes in the file," she said. "I know Anderson talked to all three of them. As I recollect, he said they were cooperative. Shocked that Terrence Dowd died in such an awful manner. But willing to do whatever they could to help no matter who was asking."

"They were all existing clients," I said. "Farrah confirmed that. Two more workers' comp cases and workplace harassment case. All still in the initial discovery phases of their cases. Nobody raised any sort of red flag."

"Here's a copy of Dowd's calendar going back three months," Eric said. "A lot of it's blacked out."

I took the papers from him. "Prosecution disclosed what they could. But there's still attorney-client privilege attached to some of Dowd's meetings."

I flipped through the dates. The names started to become familiar. He met with Runyon twice. Four summer clerk candidates. I wrote their names down. Seven other meetings all listed by name. Womack, Davis, Roberts, McCord, McCarthy, Lammers, Coleman.

Glenda looked over my shoulder. She went back to Anderson's notes. Licking her finger, she thumbed through them. "He was thorough, my Anderson. He called all seven. Here are his notes."

I read them back. Womack, Davis, Roberts were all related to the Runyon case. Other employees at the plant where he worked. McCord, McCarthy, Lammers, Coleman, potential new clients.

"You know," Glenda said. "Back when Anderson was first starting out, he couldn't afford support staff. So I'm the one who helped him stay organized. I hadn't realized how much I missed it. Watching his mind work. Having him bounce ideas off of me. But he was doing that again on the Sibley case. It was just him. A one-man band again. It invigorated him. It invigorated *me*. He was like a young man again. Oh Cass, he would have so loved working on this case with you."

"I think I would have liked that, too. I wish he would have called me."

"How's she doing?" Glenda asked. "Farrah Sibley."

"Pretty well, considering. You must know she was devastated about what happened to your husband," I answered.

"She was such a sweet girl," Glenda said. "So polite. Gosh. The first time she came here for one of Anderson's study groups, you could tell she'd never been inside a house like this. And I don't mean to sound like I'm bragging. It's just, I immediately got the impression that the girl came from poverty or tragedy. She was so appreciative. So humble. You know, over all these years, she was one I wanted to keep, you know? Just like you, Cass."

"That's kind of you. The kindness you showed her. The compassion. It meant a lot to her. It meant a lot to me too back in the day."

"But," Glenda sighed. "Anderson was never going to put her on the stand. I can tell you that."

"Did he think she did it?" Jeanie asked in her blunt way. She came and sat beside me.

"What do you think?" Glenda asked, staring straight at me.

I took a beat. "I'm not sure. That's the truth. I truly believe there's reasonable doubt. But that's not the same thing as believing she's innocent."

"You sound just like him. I think he said almost the exact same thing when I asked him that very question, Cass."

"I think she did it," Jeanie said. "I'm sorry. I just do."

Glenda pursed her lips. "I guess I won't let myself think it. Not fully."

"She made some horrible choices," I said.

"She says she loved him," Glenda sighed. "Terrence Dowd, I mean. I do believe that. But boy, that girl did some stupid things. Anderson got so frustrated with her. It was hard for him not to be paternal with her. Anderson felt guilty. He's the one who sent that girl to Dowd."

"That's not all the way true," I said. "He gave Dowd a list of five student intern candidates. Farrah was only one of them."

"Well, he still felt guilty. He respected Terry Dowd."

"I spoke with Lionel Harriman the other day," I said.

Glenda rolled her eyes. "That pompous windbag."

"Pretty much. He told me Anderson referred a few clients to Harriman Dowd."

"That was way back when. Rich Chaney and Louisa Mendoza. Asbestos claims, both of them. There were three others he referred to a firm in Oakland County. Then two more to Barry Montague in Detroit. I could get their names for you. But the files aren't here anymore. Anderson sent those on when they substituted counsel."

"It's not necessary," I said. "It all predates Dowd's murder by a number of years."

"All those cases have long since been settled. I told Anderson he should have insisted on a finder's fee. Or those firms should have offered one out of professional courtesy. Anderson did the bulk of the work. Plus, his name being attached to those plaintiffs struck the fear of God into the defendants. Those settlements were easy money. I always felt bad about that. I'm the one who pushed Anderson to retire from litigation when he did. It was after his first heart attack. He just wanted a clean break. And he told me we didn't need the money. All those lawyers he referred out? They were establishing themselves. Young lions, he called them. They owe Anderson a large chunk of their careers."

"I'm sure they know that. I know I do," I said.

"No. You'd have been fine no matter what. Even if you'd never met Anderson or walked into one of his classrooms, honey."

"Thank you," I said, feeling a bit of a lump in my throat. A pang of guilt washed over me. I would have given anything to have this conversation with Anderson Rix while he was alive. It was my fault for staying away too long.

"What else do you have for me?" Glenda asked. She squirmed in her seat. Her knuckles were gnarled with arthritis and I wondered if the time she spent hunched over in what was left of the garden was starting to catch up with her.

"The wives," Eric said. "I've been looking into Dowd's ex-wives."

I flipped to the page in Anderson's notes where he'd scrawled a few unintelligible lines. Glenda took the pad from me.

"Jennifer Dowd, Myra Dowd Mitchell, and the most recent one, Shondra Dowd. I was with him when he met with all three."

"Can you decipher those notes? I'm making arrangements to speak to them myself, but I want to avoid covering the same ground."

"They were all grieving," Glenda said. "I don't know how he did it. But he ended those marriages on decent terms with those women. And he was a serial cheater. He daisy-chained those affairs. Left Jennifer for Myra. Left Myra for Shondra."

She handed Anderson's notes back to me. Sure enough, he'd drawn an actual daisy in the margins.

"The jilted-ex theory doesn't hold water," I said. "Dowd was paying a substantial amount in alimony to Jennifer and Shondra. Myra's ended when she remarried. But when Terrence died, he was done making more money. He was more valuable to these women alive, not dead."

"Dowd golfed with her new husband. Can you believe that? I remember Myra said that. That Terry was better at divorce than he was at marriage. Shondra's the one you have to watch out for. She knew about Farrah. If you're gonna talk to any of these women again, see if you can shore her up. That's what this note means."

Glenda stood up and pointed to a few lines of indecipherable cursive from Anderson's hand. "Shondra disdain," she read.

"She made a statement to the police," I said. "She told them Dowd wanted to take a vacation for a couple of weeks. He said something about trouble at work. Shondra assumes it was to do with the voice messages Farrah had left."

"That's what Anderson was going to try to exploit if the prosecution put her on the stand. Anderson thought maybe Shondra was still carrying a torch for Terry."

"I'd like to take a look at Shondra Dowd's cell phone data," Eric said. "You might be able to subpoena that. Let me make some calls."

"You think Shondra knows more than she's saying?" Glenda asked. "You're going to want to be careful if you talk to her. She's prickly."

"Hence this," I said, turning the pad over so Glenda could see it. Anderson had drawn a cactus next to Shondra Dowd's name.

"What can I say?" Glenda chuckled. "He was a visual guy."

"This has been helpful," Jeanie said. "And we know it's not easy for you."

I was about to agree. My phone rang. I checked the caller ID quickly, intending to switch it to silent. It was a number I didn't recognize. I was going to decline it. It was probably spam. But something stopped me from doing it. A gut instinct.

I excused myself and took the call out in Anderson Rix's front yard.

"Hello?"

It was met with silence at first. Then a soft, female voice answered. "Hello. You don't know me. Please don't hang up. My name is Leighann. Leighann Sibley. Farrah's my daughter. Please. Can we meet?"

Chapter 11

"I don't like it," Eric said.

"It'll be fine. We're meeting in the food court of the mall, not some back alley in a shady part of town."

"I still don't like it."

He'd been on me since the second I told him about my phone call with Leighann Sibley. She wanted to meet with me. She wanted me to come alone.

"It feels like a setup," he said.

"You think everything's a setup."

"A lot of times it is!"

I shoved a fresh notepad into my bag and grabbed my keys out of the ceramic dish on my desk. I laid a hand against his cheek and went up on my tiptoes to kiss him.

"It's fine."

"She's afraid of something or someone. I want to know who before I feel comfortable letting you ..."

He saw the expression on my face and took a breath. "Before I feel comfortable allowing ..."

My eyes narrowed.

"Cass!" He spit out my name in an exasperated burst.

"I need you here," I said. "Doing what you're doing. Trial starts in two weeks. Keep digging into the people in Terrence Dowd's life. I need alternate suspects. I need to be able to prove Lars Eklund wasn't doing his job as well as you would have."

He grumbled, but stepped aside as I made my way down the stairs and out the front door.

I GOT to the mall twenty minutes early. Leighann told me to wait by the fountain near the bagel place. This time of day, nine o'clock on a Tuesday, the place was dead. It had been like this for a while. The Delphi Mall lost two of its anchor department stores in the last five years.

A young mom with a jogger stroller whizzed by me. Her baby was sound asleep as she got her steps in.

An old man snored in one of the massage chairs lined in front of the electronics store. His wife was undoubtedly shopping somewhere else in the mall.

Then, at two minutes past ten, a woman came out of the public restroom. She spotted me right away and looked nervously left and right. I recognized her as Farrah's mother almost immediately. The resemblance between them was striking.

Wheat-blonde hair swept up away from her face, those high cheekbones and cat-like eyes. She wore a purple cold-shoulder sweater with sequins on the front and a pair of blue jeans and pink knock-off Uggs that had seen better days.

"Mrs. Sibley?" I said, rising.

She shook her head wildly. "Just call me Leighann. I never use that name."

"Of course. Can I get you something? A coffee? Do you want to head over to the bagel place and get a table?"

"No. This is fine. Let's do this right here."

It was hard to hear her with the whoosh of the water fountain nearly drowning her out. It seemed that was the whole point. No chance anyone else could overhear us here unless they sat right down next to us.

Leighann slid her purse off her shoulder and sat on the bench beside me. She then clutched the thing to her stomach like a shield.

"Thanks for meeting with me," I said. "Though I'm curious why you called."

"How is she?"

"Farrah's okay," I said. "As okay as you can expect."

"I can't have anyone knowing I was here. Back in Michigan. I need that made clear."

I resisted the urge to tell her that would depend on what she was about to say. Her daughter was about to go on trial for murder.

"When's the last time you spoke to Farrah?" I asked.

"I wish I could smoke in here," she said. By the smell of her, she'd just finished a cigarette a few minutes before sitting down.

"I haven't told Farrah you called me. Just as you asked. But may I ask you, why the secrecy?"

"You don't know what he's like," she said.

"Victor? Farrah's father? I met him."

Leighann's eyes got big. "You can't tell him anything."

"Is that who you're afraid will find out you're in Michigan?"

"Victor is ... he always finds out. He always knows. I probably shouldn't have come. I just didn't know how else to get a message to Farrah."

She reached into her purse and pulled out a sealed envelope. She handed it to me.

"Can you see that she gets this?"

I could see through the thin white paper that she'd written several pages longhand in blue ink on lined notebook paper.

"A letter," I asked.

"I should have sent it a long time ago but I don't trust the mail in that place. They open it. Screen it, don't they? I figured if it were something her lawyer gave her, they can't look through it. Wouldn't that be unconstitutional?"

"I'll see that she gets this. But would you mind if I asked you a few questions?"

"I don't know anything. Farrah and I haven't talked in years. I wanted to reach out. I need her to know that. That's part of what I wrote in there."

"So why didn't you?"

"She still loves him. He still has his hooks into her."

"Victor?"

"Yesss! Her father. I wanted to take her with me. I can only imagine the things he's been saying to her about me."

"Leighann, Farrah and her father aren't close, if that's what you're concerned about. He hasn't been to see her since she was arrested. And as far as I know, they weren't in communication much, if at all, in the last couple of years. He wasn't supportive of her decision to go to law school."

"He wouldn't have been in support of Farrah doing anything that caused her to leave his house."

"That's the impression I got as well. You understand that your daughter will go on trial for murder in just a couple of weeks. She needs family around her. Both for her own well-being, and for how it looks to the jury. It's easier to believe the worst of people when it appears their own family has turned their backs on them."

"I haven't turned my back on her," Leighann blurted. "I think about her every day. I've written her hundreds of letters."

"She never mentioned that. She said she hasn't been in contact with you since you left the home when she was twelve."

"I didn't leave the home. Who told you that? Did Victor tell you that? Did Farrah?"

"Victor didn't tell me much of anything. He refused to talk to me. I went out there because some of Farrah's belongings were still there out in the barn. I needed to look through some things.

As far as Farrah, yes. She told me you left when she was twelve and that she hasn't spoken to you since."

"That's not my fault. It's what I need her to understand. I wanted her with me. I swear. I just couldn't figure out how. You have to understand. Victor is ... he made it impossible."

"He was abusive."

Leighann fumbled with the clasp on her purse. She reached into it and pulled out another envelope.

"This one's for you," she said. "For Farrah."

I took it from her. This envelope wasn't sealed. I looked inside and counted five thousand dollars in hundreds. It occurred to me this was exactly what her father tried to do. As if money were a substitute for them, showing up for her.

"For Farrah's defense. To help pay for it. Will that be enough?"

"She's already paid my retainer. Your daughter isn't without means."

"Are you going to win? Are you going to be able to prove she's innocent?"

"I'm going to try my very best."

"Even if you do, who do you think will hire her after this?"

"What?"

"If you win. If Farrah walks. How is she supposed to just pick up her life where it left off?"

"I don't think she's thought that far ahead."

"No one ever does. That's the problem. So take that. Put it in your trust account or whatever for her benefit. If there's money

The Client List

left over. If you win for her. Maybe it will help her get back on her feet."

"Thank you," I said. "I'm sure this will mean a lot to Farrah. The gesture as well as the money itself."

"I can get more. Tell her I can get more."

"I think you should tell her yourself. As nice as all of this is, I think Farrah would prefer to actually see you. You can visit her in jail. I can make the arrangements. And I'll tell you what I told her father. She needs family in the courtroom during her trial. The jury needs to see she has people. You understand?"

Leighann shook her head. "I can't do that. I can't let Victor know where I am. Farrah will understand. It's all in that letter."

My anger rose. "Leighann, the money is nice. I'll hold it in trust for her like you asked. But if this letter of yours is filled with excuses why you can't show up for her now, it won't do her any good."

Leighann blinked rapidly, holding back tears. My words stung. But we were well past the point of diplomacy.

"Your ex-husband was physically abusive to you?"

"It was bad," she said. "I had to get out. But he never hurt Farrah. He never laid a finger on her while I was in the home."

"Let's talk about that. While you were in the home. It would help me to understand the family dynamic. Farrah has said Victor was very religious. Very strict. When I met him, he made his displeasure with her lifestyle apparent. He didn't like that she was engaged in an affair out of wedlock."

"That's Victor. My friends used to call him the preacher. That is ... until he cut me off from them. It's taken me a lot of years.

I've done a lot of work on myself to understand what happened to me."

"He was controlling."

"He was controlling. Manipulative. About how I dressed. How I wore my hair. He wouldn't let me work outside the home. It was little things like that. He wanted my world to be smaller and smaller until it was only him. I never kept the house clean enough to his standards. The meals I cooked were never right. Then, as Farrah started getting older, he punished me every time she made a mistake. If she got a bad grade in school, it was my fault. I was too soft. I coddled her."

You left her, I thought. But I couldn't say it. Though it tore at me to think of Farrah as a little girl feeling abandoned by her mother. Left to suffer under her father's wrath all alone. But I knew it wasn't my place to judge this woman. And it would do Farrah no good if I did.

"Did he hit you?" I asked.

"Yes. He hit me. He locked me in my room for days on end. Or he locked me in that barn. Some of the other things he did. Well, it's unspeakable. And before you say it. I tried to take Farrah with me. But I knew what would happen if I tried. What he would do."

"What was that?"

"He would have killed me."

"He said that?"

"Yes. He told me if I tried to take Farrah away from him, he'd kill me. And he knew how to do it so nobody would ever know. There's a cellar under that barn. It's deep. You have to understand. For so many years I went along with him. Little by little. A thousand tiny cuts. I tried to appease him. Finally I lost myself. My world was only Victor and even that wasn't enough for him. But if he put me in that root cellar and left me to die, nobody would have known. My parents were gone. I'd been cut off from my friends for a long time by then. I could have just faded to nothing down in that hole and nobody in the world would have known. Victor would have told people I just packed up and left one day and nobody would have questioned it."

"Which is exactly what you eventually did."

"I survived. And Farrah did, too. She got out. She left him. She was thriving. I did the right thing, you see? She went to law school. She got that big job. I saw an article in the paper when they hired her at that firm. And I knew. I hadn't messed it all up. My baby was okay."

"And now?"

"Victor is still Victor. So please, just give my baby that letter and keep that money safe for her. When this is all over, maybe ..."

"She needs you," I said.

"He'll kill me."

"I can help keep you safe."

"You can't. Nobody can. Only me. I've kept myself safe for sixteen years. And my Farrah is stronger than I am. I always knew that. I knew she'd be okay with or without me. I was the problem. I was the thing Victor wanted to control, not Farrah. As soon as I left, it was all okay."

I realized this was the thing Leighann Sibley had to tell herself. The thing she needed to be true. On the one hand, I understood she was a victim in this. On the other, I couldn't stop thinking about that scared little girl she left behind.

"Mrs. Sibley ... Leighann, I really think this would all be better if you spoke to your daughter in person."

"No!" She stood up. "He's watching. Don't think for a minute he's not still watching. He's waiting for me to come back into Farrah's life. Now that everything's so public. You watch. He'll be parked outside the courtroom waiting for me. I can't give him the chance to hurt me again. I won't. I'm a survivor."

"Leighann ..."

"I know what he'll do. He'll find out who my friends are now. If there's a man in my life. Then he'll try to make them suffer for it one by one. He's done it before. I'm sorry. Farrah will understand. If you give her that letter for me, she'll understand."

Try as I might, I couldn't convince her to come with me. I couldn't convince her to stay.

I watched as she practically sprinted toward the mall exit.

Eric sent me a text. "Everything go okay?"

I slipped the two envelopes into my bag. Something Leighann said kept echoing through my mind.

He made her world small. He went after anyone she tried to get close to. She swore up and down that Victor Sibley would never have done the same to his daughter. And I knew enough about abusive family dynamics to know that was a fantasy.

I texted Eric back.

"Went fine. But I need you to look harder at Victor Sibley. I'll explain when I see you."

Chapter 12

FARRAH SIBLEY TURNED to stone as she read her mother's letter. When she finished, she neatly folded it and set it on the table between us. Today, we met in a small lawyer's room in the county jail. It was more private here. No glass between us. A guard stood outside.

"I debated bringing that to you today," I said. "Because your focus needs to be on the next couple of weeks. Exclusively."

Farrah laid her hand flat on the table. I'd only gotten to know her since she'd been behind bars. Though I'd seen pictures. Professional headshots taken for the Harriman Dowd website. And those Terrence Dowd had taken of her on his phone. In those, she'd been beautiful, confident, luminous. She still was in her own way, but the last few months had taken their toll. Now, her bird-like wrists looked thin enough to snap with just a touch. Her cheekbones jutted out, giving her an almost ghoulish appearance.

"No," she said. "I'm glad you brought it. It ... clarifies a few things for me. And I wondered, you know? My case has made the news. I've been thinking a lot about ... God. All I do is think. That's the hardest part about being in here. I'm used to staying busy. Type A. My top CliftonStrength is Achiever. Now I just have all this time to stare at walls and be inside my own head. So I've wondered about my mom. If she knew. If she cared. I didn't know how to get a hold of her. Now I know. She cares in her own way. But that letter is all about her."

"That was the gist of my conversation with her as well. Just put it aside. Later, when this is over, you can decide what kind of relationship you want with her."

Farrah slid the letter toward me. "Take it. Throw it out. Burn it. I don't need to read it again."

I took the letter and slipped it into my bag. I wouldn't burn it. I'd keep it for Farrah if she ever changed her mind.

"Your mother said some things about your dad. How controlling he was. That he was physically abusive and threatened to kill her. She left you in that environment. I know this is tough to talk about. I don't want to be insensitive, but it could be important at trial."

Slowly, she lifted her eyes to meet mine. "You want to know if my father ever hit me? If he transferred that need to control to me. The answer to both your questions is yes. But I don't want to talk about it. It doesn't matter. There won't be a shrink taking the stand in my defense. I've never submitted to one."

"Your mental state is at issue in this case. Your medical records might come in. The prosecution is arguing this was a crime of passion. So ..."

"I didn't kill Terry. You've never actually asked me that. I understand why. And until this second, I didn't care whether

The Client List

you believed I had or not. That letter from my mother? Maybe don't throw it away. You should read it yourself. She thinks I'm guilty. She assumes Terry was just like my father. She talks about how many times she fantasized about putting a bullet through him for what he did to her. She can't see past her own nose. It wasn't like that between Terry and me. There was no crime of passion. There was no crime at all. I didn't kill him. But you don't want my mother anywhere near this. You better hope the prosecution doesn't drag her into court. Because she's going to get on the stand and tell that jury she thinks I'm capable of this."

If I could have set fire to that letter right then and there, I might have. Farrah was right. The prosecution would absolutely make hay with it if they got a hold of Leighann Sibley. I hoped she slipped quietly back into the woodwork.

"I'm sorry." I said. "You didn't deserve a mother like that. Or a father."

"You know something about that, don't you?"

"What do you mean?"

"You didn't have a mother either. Or much of a father."

"No."

"It's hard being the one who has to take care of everything all the time. I've been thirty years old since I was five. Do you know what that's like?"

"Yes. I do."

"I thought you did. I can tell. Terry? He took care of things. He was a grownup. I'm sure a shrink would have a field day analyzing all that. I've got daddy issues. Terry was the father figure I craved, blah blah blah. I suppose that's all true. He's what I needed. But I was what he needed. It wasn't one-sided. He wasn't predatory. Neither was I. And now, nobody's ever going to hear about that. They won't understand. They're going to reduce what we had to a series of awful texts and voicemails I sent because I was hurt. Because people like Lionel Harriman got in Terry's ear and made him question everything. I didn't kill Terry. But I should have killed Lionel."

"He's going to take the stand. Probably one of Bailey's first witnesses. All this anger you have. You need to bottle it. You need to keep that hatred out of your eyes and not react when he says all the terrible things you hate him for. Do you understand me?"

Her face changed. In an instant, the deep lines of worry and despair disappeared. She lifted the corners of her mouth, letting the light come into her eyes.

A chameleon. A changeling.

It sent a cold stab of fear through me. I wanted to believe her. But as I looked into Farrah Sibley's eyes, I saw nothing there but blackness.

"You'll cream the detective," Jeanie said. We sat around the conference room table staring at the mound of copies of exhibits Jason Bailey would introduce. I'd written a list of his most likely witnesses on the whiteboard. He'd provided a formal witness list weeks ago, but in typical lawyerly fashion, had kitchen-sinked it.

The Client List

"Eklund's decent on the stand," Eric said. "He's been around a long time. The prosecutors love him. You're gonna wanna be careful how you handle him. He won't be rattled by the obvious things."

"He's convinced Farrah's guilty," I said. "He's got tunnel vision. I'll exploit that."

"The work was solid," Eric said. "Eklund's methodical. He's going to anticipate where you're headed with that."

"Do you put Farrah on the stand? Have you decided?" Jeanie asked. She was coming to Ann Arbor with me for this one. With Tori still not completely up to courtroom work, I needed eyes in the back of my head. Jeanie would be that.

"I can't trust that she'll hold up under cross. She gets these flashes where you can see her wheels turning. It could come across as cold. Calculating. The safer play is to keep her away from Bailey."

"Those voicemails are going to be the killer." Tori came in. She was steadier on her feet than I'd seen her in weeks. Her hard, grueling work in physical therapy had started to pay off.

"It might be good to let the jury hear Farrah in real time," Eric said. "Give them a different impression of her. Because Tori's right. Those voicemails are bad."

"There's no way to keep them out?" Miranda stood in the doorway, sipping a coffee from a Sesame Street mug one of her nieces gave her.

"Rix tried," I said. "Motion to suppress got shot down. It's one of the last things he did before his heart attack."

"He knew he was gonna lose," Eric muttered.

I swatted him in the arm. "Hey. Ye of little faith."

"I'm sorry. You're gonna give this girl a fighting chance. I've seen stranger things happen, but if I'm betting, Eklund and Bailey have the better case. There's just something about that woman. She just reads guilty, you know? And that's without her even saying a word."

"Lucky for her, *reading* guilty isn't the burden of proof."

Eric raised his hands in surrender. "I'm just saying. Prepare yourself. Anderson Rix handed you a hot steaming pile of garbage. This wasn't exactly a gift."

"Cass has won harder cases than this one." Tori came to my defense.

"Thank you," I said.

"I said I'm sorry. But do you want me to just blow smoke up your ass or do my actual job?"

"It's okay. I appreciate the perspective. And I know what you mean. Farrah's a problem. Sometimes I see how vulnerable she is. When she told me she didn't kill Dowd the other day, I believed her. I really did. Then a second later, something just came into her eyes and it sent a chill through me. She's cunning. If the jury sees even a hint of that, she's sunk. I think Rix knew that, too. I think in the end the stress of this one got to him."

"Just don't let it get to you," Eric said. He leaned over and kissed me on the cheek. "I'll also make it my job to try to alleviate some of that stress. Whatever you need."

"Your honest opinion. That's what I need. And you gave it. What about the rest of you? Jeanie? Miranda? Tori? Do you think she's guilty? Do you think I've got a shot at winning this thing?"

Jeanie smiled. "And you're smart enough to know those things aren't mutually exclusive."

"That's not an answer," I said. "I'll come back to you. Tori?"

Tori looked at the whiteboard. "I think you've got reasonable doubt. And I've seen you in action enough to know Bailey is sitting in his office right now more nervous than you are. He should be. As to the rest of it? I don't know if I think she actually did it. Anderson Rix believed in her. So I'm gonna go out on a limb here and say I think she's actually innocent."

Miranda came further into the room. She picked up a copy of the crime scene photo showing Dowd laying half in and half out of his car.

"I think she's innocent. I don't know. I just think if this were a true crime of passion, she would have shot him more than once. I don't know why I think that. It's not scientific. But that's my gut. Oh, and you're gonna win. Bank on it."

"Thanks. That just leaves you, Jeanie. Give it to me straight."

"The case is winnable," she said. "If anyone can, it's you. Tori's right. Bailey knows that. Anderson Rix's untimely demise was the worst thing that's happened to Bailey's career. But I gotta be honest. That girl? She did it. She killed Dowd. I mean ... probably."

Miranda put down the crime scene photo right in front of me. At this angle, Dowd seemed to be staring right through me, his face frozen in time as he died possibly looking at his killer.

I just hoped my instincts were right this time.

Chapter 13

THE HONORABLE CLAUDIA MCGEE ran a tight courtroom. She took the bench at exactly 8:00 a.m. and ran us through voir dire with minimal drama and fair rulings. By 11:30, we had our jury. In all my years trying cases, it was one of the most well-balanced panels I'd ever seen. Six men. Six women. Four baby boomers, four millennials, four members of Gen Z. A true cross section of socio-economic and education levels. Though it all looked good on paper, Jeanie slipped me a note as Jason Bailey rose to deliver his opening statements one minute past noon after we'd come back from lunch.

"Front row," it read. "Juror numbers two and five. They already hate Farrah. Watch out for them."

I crumpled the note quickly. Farrah didn't see it. She sat with her head down, her pen poised over the notepad I'd given her. She had strict instructions not to react to whatever Bailey was about to say.

She looked pretty today. Dressed conservatively in a muted blue suit, her hair pulled back in a matching headband. She wore little makeup and it made her look young enough to be a teenager.

"Good afternoon," Jason Bailey started. I watched the jury. He'd played well with them all morning. Gone was the smarmy attitude he'd shown me in his office all those weeks ago. He was young. Fresh-faced. Eager. He practically vaulted out of his seat and over to the lectern. He gushed a little. Seemed out of breath. But I watched his hands as he turned the pages in his trial binder. Steady. Not a hint of a tremble.

"Ladies and gentlemen, there's a famous quote from Maya Angelou. I believe it was, when someone shows you who they are, believe them. Throughout this trial, you're going to see evidence of Farrah Sibley showing us who she was."

He paused, looking straight at Farrah, which forced the jury to. Farrah sat still as a stone, keeping her gaze forward, not looking toward the jury.

"Terrence Dowd was a complicated man," Bailey continued. "A brilliant legal mind. Savvy businessman. A cunning and zealous advocate for the clients he represented. And you should know a little bit about those clients. Terrence made his career championing cases against some of the largest employers in the state. If you were injured at work, he's the man you'd want standing in this courtroom fighting for you. I had the pleasure of seeing him in action a time or two delivering opening statements, grilling some corporate executive on the stand ... it was something to see. There's no question that Terrence Dowd was one of the best lawyers in the state. I for one will miss him, though I didn't know him on a personal level."

Bailey moved out from behind the lectern. He paused in front of his table. Sitting directly behind it were two of Dowd's ex-wives.

The Client List

The third, Shondra, had been kept out of the courtroom. Later, she might take the witness stand for the prosecution. As if on cue, ex-wife number one, Jennifer Dowd, dabbed her eye with a hanky.

"In his personal life," Bailey continued, "Terrence was less artful. He was bad at relationships. Bad at marriage. His former wives will tell you he was much better at being an ex-husband."

This got a smattering of laughs throughout the courtroom. Bailey smiled, pleased that his joke landed.

"Terrence made bad decisions in his love life. And unfortunately, the last one ended in his murder."

Bailey walked between the prosecution and defense tables, pausing right next to Farrah. She stayed stock still beside me, folding her hands in her lap.

"Farrah Sibley was a star pupil in law school. Top of her class. She had the potential to be as good in the courtroom as Terrence was. He was her mentor, after all. Cunning. Intelligent. A genius level IQ, Terrence once wrote about her. She had her pick of law firms when she graduated from U of M. Harriman Dowd was a plum placement. Highly competitive. Lionel Harriman and Terrence Dowd were only interested in the best of the best. They could afford to be selective. But Terrence chose Farrah Sibley on the strength of her academic work and her impressive performance in a mock trial competition he judged. He said she was a master at delivering her closing arguments. That she had a keen sense of the jury's attitudes toward her. A skill Terrence Dowd said couldn't be taught. But Farrah Sibley has it."

It was a good technique. Bailey was trying to convince the jury Farrah was capable of manipulating them before they even heard a shred of evidence.

"Ladies and gentlemen," Bailey said. "Over the course of this trial, you're going to hear the story of how Terrence Dowd took Farrah Sibley under his wing. You'll understand what he saw in her. What he hoped they could accomplish together. But you'll also hear how Terrence could never live up to Farrah's expectations. As their relationship went on, she wanted more and more from him. How over and over, Terrence tried to appease her to no avail. How she stalked him. Threatened him. Tried to cut him off from friends and family. And in the end, nothing he did was enough for her.

"You'll hear Farrah's own voice on the dozens of disturbing voicemails she left him. And how each time, Terrence tried to help her. To give her what she wanted. In the end, to simply love her. But none of it mattered. And when Terrence finally realized the relationship was unsalvageable, that his very career, the thing he'd worked his whole life to build, was in jeopardy, he tried to end things. He wasn't a perfect man. He had flaws like all of us. He came to realize involving himself romantically with Farrah Sibley was a mistake. A fatal one.

"You can see the ending to this story coming almost from day one of their relationship. Everyone could. Terrence Dowd's business partner, his friends, his ex-wives. Everyone close to him tried to warn him. Even Farrah herself tried to warn him. But in his personal relationships, Terrence led with his heart.

"You'll hear the final message Farrah left for Terrence. It will chill you to the bone. Farrah told Terrence exactly what she planned to do to him if he insisted on ending their romance. If she couldn't have him, no one would. Then Farrah made good

The Client List

on that threat. She took a loaded handgun that she'd purchased legally some years before. She approached him alone in the parking lot of the law firm. We don't know what she said to him that night. Or what he said to her. But whatever it was, Farrah Sibley shot Terrence Dowd at point-blank range in the chest. Then she left him there, bleeding out, and drove herself home.

"It's a story we've all heard before. It's simple even as it's horrific. Farrah Sibley was a master manipulator. It was the thing she trained for as a lawyer. The thing that set her apart and brought her into Terrence Dowd's life. And ultimately, tragically, it was the thing that cost Terrence Dowd his life and deprived him from the rest of the world. Just as Farrah Sibley warned him it would. She showed Terrence who she was. She showed her coworkers, her family, and her friends. During the course of this trial, the evidence will show you who she is as well. All I'm asking is that you believe her."

AFTER MY OPENING, things were about to get terrible. I knew it. I'd done what I could to prepare Farrah for it. Now, the only thing I could do was try to prepare the jury for it.

"Good afternoon," I said. "I want to start by thanking you. You have an unenviable job. Over the next few days, you're going to be drawn into a tragedy. Terrence Dowd's loss has left a hole in the lives of the people who loved him and to this community. You didn't ask for this. But you're here. You're serving your duty and I appreciate it more than you know.

"At the end of this trial, after you've heard all the evidence. Sat through the testimony of witnesses who will make you cry. Frustrate you. And soon you'll have to look at images that will stay with you for the rest of your lives. I have no doubt you will walk out of this courtroom as different people than when you walked in."

I paused in front of the lectern. A quick scan of the jury and I had all of their eyes. Their attention. I saw Jeanie in my peripheral vision. She leaned over and whispered something to Farrah who still stared straight ahead. Stoic. That was good. For now.

"Mr. Bailey wants to tell you a story. He said as much. He has a good one. The kind they make movies about. With a beautiful femme fatale. A tragic victim. Money. Power. Intrigue. It's all so very compelling. Sells tickets. Keeps you turning the pages. I could almost hear the soundtrack Mr. Bailey wants playing in the background. A full orchestra maybe. A dramatic crescendo.

"The problem is, that's not why you're here. You're here to judge facts. You're here to make sure that Mr. Bailey does his job. Justice demands that you ignore storytellers. That you decide whether Jason Bailey has met his burden of proof. It's not about ticket sales or music scores. It's about facts. It's about whether Mr. Bailey can prove his case beyond a reasonable doubt.

"I only ask that you remember that. When Mr. Bailey's witnesses take the stand, ask yourself. Even if what this person said is true, does it prove beyond a reasonable doubt that Farrah Sibley committed the crime for which she's been charged? If the answer is no. Or even if the answer is I'm not sure. Then Mr. Bailey has failed.

"Farrah Bailey didn't murder Terrence Dowd. She did a lot of things wrong. Things she's not proud of. But love is messy sometimes. Breakups are painful. Ugly. We say things we don't mean in the heat of passion. We hurt people when we're hurt. But it's not proof of murder. Remember that. It's only proof of being human.

"During the last month of Terrence Dowd's life, Farrah Sibley wasn't her best self. Neither was Terrence Dowd. But the only thing Farrah Sibley is guilty of is handling a breakup badly. At most. And that's the thing you have to keep in your mind as you hear some of the evidence in this case. If it were you. Or your daughter. Your sister. Your best girlfriend. After everything, Terrence and Farrah were to each other? Would you, would they have had moments of weakness where you said something you didn't mean? Have you ever? Think about that. Think about the very worst thing you've ever said or texted to someone you cared about when you were angry. You might regret it later. You might wish you could have taken it back. We're all guilty of that, I think. But it's not proof of murder.

"Farrah Sibley isn't guilty of murder. She didn't kill Terrence Dowd. Did she hurt him? Yes. As he hurt her in the end. But Farrah is nothing more than a convenient, if not compelling story in the eyes of the prosecution. Because that's all he has. A story that might play on your emotions. He wants you to be angry. He wants you furious and wishing to avenge Terrence Dowd. That's understandable. We want answers. We want to make sure whoever did this to Mr. Dowd pays for it. We want to make sure it never happens again. But none of those things have anything to do with your duty in this case. As much as you may think you have a duty to Terrence Dowd, your real duty is to Farrah Sibley. Don't let Jason Bailey get away with convincing you otherwise.

"Reasonable doubt. Is what you're about to hear proof of murder? Or is it merely proof of bad breakup behavior? That's the real question ... the only question you need to keep in your mind. When you do that. When you refuse to allow yourself to be sucked in by a story, I'm confident you'll see it for what it is. Nothing more than a fairy tale. Thank you."

"Mr. Bailey?" Judge McGee said before I'd even gotten back to my table. "You may call your first witness."

Jason Bailey stared a hole through me as I passed him. He straightened his jacket, cleared his throat, and called out the name of his first witness.

"The state calls Detective Madeline Tate to the stand."

Yes, I thought. Things were about to get very terrible very quickly.

Chapter 14

Madeline Tate would prove a formidable witness. I knew this going in. The woman had been a digital forensics detective before there was even a term for the word. And Bailey was smart, taking her through her background and foundational testimony in a conversational style.

"You've been at this for a while?" he asked.

"A minute or two." Detective Tate smiled. "When I started, cell phones weren't even used for texting. Now, they've become an even more critical piece of evidence at murder scenes than an actual smoking gun, so to speak."

"I see," Bailey said. "And will you explain to the jury how you came to be involved in this case?"

"I was contacted by Detective Lars Eklund, of the Ann Arbor Police. He is the lead investigator in the Terrence Dowd murder. He had collected the cell phone found at the scene. We established it belonged to the victim, Terrence Dowd. Detective Eklund asked me to perform a forensic analysis of the data on that phone. And so I did. A day later, he asked me to do the same for the phone belonging to the defendant, Farrah Sibley."

After going through her credentials, Bailey quickly pivoted to the meat of Detective Tate's testimony.

"Detective, what kinds of information were you able to retrieve from Terrence Dowd's cell phone, if any?"

"Well, first, I focused on the location of the phone and its movement in the twenty-four hours prior to the discovery of Mr. Dowd's body."

"What can you tell me about that analysis?"

We had already stipulated to the entry of Detective Tate's report. Bailey pulled up a few critical pages from it and projected it on the large screen pointed toward the jury. Tate used a laser pointer to indicate which lines of data she was speaking about at any given time.

"The closest tower to the Belz Building, the parking garage in which the victim was found, is located at Chaney Park off State Street. So if the phone was at Belz Building, it would ping that tower. I have it doing just that beginning at 7:47 a.m. on the morning of July 17th. And that's where it stayed until Detective Eklund's people retrieved it after the discovery of Mr. Dowd's body the next morning at 8:17."

"So for twenty-four hours, the phone didn't leave the Belz Building?"

I readied myself to object, but Madeline Tate was a beat ahead of me. "That's not my testimony," she said. "I'm saying the phone pinged the Chaney Park tower from the morning of July 17th to the morning of July 18th. So it was in the general vicinity of the Belz Building. That's the scope of my testimony."

The Client List

I slowly sat back down. I liked the woman. She'd given me an opening. But I knew it would make the rest of her testimony that much easier for the jury to accept.

"Okay," Bailey said. "Were you able to retrieve a call list or text history from Mr. Dowd's phone?"

"Absolutely."

"Let's focus on the texts in the forty-eight hours before Mr. Dowd's body was discovered. What can you tell me?"

"Mr. Dowd wasn't much of a texter. I can tell you that. He sent two texts in the three days prior to his murder. One to a person in his contacts listed as Liddy. We tracked that contact down to Lydia Whitford, Mr. Dowd's legal secretary. This went out at 7:08 p.m. on the evening of July 17th."

"What did it say?"

"Coming in early tomorrow to work on Runyon. Do I have interrogatories on my desk? And she responded yes two minutes after that text was sent."

"What was the other text sent out in the days before he died?"

"He responded to confirm a dentist appointment on July 20th, which would have been three days after his date of death."

"Okay. So those are the outgoing texts. What about incoming texts?"

"Mr. Dowd received quite a few incoming text messages in the three days prior to his death."

"Can you tell us what those were?"

"Two were responses to the outgoing texts which I've already described. His dentist's office. His legal secretary, Lydia

Whitford, regarding the Runyon matter. But he received seventeen text messages from July 14th to July 17th. All originating from Farrah Sibley's phone. They begin on July 14th at 6:42 p.m."

Bailey paused. He flipped to a new screen on the overhead. This one had blown-up screenshots from Terrence Dowd's phone.

"Detective, would you read these texts into the record?"

"Of course."

> I'm sorry.

> ?

> Terry, I'm sorry. I didn't mean to lose my temper. I can do better.

> Terry, talk to me. We can't talk about this at the office. There are too many ears.

> I love you, okay?

> ?

> Goddammit, Terry. I'm not going to be ghosted. I don't deserve that.

> Terry, please call me. Or answer your phone. You know what? Fuck you. I don't deserve this. I'm sorry about the voicemail I left. I was angry. I didn't mean it.

> You know what? You are the person everyone warned me about. You're a vindictive asshole.

> Terry, please. I love you. You know that. I know you love me too. Don't throw this all away over nothing.

> Are you a child? Lionel's not your daddy. The way you suck up to him. Grovel to him is sickening. You're sick, Terry. You need help. Lionel is nothing without you, not the other way around. He's threatened by me. Can't you see it? Fuck you for not being able to see it. You're a little boy. You're weak. Time for you to be a man. I'm the only person in your life who treats you like one. I guess you can't handle it after all.
>
> Terry? Where are you? I'm getting worried. I drove by your house so we could talk face to face. Please, please call me back.
>
> I love you. I'll see you at the office in the morning. Maybe we can talk.

Tate looked up. "That last one, starting with I love you. That was sent on July 16th, Sunday night at 11:38 p.m."

"Thank you," Bailey said. "What about incoming or outgoing calls on Dowd's phone?"

"There was one outgoing call the day before his murder to Barton Hills Golf Course. As far as incoming, there are fourteen missed calls from Ms. Sibley's phone number in the seventy-two hours prior to the discovery of Mr. Dowd's body. In one of them, she left a voicemail."

"When was that voicemail sent?"

"At 9:17 p.m. on Sunday the 16th."

"So that's the day before the murder?"

"Objection," I said. "This witness isn't qualified to testify about the time of death."

"Sustained," Judge McGee said.

"Withdrawn," Bailey said. "Your Honor, I'd like to play the voicemail in question admitted as State's Exhibit 11."

"You may proceed," she said.

Farrah Sibley might not take the stand. But over the next thirty seconds, the jury heard her voice loud and clear.

"You think you're being cute, Terry," she said in the recording. Her voice bounced off the tile floors. "You have to deal with me sooner or later. But you have to deal with yourself first. Unless you plan on being under Lionel Harriman's thumb forever. That's what he wants, you know. To control you. To make you his little dancing monkey. And you've let him. You make me sick, you know that? A little boy when I thought I was getting a real man. I'm the best thing that ever happened to you. You're at the top of your game with me. Let's see how well you do without me. You'll be miserable. Just Lionel's little lap dog. But maybe that's what you like.

"Terry, I know you're screening me. I don't appreciate it. I need you to pick up the phone and deal with me. You're acting like a little baby. I've put up with about as much as I'm going to. You don't get to screw me over like this. Terry? Terry! I'm done playing around. You got that? You will deal with me. I can make things difficult but I don't want to do that."

Her voice trailed off. For ten seconds, the courtroom filled with the sounds of Farrah's sobs.

"I love you," she blurted on the recording. "I'm the only one who will ever love you the way you need to be loved. I know you love me. I know it. You're letting other people get into your head. Believe ME. Trust ME! If you don't ... if you keep shutting me out ... I will not allow it. You hear me? I will not. You're gonna see it, Terry. Soon. I'll make you feel it. You're gonna be so sorry for crossing me. You don't know what you're throwing away. So I'll show you, okay? I'll fucking show you! You WILL deal with me, Terry."

The rest of the message was unintelligible sobbing.

Bailey waited a good thirty seconds, letting the last echoes of Farrah Sibley's hysterical message settle in the jury's mind. He stood in front of the lectern, arms crossed, gazing downward.

"Thank you, Detective," he said. "When was that message sent again?"

"9:16 p.m. Sunday the 16th of July."

"So approximately eighteen hours before the discovery of Mr. Dowd's body?"

"I believe so."

"Did he return that call?"

"He did not."

"Objection," I said. "That's beyond the scope of this witness's qualifications and report."

"Sustained, Mr. Bailey. The jury will disregard that last answer."

"Detective, was the phone call from Ms. Sibley returned from Terrence Dowd's cell phone?"

"There were no other outgoing calls from Dowd's cell phone from Saturday onward. So no. He didn't return that call on his cell phone."

"Thank you. Did you also run a forensic analysis of Ms. Sibley's cell phone?"

"Yes, incident to a warrant written by Detective Eklund. We retrieved Farrah Sibley's phone on Tuesday, July 18th."

"The day after the murder."

"The day after the discovery of the body, yes."

"Okay. I won't belabor the jury by having you read the texts from Ms. Sibley's phone that were included in your recitation of those from Mr. Dowd's phone. But let me ask you this, were you also able to triangulate the position of Ms. Sibley's phone in the days before Mr. Dowd's murder?"

"Yes."

"What can you tell me about her movements?"

"Objection," I said. "Again, this is beyond the scope of this witness's knowledge."

"I'll rephrase," Bailey said. "What can you tell me about the location of Ms. Sibley's phone in the days prior to Mr. Dowd's murder?"

"The Thursday and Friday prior to the murder, Ms. Sibley's cell phone pinged the tower at Chaney Park from 8:00 a.m. to 7:00 p.m. both days. This is indicative of Ms. Sibley being present in the office building ... the Belz Building. Both evenings, the phone traveled in a path, pinging the towers along State Street. From 7:30 to 8:30 p.m., the phone pinged the tower on Lohr Road. This was consistent with two scans of an app on the phone to Fitness Universe. There is a gym on Lohr close to that tower. Then the phone traveled again after 8:30 on both those Thursday and Friday nights ..."

"Objection," I said. "Your Honor, I fail to see the relevance of Ms. Sibley's gym habits days before the timeline in question."

The Client List

"I agree, please move on, Mr. Bailey."

"All right. Detective, was there anything significant about the location of Ms. Sibley's phone the weekend of July 15th?"

"The morning of July 15th, Saturday, the phone was on the move and traveling north on N. Main Street. At 10:57 a.m. the phone stops moving and remains stationary, pinging the tower nearest Barton Hills."

Detective Bailey showed the tower on the map.

"Is there anything significant about that tower?"

"It's the tower closest to Terrence Dowd's residence on Parkridge Drive. Ms. Sibley's phone remains there for twenty-two minutes, then travels south on Main Street before becoming stationary again, pinging the tower near Kerrytown, consistent with Ms. Sibley's home address on Beakes Street. It doesn't move again until Monday morning when it travels back to the Chaney Park tower for the remainder of that business day."

"We're talking July 17th. The last day of Mr. Dowd's life?"

"Yes."

"How long was the phone at the Belz Building?"

"From 8:02 a.m. to 9:33 p.m. that Monday evening. From there, it travels the same path back to the tower near Ms. Sibley's home. It remains there through the night until the next morning where it travels back to Chaney Park near the Belz Building at 7:47 a.m."

"So on July 17th from say 5:00 p.m. to 9:33 p.m., you're saying Ms. Sibley's phone is stationary?"

"Yes," Detective Tate said. "Pinging the Chaney Park tower."

"And where was Mr. Dowd's phone located at this same time?"

"Also pinging the Chaney Park tower."

"And his doesn't move again?"

"Correct. It never moves again."

"Can you clarify again? What is the date and time of the last text from Ms. Sibley's phone to Mr. Dowd's?"

"That message on July 16th at 9:16 p.m. was the last communication from Ms. Sibley's phone to Mr. Dowd's."

"She didn't call or text him on July 17th?"

"Not from her phone, no. But as I testified, both of their phones were pinging the same tower all day on the 17th."

"She wouldn't need to text him. She could have talked to him face to face."

"That's not for me to speculate."

"Fair enough. But there are no calls or texts on the evening of July 17th, after Ms. Sibley's phone was back near the tower by her home."

"No. Not to Mr. Dowd or anyone else."

"In the preceding, say, two weeks, was she calling or texting him every evening?"

"Yes. There's at least one text to Mr. Dowd every evening from July 1st through July 16th after Ms. Sibley's phone is closest to her home tower."

"Every single night. But not on July 17th after she left the Belz Building."

"Objection," I said. "Counsel cannot establish that Ms. Sibley was in the Belz Building, only where her cell phone might have been."

"I'll rephrase. She didn't text or call him the night of the 17th even though you've got records that she did every previous night the entire month of July?"

"That's correct."

"Thank you, Detective. I have no further questions."

"Your witness Ms. Leary," the judge said.

"Detective Tate," I started. "I just want to clarify a few things from your direct testimony, then I'll have you on your way.

"You have no idea whether Farrah Sibley was at the Belz Building on the evening of July 17th when this murder was alleged to have taken place, do you?"

"No, ma'am," she said. "I can only tell you where her cell phone was."

"And from the period of 5:00 p.m. to 9:33 p.m. that night when you say it left the range of the Chaney Park tower, were there any outgoing texts?"

"No."

"Outgoing phone calls?"

"No."

"Any emails sent out from Ms. Sibley from the phone at that time?"

"No."

"Any other indication from the phone or Ms. Sibley's computer that she was actively using that phone during that timeframe?"

"Other than it being turned on, connected to Wi-Fi, and located in the vicinity of the Belz Building, no."

"The vicinity of the Belz Building," I said. "I'm glad you brought that up. What is the approximate range of the Chaney Park tower?"

"It's about a half-a-mile square."

"Looking at the tower map, there are other office buildings in that half-a-mile area, correct?"

"Yes."

"Other restaurants. A dry cleaner."

"I believe so, yes."

"How many city blocks are we talking about?" I asked.

"I believe four."

"Ms. Sibley's phone could have been at any of those locations within that half-a-mile radius within that timeframe, correct? And it would still ping the Chaney Park tower?"

"That's correct."

"Thank you."

I folded my hands and rested them on the lectern.

"You have no idea what, if any, response Mr. Dowd might have made to any of Ms. Sibley's voicemails, correct?"

"I don't know what you mean."

"I mean, he might have called her from another phone. You're saying you tracked her phone to a tower near Mr. Dowd's home the previous Saturday morning. You have no idea if they spoke or what was said."

"Of course not, no."

"So, in that sense, isn't it true that your digital forensic analysis is limited?"

"Of course."

"Texting itself is limited, isn't it? Meaning ... you can't always know the context of messages sent, isn't that right?"

"That's correct."

"Whether the sender was joking. Or using sarcasm."

"I can't tell that, no."

"And you have no idea what the intent was behind any of the texts sent, do you?"

"I'm not a psychologist, no. It's not my job to interpret emotions."

"You found no messages on Ms. Sibley's phone to anyone else regarding her relationship with Mr. Dowd, did you?"

"She doesn't appear to have texted anyone else about him, no."

"And he didn't text anyone about her, did he?"

"No."

"I see."

I tapped my pen on my notepad. "Thank you, Detective Tate. I have no further questions."

"Any redirect, Mr. Bailey?" Judge McGee asked.

Bailey rose, still staring at his notes. He leaned over and whispered something to his paralegal. Nodding, he looked back up at the judge. "No further questions, Your Honor."

"You're free to go, Detective Tate. We have time for one more witness today, Mr. Bailey."

"Thank you, Your Honor. The state calls Lydia Whitford to the stand."

The bailiff opened the courtroom door and ushered Terrence Dowd's legal secretary to the stand. She gave Farrah a cold stare as she passed her, then raised her hand, crisp as any soldier, and took her oath.

Chapter 15

"Ms. Whitford," Bailey started.

"It's *Mrs.* Whitford. I'm sorry, but I am a happily married woman and proud of it."

"Of course, Mrs. Whitford."

"My Ronnie passed away eight years ago," she said. "But in the eyes of the Lord we are still married. I'm still his wife."

"Of course, I'm very sorry for your loss."

Farrah scribbled something on her notepad and angled it so I could read it.

"See what you're gonna be dealing with?"

I gave her a pursed-lipped, slight nod.

"Mrs. Whitford," Bailey restarted. "Will you please tell the jury what your role is with Harriman Dowd and how you came to know the defendant and Mr. Dowd?"

"I'm a legal secretary, though that particular term is frowned upon nowadays. I never minded. I started working for Mr. Harriman thirty years ago at his former firm. When he decided to branch out and start the firm with Mr. Dowd, he asked me to work for him there. He took me and his paralegal at the time, Greg Lilly. That was it. Barebones staff. I started out doing general secretarial duties because of the lack of bodies. But as we expanded, Mr. Harriman hired a couple of receptionists and office administrators. I was able to move back into an actual legal secretarial role. When that happened, I began to work exclusively for Mr. Dowd in my day to day."

"What types of things did you do for Mr. Dowd?"

"I kept track of his docket. Made his appointments. Prepared his pleadings. Wrote correspondence for his signature. On occasion, he'd have me take on some light research. Pull statutes and case law, that sort of thing. Mr. Dowd always did his own legal research and wrote his own briefs. Even up until the day he died."

"What about Ms. Sibley? When did you become acquainted with her?"

"She was hired as a summer clerk four years ago. Mr. Dowd always took on law students between their second and third years. That was true of Ms. Sibley. If those clerks worked out, they were offered part-time employment during their third year. He offered her that position and she took it. Then after she graduated, the firm hired her as a full-time clerk then an associate, pending her passage of the bar."

"And she fulfilled those requirements?"

"She did. She was promoted to full-time junior associate going on three years ago."

"What were her duties as Mr. Dowd's associate?"

"She had a supportive role. She didn't take on clients of her own. She helped Mr. Dowd manage his existing clients. She sat in on meetings with them in the beginning. Eventually, she would meet with certain clients on her own. She helped Mr. Dowd complete legal research, though as I said, he would always write his own briefs. She began to appear in certain hearings on Mr. Dowd's behalf. Then eventually, she would serve as second chair if he went to trial."

"So, would you say they had a close working relationship?"

"Oh yes. Mr. Dowd started to refer to Ms. Sibley as his right arm. Though if you ask me, that's an exaggeration."

"Why do you say that?"

"Terrence Dowd was a brilliant lawyer. He didn't need a separate right arm. He didn't need help. Did it make his life easier? Sure."

"Mrs. Whitford, was there ever a time when Mr. Dowd and Ms. Sibley's relationship turned into something other than simply professional?"

Lydia Whitford squirmed in her chair. "Yes." She barked out the word.

"Can you explain what you mean?"

"You have to understand a little bit about Terrence Dowd the man. He had his flaws."

"Such as?"

"I said he was a brilliant lawyer. He was. Professionally, nobody could match him. Personally, his conduct could be questionable."

"What do you mean?"

"He was known as somewhat of a womanizer. Understand, I worked side by side with him for over twenty years. In that time, he went through three divorces. I was friendly with all of his ex-wives."

"Okay, but going back to Ms. Sibley. What did you mean when you said their relationship became something other than professional?"

"They became romantically involved."

"And how did you know this?"

"Well, if you'd let me finish a thought."

"By all means."

Mrs. Whitford's nostrils flared with annoyance. She was doing a lot of my work for me simply with her attitude. I had a good idea how to exploit that on cross.

"Mr. Dowd liked the pretty ones," she said. "I knew there was going to be trouble the second he hired Farrah Sibley. She was his type."

"His type?"

"Yes. Blonde. Thin. Buxom. And she was completely enamored of him."

"Objection," I said. "We're veering into speculation here. If the witness could be instructed to keep her testimony to what she personally observed."

"Sustained. Mrs. Whitford, if you would please refrain from speculating on the motives of the defendant or anyone else."

"Fine," she said. "But what I'm telling you is that Terrence Dowd had a pattern with the type of women he chose to romance. Take a look at the front row. Two of his ex-wives are sitting behind Mr. Bailey's table. You see what I mean? Blonde. Thin. Pretty."

"Objection," I said. "The witness is unresponsive."

"Mrs. Whitford," Judge McGee said, her irritation rising. "You will answer questions when asked, not provide off-the-cuff commentary. Do you understand?"

"Fine."

"Ask your question, Mr. Bailey," the judge said.

"Mrs. Whitford, when did Mr. Dowd and Ms. Sibley become romantically involved, if you know?"

"It was sometime the summer before last. We have a firm picnic at Gallup Park. It's an annual thing. Everyone brings their families. Well, I went to the restroom and I saw Mr. Dowd and Ms. Sibley kissing each other behind a building. They were all over each other."

"Was that a surprise to you?"

"It was not. There had been a flirtation before that. I just knew how Mr. Dowd operated. Joking. Calling Ms. Sibley into his office several times a day, then shutting the door. Bringing her coffee. Hovering near her when she went to the copier. Taking extended lunches with her. Then they started arriving together. I saw them getting out of his car when he came into work earlier that spring. But you asked me when I knew for sure they were romantically involved. It would have been at that summer picnic when I saw them kissing. After that, they were far less discreet as they saw me. They knew I was already aware."

"Did Mr. Dowd or Ms. Sibley ever speak to you about their budding relationship?"

"No. Not then."

"But later?"

"Yes."

"What happened?"

"Mr. Dowd, as I said ... his professionalism was impeccable. Or it was, up until he started seeing Ms. Sibley romantically. But as the year went on, there were certain behaviors I observed that were disturbing, to say the least."

"Like what?"

"Like they started carrying on in the office. That wasn't normal for Mr. Dowd."

"What do you mean by carrying on?"

"I mean they were having carnal relations in the office. I caught them. That's not something Mr. Dowd would have ever engaged in before. So I have to assume Ms. Sibley put him up to it."

"Objection!"

"Mrs. Whitford, again," the judge said. "Please stick to what you actually observed, not your conjecture."

"Mrs. Whitford," Bailey said. "What did you observe?"

"You want me to say it?"

"I do."

"Fine. This was right around Valentine's Day last year. I walked into Mr. Dowd's office to drop off some papers he needed to sign. I thought he'd left for lunch. I was mistaken. I swear I never would have opened that door if I knew what was going on behind it. But I opened it. I saw Mr. Dowd and Ms. Sibley. They were ... cavorting. On his desk. They were, well, in a state of undress, if you know what I mean. And everything on his desk was scattered all over the floor. Like he swept it all off like in some cheesy romance movie and ravished her on the desk."

"I see. Did you speak to Mr. Dowd about it?"

"Heavens, no. I shut the door and tried to mind my own business. I don't think Ms. Sibley saw me. Er ... the way she was angled, only Mr. Dowd saw me open the door. This is ... do I have to talk about this?"

"How about you just answer my question about whether you discussed it with either of them after the fact?" Bailey said.

"Mr. Dowd came to me the next day. I could tell he was embarrassed. As well he should have been. He apologized. But he told me not to come into his office again without knocking. I can tell you, that wasn't going to be happening anyway."

"Of course." Bailey walked back to his desk and reviewed his notes.

"Mrs. Whitford, you said this was February of last year. Did you ever become aware of a breakup between Mr. Dowd and Ms. Sibley?"

"Yes."

"How so? How did you become aware of it?"

"Mr. Dowd's behavior toward Ms. Sibley began to change. He stopped having lunch with her. Stopped having her come to his office. He froze her out."

"What do you mean?"

"I mean he started giving her the silent treatment. Started giving me notes. Things he wanted communicated to her but didn't want to tell her himself. He expected me to be some kind of go-between. Well, I wasn't having it and I told him so."

"What happened next?"

"This was, I believe, in late May or early June. Ahead of the firm picnic. Ms. Sibley became volatile after that."

"How so? What did you observe?"

"She would snap at him. Insult him right in front of me and the other staff. And even though he stopped calling her into his office, she'd go in uninvited. On one occasion, this was May 9th last year. I know that because it was the day before a major trial Mr. Dowd had. Ms. Sibley was originally going to serve as second chair but he took her off it. Well, she marched right past my office and went into his. She started screaming at him. Told him you can't do this to me. You'll pay for this. I'll make you sorry you treated me like this."

"Those specific words? That's what you heard?"

"Yes, sir. She said I'll make you pay for this. I'll make you sorry you treated me like this. She said that for sure. Then she stormed out. She slammed his door so hard the walls in my office shook."

"Okay. Mrs. Whitford, I know this is hard, but I need to take you back to the morning of July 18th. Can you tell me what happened that day?"

She gripped the witness box as if she were afraid she'd fall out of it.

"That was the morning I found Mr. Dowd."

"Found him where?"

"He had texted me the night before that he was going to come in early that morning to work on a case. He asked if I'd left paperwork for him related to it on his desk. I told him I had. Well, he didn't ask me to come in early but I figured it was a good idea to arrive at the office at 8:00 a.m. I park my car on level 3, all the support staff does. But I park by the stairs and walk up to level 4, which is the stairwell door that opens to the elevators. Anyway, I walked up to level 4 and right past where the senior partners have their reserved parking. I saw Mr. Dowd's car parked in his usual spot but the driver's side door was open. I walked up to his car. That's when I found him. He was dead. He was lying in the doorway of his car and there was blood everywhere. All over his shirt. He was white and stiff and his eyes were still open. It was so awful."

"Mrs. Whitford, may I direct your attention to State's Exhibit Number 12? Can you describe what it is?"

"It's a photograph. A horrible photograph of Mr. Dowd as I found him."

"Is it a clear and accurate representation of what he looked like when you discovered him on the morning of July 18th?"

"I just said it was."

"I'd like to move for entry of State's Exhibit Number 12."

"No objection," I said.

Bailey displayed the image of Terrence Dowd lying half across the front seat of his car, shot through the chest.

The jury took it in. Liddy Whitford dabbed her eyes with a hanky.

"What did you do then, Mrs. Whitford?"

"After I got done screaming, I pulled out my cell phone and called 9-1-1."

"Okay. Thank you. I know this is hard. I'd like to ask you about a few things the day before. Monday. Are you familiar with the billing software used by Harriman Dowd?"

"Of course."

Bailey went through the dance of authenticating certain business records Lydia Whitford kept.

"Mrs. Whitford, I'd like to direct your attention to the entries on page four of State's Exhibit 14. Can you tell me what that shows?"

"These are entries from various copy jobs. We keep the central printer near my desk. Every employee has their own copy or print code. When documents have to be physically printed, whether it's a word document from one of the workstations or from Lexis/Nexis, they come out the main printer. That's how we keep track of which client to bill."

"You're saying each employee has their own print and copy code unique to them?"

"That's correct."

"At 8:27 p.m., there's an entry. Can you explain what that means?"

"There was a print command sent to the main printer. Three court opinions from Lexis, then a memorandum of law. See, Mr. Dowd preferred physical copies of things. He hated reading from a screen."

"Okay. Whose code was used to print these items?"

"Farrah Sibley's."

"At 8:27, you're saying a print job was sent by Farrah Sibley."

"Yes."

"Is there any way that job could have been sent from an offsite location?"

"Like from her house? No. We don't authorize that. I mean, you could theoretically email yourself something as an attachment. But to physically print it, you have to be in the office."

"Thank you, Mrs. Whitford. I have no further questions."

"Ms. Leary?" Judge McGee said.

I grabbed my notes and stepped up to the lectern.

"Mrs. Whitford, a couple of things. I'll start with this business of the print codes as it's probably most fresh in everyone's minds."

"Certainly."

"You don't know who actually sent this print command, do you?"

"What do you mean?"

"I mean, you only know that this code was currently assigned to Farrah Sibley, right?"

"Who else would have sent it?"

"Well, anyone who has that code, correct?"

"But it was Ms. Sibley's code."

"Why was it Ms. Sibley's code?"

"What?"

"Well, isn't it true that code was actually assigned to the summer intern? As in, that's how she got it?"

"That's when she might have gotten it, yes?"

"In fact, those two letters at the beginning of the code, SI, that stands for summer intern."

"Yes."

"And isn't it true that prior to Ms. Sibley's employ, every summer intern was given that exact code? It was associated with the position, not the person, correct?"

"That's correct, but none of the previous summer interns still worked for us."

"She kept the code because she kept her job, right?"

"Right."

"But she wasn't the only person with access to that code, correct? She wasn't the only one who knew it."

"I suppose."

"Do you know when that particular code was first issued?"

The Client List

"We started using that system nine years ago during a security upgrade and when we converted to new billing software."

"Nine years ago. So there were at least five other interns who used that precise code before Ms. Sibley. Because you said she was first hired as a summer clerk four years ago, right?"

"Yes, but as I said, none of them still work for Harriman Dowd, only Ms. Sibley."

"You weren't in the office at 8:27 p.m., right?"

"No. I wasn't."

"So you don't actually know who punched in that code."

"No."

"Mr. Harriman could have even done it, correct?"

"Why would he? He had his own code."

"One that he often forgot, isn't that right?"

"Oh, he forgot it all the time."

"And in those circumstances, you'd print things for him, right, using your code?"

"Sometimes, yes."

"So it's true that different people used different codes, correct? It wasn't a foolproof system, was it?"

"It was as foolproof as the people using it."

"Thank you. I'll move on. You testified about an argument you overheard Mr. Dowd and Ms. Sibley had on May 6th, correct?"

"Yes."

"You claim you heard Ms. Sibley shouting you'll pay for this, you'll be sorry, is that right?"

"Yes."

"But you were in your office. You said the walls shook when she allegedly slammed the door."

"Correct."

"Isn't it true that your office is actually located at the opposite end of the hallway from Mr. Dowd's?"

"What do you mean?"

"Well, I mean his office is right near the elevators, right?"

"Yes."

"And your office is in the opposite corner, right?"

"Yes."

"And how many offices are in between?"

"I think five."

"Five offices down. Got it. Were you in the office working with Mr. Dowd and Ms. Sibley on Monday, July 17th?"

"Of course I was."

"You didn't hear any arguments between them that day, did you?"

"What? No. I don't think so."

"In fact, they were cordial to each other, weren't they?"

"I don't recall."

"You don't recall. But you told the police in your statement that it was a normal workday. Nothing out of the ordinary. That you couldn't believe this happened because you were just talking to Mr. Dowd and he seemed fine. You said he was in a good mood, isn't that right?"

"It's right that I said that, yes."

"And isn't it true that you ate lunch with Ms. Sibley that day in the break room?"

"We ate lunch at the same time, yes."

"Did you speak to her?"

"I'm sure we engaged in small talk, yes."

"You didn't just eat at the same time. You sat at the same table, even though there were other places for you to sit, right?"

"We sat at the same table, yes."

"And Mr. Dowd joined you both, didn't he?"

"He came in at some point, yes. There was some leftover birthday cake from his party a few days before."

"And all three of you ate it together. Isn't that right?"

"I believe so. Yes."

I paused and looked through my notes. "Mrs. Whitford, you mentioned on direct that you've remained friendly with Mr. Dowd's ex-wives, isn't that right?"

"Yes."

"But you're particularly friendly with Shondra Dowd, Mr. Dowd's most current ex-wife. Isn't that right?"

"We are friends, yes."

"She's a frequent travel companion of yours, isn't she? You've gone to Hershey, Pennsylvania with her, Shipshewana, various casinos around the state of Michigan. Isn't that true?"

"We've done those things, yes."

"You weren't happy when Mr. Dowd divorced her, were you?"

"I don't know what you mean."

"Well, I mean, she's your friend. You've testified that you were aware of what you described as Mr. Dowd's philandering ways. When Ms. Sibley was hired, he was still technically married to Shondra, wasn't he?"

"They were separated but trying to work it out."

"And you weren't friends with Farrah Sibley, were you?"

"No. We worked in the same office."

"You don't like her much, do you? I mean ... before Mr. Dowd's death."

"She wasn't my favorite person, no. But if you're implying I'd lie to make her life difficult ..."

"I'm not implying that at all. I'm just trying to understand your relationship to Ms. Sibley, Mrs. Dowd, and the former Mrs. Dowd. You were angry with Ms. Sibley for carrying on with Mr. Dowd, weren't you?"

"I didn't like it."

"You felt she was being predatory, didn't you?"

"I don't know what you mean?"

"You said you spoke to Mr. Dowd about his relations with Ms. Sibley in the office. Did you ever speak to Farrah?"

"We had words."

"Words. In fact, you told her you had your eye on her, didn't you?"

"I may have said something like that. My memory is that it was more she should be discreet. More professional."

"You called her a name, didn't you?"

Lydia Whitford frowned at me. "What name do you mean? Why don't you just come out and say it?"

"Why don't you?" I asked. "What did you call her?"

"I told her she was acting like a slut. Something like that. Or that people would think that's what she was if she carried on at work like that."

"And you thought that's what she was, didn't you? It's what you still think."

"Objection," Bailey said. "I believe Mrs. Whitford has fully answered this line of questioning."

"I don't care for those kinds of shenanigans at work and I told Ms. Sibley that. I'd tell her or anyone else doing those things the same thing. It doesn't mean I'm lying today."

"Sustained," Judge McGee shouted. "Move on, Ms. Leary."

"Got it," I said. "Thank you. I have no further questions."

"Mr. Bailey?"

"I think she's done just fine. No more questions from me."

"You can save the commentary, Mr. Bailey," Judge McGee said before I could voice my objection.

"All right. You may step down, Mrs. Whitford. Thank you. With that, we're adjourned until tomorrow morning."

When Lydia Whitford walked by our table, she leaned down and whispered to Farrah, "I know what you're trying to do. And God knows what you're trying to do. You won't win."

I rose from my seat. The jury was still filing out. I put myself between Farrah and Lydia Whitford. The deputy assigned to Farrah rushed forward. But Lydia raised her hands in submission, backed away, and stormed out of the courtroom.

Chapter 16

JEANIE and I had twenty minutes to talk to Farrah alone before she was transported back to the jail. Once the jury left the room, she was cuffed and led into the conference room across from Judge McGee's chambers.

"Do you see what I'm dealing with?" she said. "Lydia Whitford has had it out for me since the second I got hired. It started with a thousand microaggressions. Comments on my clothes. My hair. Then she'd become more overt, lecturing me about putting it out there. She actually said that to me once. I complained to Terry about it but he revered that woman. She was a kind of mother figure to him."

"I think she did a good job showing her true colors to the jury," I said. "The younger members for sure caught on. I don't think she came across as very likable at all."

"But will they believe her? Will they believe all of that crap she said about me threatening Terry? I would never hurt Terry. I never meant that. I just wanted him to stand up for himself. He relied on Lionel too much when he didn't need to. That was the biggest thing we used to fight about. Lydia was in lockstep with that. They treated Terry like a child sometimes when neither of them would have had anything without him. He was the star. That firm wouldn't have existed without them. I mean, it doesn't now that he's gone. I've heard there's been a mass exodus of Terry's clients. You watch. Within a year, Harriman's going to have to close up shop. Lydia's gravy train left when Terry died."

"You did good today," I said. "You kept your composure. You didn't let Lydia rattle you. You're going to need to do the same thing tomorrow and every day after. I believe Bailey's calling Lionel Harriman next. He'll confirm what Lydia said. I'll do my best to show his bias against you as well."

"Those voicemails are what hurt you today," Jeanie said, blunt as always.

"But we knew that going in," I added.

"They're out of context," Farrah said, waving a dismissive hand. "You said all the right things in your opening. I bet there's not a person in that courtroom who hasn't sent awful texts or voicemails to someone they loved but were arguing with."

Jeanie caught my eye. I didn't agree with Farrah, but there was no point saying so. I needed her to stay positive. I needed her to stay calm.

"I'll do what I can to show that," I said. "The context. Lydia admitted that her last observations of the two of you weren't fraught with tension. The jury won't be permitted to assume anything."

"They're going to assume everything," Farrah said. "I can already feel it. The way some of them look at me. Especially the older ones. They're all like Lydia Whitford. God. I've been battling the Lydia Whitfords of the world my whole life. Terry was the only one who saw me for who I really am. Who believed in me and my potential. Terry and Anderson Rix." She choked up. It was one of the rare times I'd seen Farrah show emotion.

"Thank you," she said. "If I forget to say it. It means everything to me that you're sticking by me, Cass. I know you didn't have to. Despite what Rix wanted, you didn't have to take over my defense. I know that."

"It's okay," I said. "And this is only the beginning. There's a lot more trial to get through. Just try to get a good night's sleep, if that's even possible over there. It's going to be another long day tomorrow."

"I should give you the same advice," Farrah said. The vulnerability she'd shown completely vanished. In its place, she gave me a cold stare. "I need you at the top of your game. I need you to be the person Anderson Rix saw."

A knock on the door saved me from having to respond.

"Time to head back, Sibley." The deputy came fully into the room. Farrah dutifully rose. They took her by the arms and led her out, leaving Jeanie and me alone for a moment.

"You know," Jeanie said. "Most of the time I believe her. Then she'll change like that and I swear I feel like I'm staring into the face of the last person Terry Dowd saw before she pumped a bullet into his chest."

"Lord," I said. "Keep that to yourself."

As I gathered my things, I knew exactly what Jeanie meant. Because the same feeling settled over me as we walked out of the courthouse together.

"Please raise your right hand. Do you swear to tell the truth, the whole truth, and nothing but the truth, so help you God?"

"I do." Lionel Harriman's booming voice filled the courtroom the next morning. "So help me God!"

He gave the briefest glance at Judge McGee. A look came over his face and I wondered if he imagined himself sitting in her chair and wearing that robe. I'd heard it had once been his aspiration.

"Will you state your name for the record?" Bailey asked.

Harriman leaned forward, practically kissing the small microphone in front of him. "Lionel Edgerton Harriman."

"Thank you. And can you tell the jury how you came to be associated with the victim in this case?"

"We were law partners. Had been for over twenty years. And I considered Terrence Dowd a close personal friend. No. It was more than that. I considered him family. He was like a brother to me."

"Well," Bailey said. "I'm sorry for your loss."

Bailey spent the next half hour taking Harriman through his background and the history of the Harriman Dowd law firm as well as his current role as more of a figurehead to Dowd's doing the heavy lifting.

"Do you recall when you first became aware of Farrah Sibley?" Bailey asked.

The Client List

"No. I can't say that I recall that. She was one of Terrence's summer clerks. Then he offered her a permanent position."

"Is that something he had to consult with you about?"

"It was something we would have discussed at a regular corporate meeting. But Terrence was free to make his own hiring decisions. So it would have been more that he informed me of hiring her rather than asking for my input. I trusted Terrence in those matters and I've never been someone to micromanage other people. I firmly believe the way to win at business is to hire the best people, then get out of their way and let them do their jobs."

"I see. Can you tell me what interaction, if any, you had with Ms. Sibley in the office?"

"Very little. I mean, I knew her to say hello. In more recent years, after she became an attorney, she attended some of the staff meetings. But her role was subordinate. She worked under Terrence."

"She didn't have clients of her own?"

"No. She assisted with Mr. Dowd's."

"How did you find her? Did you form an impression of Ms. Sibley?"

"Not really. I found her unremarkable for the most part. But as I said, I didn't have much interaction with her. She was Terrence's girl."

I cringed at the reference. So did at least three members of the jury.

"Understood," Bailey said. "Was there ever a time where you had discussions with Terrence Dowd regarding Ms. Sibley?"

"Yes."

"What happened?"

Harriman let out a sigh of disgust and trained a pair of cold eyes right at Farrah. "First, I want to make it very clear that I find this whole thing distasteful. I'm being asked to share dirty laundry and be indiscreet in a way I find ..."

"Objection," I said. "The witness is unresponsive. He's making speeches."

"Sustained," Judge McGee said. "Mr. Harriman. You know well how this works. You're to answer direct questions asked of you unless there's an objection, in which case you'll remain silent until I've ruled. Understood? Let's not go too far off the rails here."

"Of course, my apologies. What was the question, Mr. Bailey?"

"Did Mr. Dowd ever wish to discuss Ms. Sibley with you?"

"Yes. He did."

"When was that?"

"I'd say it was late spring of last year. I don't have a specific date. This wasn't part of any formal firm meeting where minutes were taken or something that would have been marked on my calendar."

"Okay. Mr. Dowd had walk-in privileges to your office?"

"Yes. As I did with him. Though most of the time, when Terrence wanted to talk to me, he came to my office. I had the bigger one with a formal sitting area. We often had coffee together in the morning before the workday officially started.

That's when we would discuss things on either Terrence's or my mind that were more informal."

"So you spoke about Ms. Sibley during your morning coffee talk?"

"I believe so, yes."

"And this was late spring of last year."

"Yes. In early May."

"Early May. Okay. Do you recall the substance of what you spoke about?"

"Terrence had some concerns about Ms. Sibley he felt he needed to bring to my attention."

"What type of concerns?"

"Terrence wanted to inform me of a potential human resource issue he might have with Ms. Sibley."

"A human resource issue?"

"We have a formal harassment and discrimination policy in place at Harriman Dowd. Terrence raised some concerns about the implementation of that policy as it related to Ms. Sibley."

"Can you be more specific?"

"Terrence felt he might have exposed the firm to a lawsuit where Ms. Sibley was concerned. He sought my advice on how best to deal with it."

"What kind of lawsuit?"

"Terrence brought it to my attention that he and Ms. Sibley were engaged in a romantic affair."

"They were sleeping together?"

"If you want to put it that way, yes."

"What did he say, specifically, if you recall?"

"Objection. The answer calls for hearsay."

"Your Honor, we've been through this in pretrial. Mr. Dowd's statements to Mr. Harriman are being offered to show Mr. Dowd's state of mind."

"They're being offered to show the truth of the matter asserted," I said. "To prove that, according to this witness, Terrence Dowd said them."

"I don't agree," Judge McGee said, in a ruling I anticipated. Anderson Rix had filed a formal motion to suppress Harriman's statements and been denied in a written ruling. But I had to make the objection for the record anyway.

"You may answer, Mr. Harriman."

"I don't recall Terrence's exact words. But he told me he was involved with Ms. Sibley. That it had become complicated and he wanted to end it. He told me he was concerned that she might make trouble for him or the firm and he wanted me to have a heads-up. And he apologized. I know he felt some embarrassment that he'd let things get as far as they had with her. There was one thing he said that I do remember his exact words and this is what I told the police. He said Harry, that was a nickname he had for me. A term of affection. He said Harry, this girl is off her rocker. If anything happens to me, just keep that in mind."

"What did he mean by that?"

"Objection. Calls for speculation. And I'd like to renew my objection that this statement is hearsay in that it's being offered for the truth of the matter asserted."

"I'll renew my ruling."

"Your Honor," I said. "I'd like a sidebar."

She waved us forward.

"Your Honor," I said as Judge McGee covered her microphone with her hand. "This statement has two parts. First, Mr. Harriman just told the jury Terry Dowd said my client is off her rocker. I want that stricken. As to the second part about if anything happens to him ..."

"If the entire statement goes to state of mind, then the entire statement comes in," Bailey said. "We've been through this. Ms. Leary's argument is no more compelling than her predecessor's in his motion to suppress."

"I agree," McGee said. "This matter is settled as far as I'm concerned. Your motion is once again overruled. Let's get on with this."

Bailey stormed back to the lectern. "Mr. Harriman. What did you take Mr. Dowd's statement to mean?"

"That he was concerned about Ms. Sibley's emotional stability. And that he was concerned she might do something to hurt him."

"Hurt him how?"

"In any way she could. Obviously, professionally. Terrence was deeply apologetic to the extent he'd exposed the firm to liability. But he said, if anything happens to me, indicating Ms. Sibley would be the cause of it."

"Did you take him seriously?"

"I most certainly did."

"What did you do next?"

"I asked him what he wanted me to do. He said nothing. Not at that time. He said he believed he had things under control but didn't want me blindsided just in case."

"What did you tell him?"

"I told him I trusted him. And I did. And I said ... and I regret this now. I regret a lot of things. I told him that he had my support. If he wanted to make a preemptive settlement, I'd support that. Whatever Terrence felt was best."

"Were you concerned?"

"Of course. And I was a little angry with Terrence. I didn't condone the way he conducted his personal life. I don't believe in divorce. I don't believe in affairs out of wedlock. But I also don't believe it's my place to judge someone else, especially when they ask for forgiveness. Which Terrence did. I hoped that he was on a better path after that meeting. I hoped ..."

Lionel Harriman began to cry after that. He composed himself quickly.

"Would you like to take a break?" Bailey asked.

"I would not."

"All right. I have no further questions."

"Ms. Leary?"

I couldn't unring the bell. But I held a copy of Lionel Harriman's statement to the police in my hands.

"Mr. Harriman. A couple of things. When was the last time you spoke with Mr. Dowd?"

"I saw him on the morning of July 17th. We had our coffee together like normal."

"Like normal. Did he mention Farrah Sibley?"

"Not that I recall."

"He never mentioned her to you again after that meeting in May, did he?"

"Not that I recall."

"And you never asked him about her after that, did you?"

"Not that I recall."

"You never deemed it important enough to intervene after that May conversation, did you?"

"Intervene how?"

"You tell me."

"I trusted Terrence could handle his own affairs as he promised he would."

"Did you speak to Farrah Sibley?"

"When?"

"Ever."

"Well, I suppose I said hello in passing."

"But you never approached her to get her side of the story on her relationship with Terrence Dowd, did you?"

"Certainly not."

"She was your employee though too, right?"

"Technically, yes."

"And you're the senior partner at Harriman Dowd, are you not? I mean, that's your name first on the letterhead, right?"

"Yes."

"So you didn't take Terrence's so-called revelations seriously enough to reach out to outside counsel?"

"I didn't reach out to outside counsel on it. That's not the same as me not taking it seriously."

"But you never talked to Dowd about it again. That's your testimony?"

"That's correct."

"And Terrence told you he was ending the affair. That's your testimony?"

"That's what he said. That he was trying to end it."

"But he didn't, did he? In fact, Terrence and Ms. Sibley continued a romantic relationship all the way up until his death. Isn't that right?"

"It appears so."

"So when Mr. Dowd told you he had ended their relationship, he wasn't being truthful, was he?"

"I don't ... I'm not privy to that."

"All right."

I turned to the relevant page in the police report.

"Mr. Harriman. You gave a statement to the police after Terrence's death. Isn't that right?"

"Of course. I fully cooperated with law enforcement."

"I understand. And you told them about this conversation you had with Terrence Dowd. The one in May pertaining to Farrah Sibley."

"Yes, ma'am."

"Did you volunteer it or did you have the impression they were already aware of the romantic relationship between Ms. Sibley and Mr. Dowd?"

"I believe they asked me if I knew about a romantic relationship between them, yes."

"Okay. And in your statement when Detective Eklund asked you if you knew Terrence Dowd was sleeping with Farrah Sibley, you said yes."

"Yes."

"And then you volunteered your interpretation of this conversation in May."

"Yes."

"But you didn't remember that it was May, did you?"

"What do you mean?"

"Do you remember what you told the police regarding the timing of this conversation?"

"I don't recall what I told them. But I know the conversation was in May because it was before my annual vacation to my timeshare in Aruba. I always leave the second week in May.

And Terrence specifically told me to go enjoy myself and that he'd handle all of this."

"Terrence Dowd was shot on July 17th, more than two months after he came to you about Farrah Sibley."

"Yes. That's correct."

"And you claim he told you if anything happens to him, Farrah would be responsible."

"Yes."

"But you certainly weren't concerned enough to cancel your luxury vacation over it, correct?"

"I resent your implication, but I didn't cancel my plans, no. That's not the same as me not taking it seriously."

"How long were you gone?"

"Three weeks. I returned the first week in June."

"Did you communicate with Terrence while you were in Aruba?"

"No."

"No calls. No texts?"

"No."

"Never checked in to see if he was all right? I mean, if he was concerned enough to tell you if anything happened to him, right?"

"I answered your question. I didn't have contact with Terrence while I was in Aruba."

"Your partner. The man you say you had brotherly affection for told you he was worried something might happen to him. And you left for three weeks without checking in?"

"Objection," Bailey said. "Is there a question in there?"

"My question is this. You weren't really concerned about Mr. Dowd's safety after that conversation, were you?"

"Of course I was concerned."

"About his safety?"

"Sure."

"But not so concerned that you'd change your travel plans."

"No."

"And not so concerned that you'd check in with him while you were gone, isn't that right?"

"I didn't check in."

"Because you didn't take Mr. Dowd's statement seriously, did you?"

"What?"

"You knew Terrence Dowd was only joking, didn't you?"

"I don't know."

"Or at the very least, you believed he was exaggerating, didn't you?"

"I don't ... I can't ..."

"When he made the statement that Ms. Sibley was off her rocker. That was a joke, wasn't it?"

"It might have been. I don't know."

"In fact, that's exactly what you told the police, isn't it? You said Terrence had a dry, sarcastic sense of humor. We joked all the time."

"I believe I said that. Yes."

"Because he was joking and you knew it. This wasn't some real threat of violence he was talking about. It was an off-the-cuff statement said in a sarcastic manner, and you knew it."

"Objection! Now Ms. Leary is the one making speeches."

"Sustained."

"All right. Mr. Harriman. You never called the police after Mr. Dowd allegedly told you if something happened to him Farrah did it."

"I didn't call the police. No."

"You never even discussed it with Terry again, did you?"

"No."

"Thank you. I have no further questions."

"Mr. Bailey?" the judge said.

Bailey looked distracted as he walked up to the lectern.

"I've just got one, Mr. Harriman. I'd like to give you the chance to explain why you did or didn't do what Ms. Leary is hammering you for."

"Thank you," Harriman said. He turned and faced the jury. "Terrence said he had everything under control and I trusted him. That's not to say I wasn't concerned. I was concerned. But like I said. I believe in hiring or working with good people, then staying out of their way. I believed Terrence. In all things. When he said he had things under control. And I believed him when he said if something happened to him, Farrah Sibley would be responsible. Period."

"Thank you. I have no further questions."

"Ms. Leary?"

I rose. "Mr. Harriman. How was Aruba?"

"Objection!"

"Ms. Leary?" Judge McGee gave me a stern look.

"No further questions, Your Honor," I said.

Lionel Harriman slammed the door to the witness box as he stepped down.

Chapter 17

BAILEY STARTED the next morning out with the medical examiner. The jury got its most detailed look at Terrence Dowd's lifeless body, bloody car, and the retrieval of the bullet that killed him. After that, came Eklund.

Detective Lars Eklund was an odd-looking man. Six foot eight. Reed thin. Though he had a full head of hair, it was thin, wispy, and white-blond. He had a habit of smoothing it over his brow when he spoke, keeping it from his eyes. It was hard not to start counting the times he did it as Bailey took him through his background testimony.

He was the lead detective on the Dowd murder. He had twelve years' experience investigating violent crimes. Before that, he worked on a human trafficking task force in Detroit, just as Eric remembered.

Bailey took him through all his background testimony and how he came to be involved in this case. He outlined the steps he took to secure the crime scene. Most of my cursory objections were overruled as I expected them to be. After an hour on the stand, Bailey got to the heart of Eklund's investigation.

"Detective Eklund," Bailey said. "Were you able to determine Terrence Dowd's manner of death?"

"I'll defer to the medical examiner's report regarding his specific cause of death. But he was shot at point blank range through the chest. That was evident to even a casual observer upon view of the body. We learned later, again deferring to the ME's report, that the bullet penetrated the left ventricle of his heart, severing his left main coronary artery. He bled out within a manner of minutes."

"What do you know about the wound or the type of weapon that caused it?"

"I worked with the Michigan State Police crime lab. Ballistic testing on the bullet and shell casing showed it was a 9 millimeter round fired from a Glock 19 handgun."

"One shot?"

"One shot. Yes. It was determined the shooter was standing no more than a foot away from him. He had an exit wound through his left lung, roughly a forty-five-degree angle downward from the entrance wound."

"Why is that significant?"

"Well, it means the shooter was standing above him while Mr. Dowd was seated. That's also consistent with the position in which his body was found."

Bailey went through the crime scene photos again.

"For the record, can you describe the position in which you found the body that's depicted in the photos you took?"

"Mr. Dowd was facing out. His legs were outside the vehicle perpendicular to the driver's seat. The theory is he had either been standing or sitting facing the shooter rather than in the driving position with his legs tucked under the steering wheel. It's possible Mr. Dowd was either just about to get into his vehicle or had just exited it when the shooter approached."

"Isn't the Belz Building garage under camera surveillance?"

"There are cameras that record vehicles coming in or out of the main exit and entrances. None were in position near Mr. Dowd's parking space. There is a camera pointed at the elevators inside the building but they're fixed. They only record people entering and exiting those elevators. There are no cameras in the stairwells."

"Were you able to determine an approximate time of death?"

"We know from the camera footage that Terrence Dowd exited the elevators at 7:46 p.m. on July 17th."

Bailey played the security footage. Terrence Dowd was shown exiting the elevator alone. He had a key fob in his hand and moved quickly out of frame toward the entrance to the parking garage. As Eklund testified, there was no footage inside the garage or near Mr. Dowd's vehicle.

"There's no footage of him leaving the garage. The Belz Building itself was primarily empty at that time, the workday having ended three hours prior. I learned later that the main doors to the building were locked at 6:00 p.m. You need a key card to get in after that. None were swiped coming back in after 6:00 p.m. that evening. All other employees, except for the defendant, left before Mr. Dowd that day. The other offices in the building were also empty by 6:00 p.m. according to the camera footage, key card access, and reporting of the office personnel."

"You're saying Ms. Sibley was the only other person in the building after 6:00 p.m. on July 17th?"

"Along with Mr. Dowd, yes. Ms. Sibley's vehicle is seen leaving the structure at 9:34 p.m."

Bailey played footage of Farrah's car exiting the south entrance at 9:34 p.m. Then later, he played footage of Lydia Whitford's vehicle reentering the structure at 8:02 a.m. the next morning. Hers was the first to arrive. Her 9-1-1 call came twelve minutes later at 8:14 a.m.

"Detective, what investigative steps did you take after securing the crime scene?"

"Mr. Dowd's cell phone was found a couple of inches away from his right hand in a charging dock in the center console. I turned the phone over to Detective Madeline Tate of the Michigan State Police for forensic analysis. I questioned Ms. Whitford and other employees of Harriman Dowd. Specifically Mr. Harriman. Both Ms. Whitford and Mr. Harriman expressed concern about a relationship Mr. Dowd was having with the defendant. When I asked them if they knew of anyone who wanted to hurt Mr. Dowd, they were consistent and immediate with their answers. They told me I should talk to Farrah Sibley."

"And did you?"

"She wasn't scheduled to come into the office that morning. Ms. Whitford advised me that Ms. Sibley had taken some personal time to go to a doctor's appointment. They expected her in after noon. I continued certain other investigative steps in the meantime. I collected the security footage from the parking garage. I interviewed other employees in the Belz Building as they came in. I worked with the crime scene investigators from the State Police. By early afternoon, I had some preliminary findings from Mr. Dowd's cell phone. I was able to hear the voicemails left by Ms. Sibley and see her text messages. Ms. Whitford and another office secretary provided me with data from the office. Mr. Dowd's billings. His schedule the day of his shooting and the days before. His call sheets. Copy machine and print commands. From all of that data, in addition to the info on Dowd's cell phone, it became clear that Farrah Sibley was a person of interest. She was in the building during the timeframe Mr. Dowd was shot. I want to say it was two or three in the afternoon and Ms. Sibley hadn't returned from her appointment. So, I called her cell phone. She answered. I asked her if she'd be willing to come to my office and speak with me. At that time, I didn't know if she was aware of what had happened at the Belz Building."

"What did she say?"

"We made arrangements for her to meet with me at 5:00 p.m. that afternoon."

"Then what happened?"

"Ms. Sibley was prompt. I took her into an interview room."

"Can you describe her demeanor?"

"Objection," I said. "Calls for speculation."

"Your Honor, as a homicide detective skilled in conducting interviews, this witness is qualified to testify as to his impressions of potential witnesses to a murder case."

"Overruled, the witness may answer."

"She seemed calm. She was dressed professionally in a blue suit. I offered her some water. She said she didn't need anything but thanked me. I asked her if she minded if I recorded our conversation. She had no objections."

"Your Honor," Bailey said. "At this time, I'd like to play the recording of Detective Eklund's interview with Ms. Sibley."

I had no grounds to object at this point. Bailey clicked the trackpad on his laptop. The overhead blazed to life. The interview room camera was set in a low corner of the room, giving a full view of a small table. Farrah walked in and sat in the chair to the left of the camera. Eklund took the one on the right. You could only see him in profile, but Farrah appeared straight on. As he described, she wore a neatly pressed blue silk suit. She crossed her legs at the ankles and met Eklund's gaze straight on.

"Ms. Sibley," Eklund said in the recording. "Do you know why I've asked you to come in this evening?"

"I believe so."

"You understand that Terrence Dowd was found dead this morning?"

"I've been told that, yes."

"You've been told that. Who told you that?"

Farrah didn't answer. Her face held no expression. A complete void. She blinked slowly and took a breath.

"Detective, I'm here at your request. But I won't be answering any of your questions without an attorney present."

"You won't be ... but you are an attorney, aren't you?"

"I am."

"I'm just asking you how you found out Terry Dowd was dead."

"And I am exercising my constitutional rights not to answer any of your questions."

"You're not under arrest. The man's dead. Murdered, most likely. Shot through the heart. I understand you and Mr. Dowd had a relationship."

No response. Just a cold stare from Farrah. She kept her hands folded in her lap the whole time.

"Ms. Sibley. You are free to leave at any time. I'm not holding you here. This isn't a formal interrogation. I'm just trying to figure out what might have happened to your boss. Your ... he was your boyfriend too, wasn't he?"

No response.

"Do you know who might have done this? Who might have wanted to hurt him?"

No response. Farrah didn't move. She barely blinked.

"I understand this has got to be hard. It's a shock. You cared about Mr. Dowd. That's the story I'm getting from the people who worked with the both of you. It sounds like you were one of the closest, if not the closest person he had in his personal life as well as at work. So that puts you in a unique position to help me today. Don't you want to do that? For Terrence?"

No response. Beside me, Farrah adopted the exact same posture as she had on the video. Shoulders back. Stone-faced. Hands in her lap. One by one, the members of the jury noted it too.

"The man is dead, Farrah," video-Eklund said. "Shot dead. Murdered. Your boyfriend. I want to play something for you."

Eklund pulled out a small recording device. The sound quality was horrible on the video, but you could make it out for what it was. Farrah's last awful voicemail message to Terrence Dowd.

Video-Farrah and actual Farrah sat completely still. An ice sculpture. No reaction.

"You want to explain your side of this? You're a smart lady. You have to know what it might sound like in light of what's happened."

"I know my rights. I'm exercising them."

"But you're here," Eklund said. "You get how this looks, right?"

No response.

"If you had nothing to do with this. If you're not the one who put a bullet into that man, I would think you'd want to say so. I mean, why even come in here at all if you're just going to sit there like a statue? I told you, you're not under arrest."

"You asked me to come in. So I came in. But I understand my rights and I'm exercising them and declining to answer any questions."

Farrah rose in the video. Eklund looked up at her.

"You're leaving?" he said. "Honey, you're not helping yourself one bit right now. You know that. You get that, right?"

"I'll send the name of my attorney. In the future, you can communicate with him or her should you need to. You said I'm free to go."

"By all means," Eklund said, the sarcasm dripping from his tone.

The Client List

Farrah turned her back on him and walked out of the interview. She left Lars Eklund shaking his head in disbelief as she closed the door behind her. I scanned the jury. They wore similar expressions of disbelief.

"Detective," Bailey said. "Obviously, you made an arrest in this case or we wouldn't be here. Can you explain how you got to that point?"

"With the statements of Mr. Harriman and Ms. Whitford. They were consistent. They both overheard Ms. Sibley making threats to Mr. Dowd. Her cell phone data put her at the scene when Mr. Dowd was shot. The surveillance footage. There was footage going back four weeks. Each day, Ms. Sibley entered and exited the building through the south elevators except for the day of the shooting. On that day, She didn't use the elevators. She had to have used the stairs ..."

"Objection, calls for speculation."

"Again, this witness is qualified to draw inferences from the evidence he collected. He just testified that he reviewed footage. It's entered into evidence. Ms. Sibley didn't levitate to the parking garage. It's a reasonable inference that she took the stairs."

"All right, all right," Judge McGee said. "And you're free to argue that in closing. For now, let's stick to the observable facts, Detective. The jury will disregard that last statement."

"Detective, what led up to your arrest in this case?" Bailey reframed his question.

"Ms. Sibley has a gun registered to her name. A Glock 19. It was not found in her apartment. It's missing. But she owns the type of weapon used to kill Terrence Dowd. The fact that all calls and texts to him stopped after the evening of July 16th. All those facts combined gave me probable cause to arrest Farrah Sibley for the murder of Terrence Dowd."

"Thank you," Bailey said. "I have no further questions."

"Your witness, Ms. Leary."

I straightened my jacket and stepped up to the lectern.

Chapter 18

"Detective, let's start on the last conclusion you made that you just testified about. The alleged murder weapon. You said Mr. Dowd was shot with a Glock 19, correct?"

"That's correct."

"Would you describe that as a unique weapon?"

"Unique?"

"In the sense they're hard to find or rare."

"No. It's not a unique weapon."

"In fact, you own a Glock 19, don't you?"

"Yes, I do."

"How many homicide cases have you investigated in the last five years that involved gun violence?"

"I can't say for sure."

I paused. Eric sat on the bench just behind Jeanie. He was directly responsible for the research I was about to lay down.

"Was it sixteen?"

"That sounds about right."

"Do you know how many of those sixteen cases involving gun violence also involved the use of Glock 19?"

"Not off the top of my head, but I bet you're about to tell me."

"I am. Would it surprise you if the number is eleven?"

"No, that wouldn't surprise me."

"So, is it fair to say that the Glock 19 is a common weapon?"

"Yes."

"It's one of the most common types of handgun purchased in the United States. Did you know that?"

"I can't say I knew it for a fact. But no, it doesn't surprise me. If you'd asked me to guess, that would have been my guess."

"Fair enough. And you never found the gun used to shoot Terrence Dowd, did you?"

"We did not. No."

"So you cannot say whether the bullet and shell casing retrieved from Terrence's vehicle came from a Glock 19 registered to Farrah Sibley, can you?"

"I can't say that, no. But that was only one piece of evidence in this case."

"It's not evidence at all because you don't have the gun, do you?"

"Objection, asked and answered," Bailey said.

"Let's move on, Ms. Leary. You've made your point."

The Client List

"Of course," I said. "But Detective, you've recited a list of suspicions you had. Your evidence. The statements from Ms. Sibley's coworkers. The cell phone data, texts and voicemails. But you have no physical evidence tying Farrah Sibley to the scene of Terrence Dowd's shooting, do you?"

"She was in the building at the time of the shooting. This we know from the security footage of when she left. The data from her workstation. Her cell phone pinged the tower closest to the Belz Building."

"The tower with a half-a-mile radius," I said.

"Is that a question?" Bailey jumped up.

"I'll ask one," I said. "Detective, you executed a search warrant of Farrah Sibley's home, correct?"

"Yes."

"You didn't find any physical evidence tying her to the crime scene incident to that search, did you?"

"No."

"No bloody clothes."

"No."

"No murder weapon."

"No."

"And when you arrested her, you found no gun residue on her hands, did you?"

"Well, she was arrested a few days after the shooting, so I'm not sure that makes a difference."

"But you questioned her within a few hours of the shooting. You didn't see any blood on her, did you?"

"No."

"No signs of injury?"

"No."

"Let's talk about Lionel Harriman, then," I said. "This investigation isn't the first time you ever met him, is it?"

"No."

"You were personally acquainted with Mr. Harriman before this case, weren't you?"

"We are friendly, yes."

"You play in a golf league with him, don't you?"

"In a league, yes. We're not on the same team. But I know him socially."

"I see. How many other suspects did you pursue in this case?"

"We had no other solid leads."

"No other solid leads. Did you interview any of Ms. Sibley's friends?"

"She didn't appear to have any. None came forward."

"She has a family though. Did you know that?"

"I'm not familiar with her family. She has no siblings. It's my understanding her mother isn't in the picture. Her father is not local."

"Not local. Where does he live?"

"I believe in Mount Pleasant."

"A two-hour drive," I said.

"Right."

"You never talked to him."

"No."

"You made up your mind that Farrah Sibley was responsible for this and that was it, didn't you?"

"That's not how I would characterize it. I went where the evidence led and that was straight to your client."

"No gun. No physical evidence. No eyewitnesses. That evidence?"

"Objection!" Bailey said. "Counsel is making her closing argument, not asking questions."

"Sustained," Judge McGee said. "You know better, Ms. Leary. So do better."

I paused for a beat. Eklund was tough. His crime scene was tight. My sense was the jury liked him. I had arguments I could make in closing, but doing too much of that with him on the stand could backfire and give Bailey the chance to let Eklund clean things up.

"Thank you. I have no further questions."

Bailey declined recross. With that, Judge McGee adjourned us for the weekend. I shared a quick word with Farrah before the deputies led her back to the jail. Gathering my things, Jeanie, Eric, and I walked out to Eric's car for the drive back to Delphi.

"That went well," Jeanie said. She slipped into the backseat. I took the passenger seat.

"I don't know. Eric, I know you hated that."

"You did what you had to do," Eric said. "Just because Eklund's a fellow detective doesn't mean he can't make mistakes."

"But you don't think he made any," I said.

"No," he said while turning onto Main Street. "Not really."

"The info about his former caseload was good," Jeanie said. "I think it played well."

A heavy silence fell. I knew what they were both thinking. I scored some points, sure. Minor ones. But the showstopper of the day was Lars Eklund's video interview with Farrah Sibley.

"He killed me today," I finally said. "That tape killed me."

"Cass," Jeanie said. "Maybe you really need to consider putting her on the stand. Give her a chance to show she's a human being. Right now?"

"Right now she looks like a cold-hearted murdering bitch," I said.

Nobody in the car disagreed with me.

"I don't know," Eric said. "Maybe they need to hear her explain herself. A lot of people have said a lot of awful things about her."

He accelerated onto the on-ramp. I understood what they were saying. Thinking. I'd turned it over in my head a thousand times. But I just kept coming back to one thing.

"I can't do it," I said. "Neither of you are wrong. But every time Farrah Sibley's been given a chance to speak for herself. Those voicemails. Her behavior in that interview. Hell, even some of the things she says to me. She makes it worse. She's her own worst enemy and has been since the beginning. I just can't open her up to cross-examination. She'll think she can outsmart Jason Bailey and the jury could see right through that. I have to find another way."

I saw Eric meet Jeanie's eyes in the rearview mirror. I could read them both. They wouldn't say it. Neither would I. But this case was getting away from me and my client ... Anderson Rix's last client ... would probably spend the rest of her life in jail.

Chapter 19

AFTER THREE STRAIGHT days of rain, I felt the sunlight on my face as I lay there debating whether I should do something crazy like get out of bed. The space next to me was empty. Eric had left early to run down some leads on a case Jeanie was working on. Since the Dowd trial started, he'd taken to staying with me every night. It was nice. He made breakfast every morning. Something I didn't usually bother with during trials. The heavenly smell of strong coffee hit my nostrils. It called to me more than the pillow under my head.

Ten minutes later and I was downstairs. I poured my coffee and walked out to the porch to drink it. My two dogs, Marbury and Madison, were sunning themselves on the dock. Marby lay on his back with his short legs up in the air, his round belly rising and falling as he snored.

"Weird dog," I whispered. Madison opened one sleepy eye, regarded me, then fell promptly back asleep.

The fishing boat was gone. Shielding my eyes from the sun, I could make it out in the distance on the northwest end of the lake. Joe was out there. I couldn't tell if Matty was. His truck wasn't here, but he sometimes liked to park it up the hill.

I sat on the wooden rocker and set my coffee down. That's when I saw it. A navy-blue and bold embossed card. Sipping my coffee, I picked it up.

"Son of a bitch," I whispered. "She didn't."

"Katherine Bishop and Thomas Loomis request the honor of your presence at a dinner reception celebrating their marriage ..."

I immediately tried to call Vangie. It went straight to voicemail. Saturday morning and she was probably sitting in the bleachers at summer volleyball camp or something.

I went back inside and checked the trash. Not finding the envelope the invitation came in, I set it on the counter and warmed up my coffee. By the time I made it back outside, Joe was tying the boat to the dock. He dumped half a dozen nice-sized crappies from the live well into the cage he kept secured to the dock.

He didn't acknowledge me. I knew that look. That furrowed brow. Deep lines around his mouth. God. He looked just like our dad sometimes. It's nothing I'd ever say to his face.

I waited for him to join me on the porch. He sat in the chair beside me and stared out at the water for a moment. Finally, he turned to me.

"Is there any of that left?"

"There's some," I said. "But I was just about to make a fresh pot. You wanna tell me what this is about?"

I waved Katie's wedding invitation at him. He looked back out at the water.

"I don't want to talk about it."

"Sure. You just left this here where you knew I was gonna see it. Did she honestly just invite you to her wedding? The ink on your divorce judgment isn't even dry yet."

"It's been a couple of months. It's not like there's a formal waiting period."

"You didn't answer my question. She invited you? Is she trying to be funny?"

"Emma brought it over. It was addressed to her."

"Is she going?"

"She claims she called Katie and told her where she can stick her RSVP. I wish she hadn't."

"Can you blame her? Emma feels like Katie cheated on her, too. Now she invites her to celebrate with the guy she left you both for? I really don't get this woman. Katie just isn't the person I thought she was."

Joe shrugged. Marbury trudged up the porch, yawning as he went. Joe reached down and rubbed his ears. Marbury rewarded him by wagging his tail and rubbing his body on Joe's leg. Then the dog settled down and slept on top of Joe's foot.

"What about you? How pissed off are you?"

I watched his jaw turn to granite.

"Joe, maybe you should talk to someone. I'm worried about you."

"Don't be. And I don't want to talk about it."

"You never want to talk about it. You just want to brood. Then you let it get to your head and you smash things. Or you drink more than you should. I'm not judging you for any of it. I'm just worried. That's all. I love you, stupid."

"I'm fine."

"Sure. Peachy. How many beers did you have yesterday?"

"I'm not Matty," he snapped. "And you're not Mom. I'll start looking for a new place so you don't have to count my beers, Cass."

"That's not what I meant. I don't want you to leave. I like having you here."

"You like hovering."

I took a breath. This wasn't going how I meant it to. It had been like this between us for weeks. I said the wrong thing. Set him off. Or I said nothing at all and quietly watched my brother in pain.

I rubbed his back. He went rigid, but let me.

"I love you," I told him once again. We sat silently for a few minutes. Madison started chasing a squirrel across the lawn. She treed it and stood at the base of my largest maple and let out her shrill, sinus-clearing bark.

"How's your trial going?" Joe asked.

I sipped the last of my coffee. "The truth? I honestly don't know. I'm pretty sure my jury hates my client and they can absolutely convict on dislike."

"I'm sorry," he said. "But you'll turn them around. You're good at that."

"Thanks."

"How's it going having Eric around full time?"

It was an odd segue.

"What do you mean?"

"I mean ... he's sitting in court with you now. He's in the office. And he's here more than he's not."

"It's nice. We make a good team, I think. Plus, it sure beats worrying about him like I used to when he was a cop."

Joe turned toward me. He had a smirk on his face I never liked. It meant he was about to skewer me with some observation. Or worse, he'd go silent and drive me crazy with it.

"What?"

"Nothing," he said. He got up and went to pour his own coffee. I followed him.

"What? You look like you want to say something. So say it."

"You're doing that thing you do."

"What thing?"

"Of course you don't want me moving out. Of course you want Eric working with you every day. So you can keep an eye on him. So you can keep an eye on me."

"What the hell are you talking about?"

"You know what I'm talking about. You don't want to have kids of your own. You just want to treat the rest of us like children. Swoop in and fix everything."

"You know what? Enough. You're in a mood. You're mad about Katie so you're doing that thing *you* do. That thing you learned from Dad."

He slammed his mug down on the counter. "What did you say?"

"You heard me. You feel bad, so you might as well make the people around you feel bad. You're a grown man. So is Eric. I'm not trying to babysit either one of you. Though in your case, maybe you need it. You're acting like a twelve-year-old."

"I don't want to get into this."

"Oh really? Seems like you do. You left that card out. You're the one who started throwing bombs the second you saw me."

"Forget it."

"Right."

I hated this. The last thing I wanted was to be out of sorts with my brother. But damned if I was going to do the thing I always did. The thing they expected of me. Make peace. Be the one to soften whatever blow and say I'm sorry even if I wasn't the one who did something wrong.

God. Our mother did that. If I'd just accused Joe of stealing from my dad's playbook, I usually stole from hers.

"You know what?" he said. "I think out of all of us, you've got the right idea."

I should have walked away. He was baiting me again. I could have kicked myself as I heard the words come out of my mouth.

"What pray tell do you mean?"

"Never getting married. Seriously, don't. If Eric comes at you with that ring someday, run. Learys are bad at it."

"Joe, stop. You said that before. And you almost said it in front of Tori."

"It's good advice. They're better off just being parents to Sean and screw the rest of it. The second you get married, it ruins everything. The Leary Curse."

I felt the hairs rise on the back of my neck. A shadow fell behind me. Eric. I didn't need to ask how long he'd been standing there.

"Great," I said. "Nice work, Joe."

Eric stood holding two grocery bags. I took one from him and started emptying it. Joe had that smirk on his face. I would kill him. Later. In his sleep. I would frigging kill him.

In true hit-and-run fashion, my brother left the kitchen and headed for his apartment over the barn.

"I'm sorry," I said, turning to Eric. "Emma brought this over."

I slapped the wedding invitation on the counter. Eric read it and whistled low. "She sent that to him? What did Joe do to piss her off this time?"

"She sent it to Emma."

"Yikes. Should I call one of the deputies to do a wellness check on Tom and Katie?"

Closing my eyes, I shook my head and put my hands up in a stopping gesture.

"You okay?" Eric said.

"How much of that did you hear?"

"All the way up to the Leary Curse."

"Ugh. I'm sorry. He's hurting. He's ..."

"He's Joe. He'll get over it. And this is shitty." Eric picked up the invitation. He folded it in half and tossed it in the trash. Then he came to me and folded me into an embrace. He felt so warm, strong, and tall. But I had to wonder how much of what my brother said weighed on him as well.

The Leary Curse. Was he right? I shook my head to clear those thoughts from it. More visions of murdering my brother in painful ways rose up in their place.

"Come on," Eric said. "It's gorgeous out there. It's been a long week. It's going to be an even longer one this next one. Let's go out on the pontoon and just float for a while. It'll do you good. You've barely been on the lake this year. This trial is your whole life."

"I love you," I said. He smiled.

"I know."

I busied myself packing a few things to take out on the boat. Eric's plan was brilliant. He went on ahead of me and started the motor. I half expected the battery to be dead. Such would be my luck. Eric scooped up both dogs and deposited them on the boat.

I changed into a bathing suit and threw a cover-up over my head. I made it out the door as my cell phone rang on the chair where I'd left it. I probably should have let it go to voicemail. But the caller ID puzzled me.

"This is Cass," I answered.

"Jason Bailey," he said. "Sorry to bother you at home on a Saturday, but I'm hoping we can meet tomorrow. I'll come to you."

Eric waved to me from the captain's chair. I held up a finger.

"What's this about?"

"Ten o'clock? You pick the place. I just need about an hour of your time."

Eric revved the engine. Madison leapt to the back of the boat. Her usual perch. She liked to look down at the water for fish.

"We can meet halfway. There's a diner in Saline off 12. I can text you the address," I said.

"I'll be there," Bailey said, then abruptly clicked off.

I looked down at my phone, then back up at Eric. I tossed the phone on the chair and headed out to the boat.

Chapter 20

Jason Bailey wasn't alone when I walked into the diner. His companion, a young man, maybe thirty, blond hair, well-built, wearing a maroon Central Michigan tee shirt, rose from his side of the booth, shook hands with Bailey, then left. He passed me as I walked in.

I knew him from somewhere but couldn't immediately place it. The CMU tee shirt though. It meant something.

Bailey saw me and rose to greet me. He shook my hand the same as his breakfast companion had.

"Thanks for coming all the way out here," Bailey said. "I would have gladly met you somewhere in between."

"It's fine," I said, looking back over my shoulder. The young man climbed into a black Range Rover and pulled away from the curb.

A name floated into my head. Kurt. Kent. Then the answer solidified. That was Kurt Sommerville. Farrah's ex-boyfriend.

Tori and Eric had tried to track him down but he refused to answer their calls or meet with them.

"What's this about?" I asked.

"Sit, please," Bailey said. "Are you hungry?" He raised his hand to get the server's attention. Any appetite I had melted away the second Kurt Sommerville's name materialized in my mind. This wasn't some casual meeting. It felt more like an ambush.

Bailey lowered his hand.

"Something's come up," he said. "You know who that was just leaving?"

"Yes."

"Okay. Well, some additional evidence has come to light and in the interest of full disclosure, I wanted to bring it to you."

"What new evidence?"

Bailey reached down and picked something up. He produced a manila file holding about a half inch of paper and a thumb drive taped to the front of it.

"Kurt Sommerville has produced some text messages that are germane to the Dowd case. I didn't know about them until yesterday afternoon. I'd frankly like to wring Sommerville's neck for withholding them. But he wasn't under any sort of formal obligation to produce them."

I didn't like it. I hated walking into meetings where I didn't know the context. I put a flat hand over the top of the file folder as it rested on the table.

"He's a jilted ex-boyfriend," I said.

The Client List

"He's more than that. Look, I know this is going to be an uphill battle with Judge McGee. But I truly had no idea these phone records existed. But Sommerville's been on my witness list from the beginning. McGee might rant and rail for a minute, but she's going to let this evidence in. I'm here as a professional courtesy …"

"Professional courtesy? You have a legal and ethical obligation to disclose your discovery, Jason. Let's not pretend this is you being magnanimous just for the sake of it."

I wanted to flip the cover on that file folder. At the same time, I'd be damned if I'd let Bailey watch me read it, looking for some reaction. Plus, I didn't need to. I could guess the flavor of what Sommerville had produced. It was likely the 1.0 version of the texts and voicemails Farrah left for Terrence Dowd. The ones she swore to me she'd never left.

"Well, be that as it may. I'm disclosing it now. I've done my duty. You're of course free to argue whatever you'd like to the judge tomorrow."

"Gee, thanks."

"This is only part of why I wanted to meet. The other part is, I've been authorized to renew a plea deal for your client. She pleads guilty to second degree, I recommend twenty years with the possibility of parole. Final offer. Take it or leave it."

"Why now? You just dropped new evidence in my lap you clearly think will turn into some bombshell for you. You haven't completed your case in chief. Do you think you're doing that badly?"

"It's not about that. I'm not playing games. It's a legitimate deal and you need to seriously consider it. Your client needs to seriously consider it. She's looking at life in prison if she goes down. I'm offering her a chance at freedom down the road. She's young. She could rebuild her life somewhere. The alternative ... well ... she's young, Cass. You and I both know what hard time does to people like her. She'll probably die in there."

He wasn't wrong. But I wasn't inclined to admit it. Not with this turd he'd just laid in my lap.

"I'll convey your offer."

"Good. And I won't take up any more of your time. Again, I'm glad you came all the way down here but I figured after you heard my offer and had a chance to look at what's in that file, you'd probably want to go straight to the Washtenaw County Jail anyway. Talk to Ms. Sibley right away."

I didn't respond. Bailey was already on his feet. "I have to head back to the office. Trial week is a 24/7 deal. You know that. I'll see you in court and if you have a reason to get a hold of me sooner, I'll have my cell on me. Call anytime."

"Thanks."

"Stick around. Try the French toast. They use Zingerman's bread."

Bailey put a twenty-dollar bill on the table for his tip, then left.

I waited until he walked down the sidewalk out of view before flipping open the file folder. I only made it past the first page before pulling out my cell phone and calling the county jail. When I got through to the right party, I said, "This is Cass Leary. I need to make arrangements to visit my client, Farrah Sibley, in the next hour."

FARRAH's whole posture changed as she leafed through the printout of Kurt Sommerville's text messages.

They were scathing. If the jury were permitted to see them ... to hear the voicemail ... it could do real damage.

Farrah shook her head. "I didn't send these."

"What?"

She shoved the papers across the desk at me. "I'm telling you I never sent those text messages to Kurt."

"It's your phone."

"It's an old phone," she said. "Look at the number. That's not my current cell phone. The one I've had for the last four years."

"But this was your phone. You admit to that?"

"I didn't send these. The voicemail, yes. I'm not proud of it. I'm sorry. I'm a hot-blooded person. I've never denied that. But the rest of that, it's not me."

"That's what you want me to go with? What do you expect the jury to believe if this gets in front of them? That someone else sent text messages from a phone you admit belonged to you?"

"I'm not responsible for what they believe. I can only tell the truth. And I have been."

"No, you haven't!" I hadn't meant to shout. But Farrah was glossing over one critical fact.

"We went over Bailey's witness list numerous times. I asked you about Kurt. Specifically asked you whether he could say anything harmful to your case. You told me no. You told me it was a normal breakup as far as those things go. That you ended amicably."

"Kurt's lying. Because he fabricated these text messages somehow."

"What possible motive would he have for doing that? Even if there was some way he could. He would have had to have access to this phone. Do you know if he did?"

She threw her hands up. "Not that I know of. But these text messages, they're years old, Cass. How can they possibly be relevant now?"

"I know you know the answer to that. You're a lawyer too, Farrah. Bailey is going to try to use them to show a pattern. To show that what happened with Terrence Dowd was an escalation in a pattern of conduct on your part. To help the jury believe that Terrence's murder was foreseeable and inevitable where you're concerned."

"Is that what you believe?"

"It doesn't matter what I believe. It matters what Bailey can prove."

"That's a cop-out. That's legal-speak. Don't do that. Not with me. I'm asking you. Right here. Right now. Do you think I killed Terry? Do you think I'm lying to you about these stupid text messages?"

I did a mental five count. I didn't want to answer Farrah out of emotion. I was angry. Livid, actually. When I felt my blood pressure start to lower, I folded my hands and rested them on the table. I met Farrah's eyes.

"I'm having a very hard time believing you didn't send those texts to Kurt. But even if you're telling the truth, it's going to be a hard sell."

"Then you have to keep the jury from ever seeing them. Can you do that?"

"I don't know. That's the truth. It's unconscionable to me that McGee would allow these in without me being able to examine the phone they were allegedly sent from. Do you have any idea where it might be?"

"No. This was when I was on my dad's cell phone plan. That summer, I was still living at home between semesters."

It raised an obvious question. "So your father had access to that phone? Could he have sent those messages pretending to be you?"

I looked at them again. Some of them had a strong, religious undertone.

"Why would he do something like that?"

"You tell me."

"No. Leave my father out of this."

"Farrah, this isn't the first time he's come up. Your mother's letter warned of this exact kind of thing."

"It won't work. You don't understand."

"So help me."

"I don't know. Maybe. It wasn't password locked. He wouldn't let me use one when he was paying for the plan. He got that phone for me when I was sixteen."

"That's something, at least. I'll make that argument if we get to that point. You have to be prepared for the fact that these texts are going to come in. The jury is going to hear them."

"Then you have to be good at giving them an alternate theory. I know you can. I trust you. I just wish you trusted me."

"Farrah, there's another reason I'm here. Bailey didn't just want to talk about the phone evidence and Kurt Sommerville. He came with a plea deal."

She put her shoulders back as if she were bracing for my next words.

"Twenty years," I said. "You'd be forty-eight when you're up for parole. You understand if you're convicted of second degree murder, you'll likely spend the rest of your life in prison."

She closed her eyes. It almost looked as if she were meditating right in front of me. Maybe it wasn't such a bad idea for both of us.

When she opened her eyes, she had the same question she'd had of me since the day we met.

"Do you believe I did this? That I hurt Terry like that?"

I wanted to give her the same answer. That it didn't matter what I believed. That my job was to put the prosecution to its proofs and let the jury decide.

"I don't know," I said. It was an honest answer.

"Cass ..."

"But I need the jury to not know, either. That's reasonable doubt. So yes. Me personally. I have reasonable doubt whether you did this."

"That's not the same thing as believing I'm innocent."

"I know."

"Rix believed me."

"I know that too."

"It mattered. Sometimes, I can't breathe thinking about how much it mattered. And it matters to me that you do too."

"I gave you an honest answer."

"I gave you one too. I didn't kill Terry. And I didn't send those messages to Kurt. I don't know why he's doing this."

"I'll do what I can. You know that. I have solid legal arguments for keeping this crap out. But you have to be prepared that they'll come in. And you have to tell me what you want to do with Bailey's plea deal. There won't be another one. It's now or never."

"No," she said without hesitation. "I'd rather spend the rest of my life in here than admit to hurting someone I loved like that. I know how this works. I know if I say yes to this deal, I have to stand in open court and say I committed this crime. I haven't lied yet. I don't plan to start now."

I waited a beat, then gathered the printouts back into the file folder and closed it.

"All right," I said. "Get as much rest as you can. You're going to need it. I'll see you in court in the morning."

Farrah remained staring straight ahead at the wall as the guard came in and let me out.

Chapter 21

AT 9:40 a.m. the next morning, I had appealable error. Rough consolation for what I knew might turn the tide against Farrah Sibley. But despite every solid legal argument I made, the Honorable Claudia McGee wasn't buying it.

"Your objections are noted," she said. "But overruled. You'll have ample opportunity to cross-examine the witness, to call your own during your case in chief, but as long as Mr. Bailey can properly authenticate these texts and messages, they'll be admitted. Your motion to suppress is denied."

Farrah took a sip from her water bottle. Her hands trembled as she did it and it was the first sign of emotion I'd seen from her in the actual courtroom. Luckily, the jury didn't. Judge McGee had them sequestered in the jury room pending the outcome of this morning's motion. A moment after we finished, she called them back in. Bailey stepped to the lectern and called Kurt Sommerville to the stand.

He'd swapped his Central Michigan tee shirt for a gray suit and red tie. He looked freshly barbered with close-cropped hair and a shave. He grabbed his own water bottle from the ledge in front of him and readied himself to answer Bailey's first questions. He never looked at Farrah, not once.

"Will you state your name and where you live for the record?"

"Kurt William Sommerville. I live in Midland, Michigan."

"Are you single? Married? Have a family?"

"I'm married. My wife is Annabelle Sommerville. We have a son, Jayden. And we're expecting a daughter in three months."

"Congratulations. Mr. Sommerville, why don't you tell me how you know the defendant in this case?"

"Farrah and I dated in college. We were both students at CMU. Both communications majors."

"How long did you date?"

"Let's see. We met our freshman year at orientation. Then she lived in Sweeney Hall. I lived in Merrill. They're in the same quad. Brother and sister dorms. We started hanging around the same circle of friends. Beginning sophomore year, we started dating. We dated halfway through senior year, then broke up."

"Could you describe the circumstances of that breakup?"

"What do you mean?"

"I mean, was it your decision? Hers? Mutual?"

"That time it was kind of mutual. Farrah was going to go to law school after graduation at U of M. I was going to go for my MBA at Northwestern. It just seemed a natural time to give each other space."

"I see. So was that the end of your romantic relationship with Farrah Sibley?"

"No. About a year later. Christmastime. After we'd both graduated from CMU. I came back to Mount Pleasant to visit friends I still had in the area. Farrah and I had kept in touch. Just talking. I texted her or she texted me. Anyway, we met for dinner and things just started up again. We were on and off again into that next year. That's when things got bad."

"Bad how?"

"I don't suppose I handled things very well. I was ... I wasn't interested in getting serious. Farrah was. I guess I didn't realize that. I tried to break things off. She didn't take it very well."

"What do you mean?"

"Well, she called me all the time. All hours of the day and night. Asking me where I was. What I was doing. Why I hadn't called her first. That sort of thing. Then she showed up unannounced at my apartment in Evanston. Just out of her mind."

"In what way?"

"Crying. Yelling. Hysterical. Wanting to know why I was blowing her off. It got scary. That's when things, at least in my mind, were done for good."

"When was this?"

"This would have been in February, four years ago. It was the weekend near Valentine's Day. That's what seemed to have set her off. That I hadn't made plans with her. It really threw me."

"Why's that?"

"Because I'd told Farrah we were done. That I couldn't see her anymore. She just wouldn't take no for an answer. She turned pretty psycho."

"Objection," I said.

"Mr. Sommerville," Judge McGee said before Bailey could even respond. "Let's watch our word choice, shall we?"

"Sorry," Kurt said. "But that's my impression."

"Mr. Sommerville," Bailey said. "What about Ms. Sibley's behavior concerned you?"

"Well, her showing up unannounced was weird. Then some strange things started happening. My tires were slashed. My car got keyed with the word cheater."

"Did you file a police report?" Bailey asked.

"No. I didn't want to make an issue out of it. I didn't want to get Farrah in trouble. I just wanted her to leave me alone. So I told her that the next time she called."

"How did that go?"

"Not well."

"In what way?"

"She left this threatening voicemail."

"When was that?"

"March of that year. Four years ago."

"Do you still have that voicemail?"

"I do."

"Why did you keep it?"

"I was worried. I thought ... some of the things Farrah said to me got really nasty and threatening. I thought ... if something happened to me, I wanted to keep that voicemail."

"Your Honor, we'd like to mark State's Exhibit 57 for identification. Mr. Sommerville, do you still use the same cell phone number as the one you used four years ago?"

"Yes."

"You received a voicemail to this phone number on March 12th, four years ago?"

"That's right."

"Do you know who placed the call?"

"Yes. It showed up on my caller identification as Farrah Sibley."

"Did you listen to the voicemail?"

"Yes."

"Did you recognize the voice?"

"Absolutely. It was Farrah. She left me voicemails a lot over the course of our relationship. I know her voice. We dated and knew each other for years."

"At this time, I'd like to enter State's Exhibit 57 into evidence and play it for the jury."

"Objection as to improper foundation, and the fact that this exhibit's prejudicial effect outweighs its probative value. Ms. Sibley has not been charged with anything pertaining to Mr. Sommerville. Prior bad acts are inadmissible."

"As I indicated in my written brief," Bailey said. "This evidence is being introduced to show a pattern of behavior that is wholly relevant to the issues in this case."

"Your objection is noted and overruled," Judge McGee said to me. "You may proceed, Mr. Bailey."

There was a brief pause. The room filled with the sound of static. Then Farrah Sibley's voice came through loud and clear.

"You think you can treat me like this? You son of a bitch. I know where you live. I know where you stick your puny little dick these days. Nobody gets away with treating me like this. Nobody. You know I can make you sorry for trying to blow me off, Kurt. You hear me?"

As the recording went on, Farrah's voice sounded more unhinged. It cut off at the end.

An arm came over my shoulder. Eric stood right behind me. He put a folded piece of paper in front of me, then sat back down. I quietly opened the note. He wrote, "Go hard at the kid about Victor Sibley. As hard as you can."

I nodded, then folded the note again. Farrah looked at me, but I didn't show her the note.

"Was that the only message like that you got from Farrah Sibley?" Bailey asked Sommerville.

"The only voicemail. There were lots of texts though after that. They got weirder and weirder."

Bailey moved to enter the texts over my objections. McGee overruled me. A moment later, Bailey projected a screenshot showing a series of unanswered texts presumably from Farrah.

> Don't ignore me or else, Kurt. I'm not some plaything you can throw away. I've got feelings. And receipts. Remember that.

There was nothing for a few weeks. Then ...

> You're a sinner. God says Thou Shall Not Commit Adultery. Hell is waiting for you.
>
> The body is meant for the Lord and the Lord for the body.
>
> The fiery lake is waiting for you.
>
> You will reap what you sow, Kurt.

"Mr. Sommerville," Bailey said. "This text on April 17th, about reaping what you sow. Is that the last one you received from Ms. Sibley?"

"I blocked her contact after that. And I moved a few weeks later after I graduated from Northwestern. I went out to live with a cousin in Denver. As far as I know, Farrah didn't know where to find me after that. I told all of our mutual acquaintances to keep that quiet. I really thought she'd try to follow me out to Colorado. But I didn't hear from her again after that summer. I heard later she got a job at some big law firm in Ann Arbor. And I heard she was maybe dating someone she worked with there."

"How did that make you feel?"

"Relieved. Like I'd dodged a bullet."

"Did you ever see Farrah Sibley again after that?"

"No. I got married the next spring to my wife. I moved on. I assumed Farrah had too. Then ... all this started. I heard on the news she'd been arrested for murdering her boss."

"How did you feel about that? When you heard."

"I was shocked and not shocked. That's all I can say."

"Were you contacted by the police?"

"Yeah. I got a phone call from some detective, but I didn't return it. I'd moved on. This is all ... it's uncomfortable for me. And it's caused problems in my personal life."

"In what way?"

"Look, I'm not proud of this. But there was some overlap between Farrah and my wife. I wasn't completely honest with my wife about that. But I was ending things with Farrah. There was never any question in my mind who I wanted to be with."

"Why didn't you show the police these texts and voicemail after you heard about Farrah's arrest? If you weren't surprised, as you say."

"I'm ashamed of that now, okay? But they'd arrested her without anything to do with me. So I figured they had whatever evidence they needed. I told you they called and I ignored them. Then they stopped calling. So I figured they didn't think I was important. Nobody asked to see my phone. I haven't done anything wrong. I really didn't want to get dragged into this. It's upsetting for my wife. It's dredging up past history I'd have rather just left behind. Farrah's not in my life now. At all. That's the way I wanted to keep it."

"Thank you," Bailey said. "I have no further questions."

"Ms. Leary?"

I wanted to look at Farrah. See how she was holding up. I could feel the tension emanating from her. Keep it together, I thought. Just keep yourself together.

"Mr. Sommerville," I said. "If I understand your testimony, you were lying to Farrah Sibley about seeing other people during your relationship, weren't you?"

"What?"

"Well, you just admitted there was some overlap, as you called it, with your current wife Annabelle and Farrah Sibley. You were dating both women at the same time. Is that correct?"

"It's not how you're making it sound."

"Well, how is it then? Were you sleeping with Farrah Sibley and Annabelle during the same timeframe?"

"I don't … I wasn't … do I really have to answer that?"

"Yes or no," I said.

"Yes. There was overlap. That's what I said. How many ways can I say it?"

"Did you tell Annabelle you were continuing a sexual relationship with Farrah?"

"I'm not proud of how things went down during that time. I've never claimed I was."

"That's not my question. My question is whether you told Annabelle Gordon that you were still intimate with Farrah Sibley?"

"No. I didn't tell her. I didn't see the need since I was ending it with Farrah."

"Did you tell Farrah you were still seeing Annabelle?"

"Not at first, no. But she found out somehow. I think she followed me."

"Did she confront you about it?"

"Yes."

"She confronted you about it when she came to visit you that February, isn't that right? Isn't that what caused her to be upset with you that day? Because she found out you were having an affair with Annabelle while you were with her."

"That's not how I'd describe it."

"But you were lying to both women, weren't you?"

"Yes."

"You claimed that you hadn't seen or spoken to Farrah in nearly four years prior to today's proceedings, isn't that right?"

"That's right."

"Or three and a half years since your breakup to the time you heard about her arrest, correct?"

"About that, yes."

"You saved what you describe as threatening voicemails on your phone. For three and a half years. And yet you expect this jury to believe you didn't feel compelled to come forward."

"I can't control what they believe. But I'm telling you the truth."

"The truth. Got it. And when Detective Eklund reached out to you, you never bothered to call and tell him about this alleged incident with your tires being slashed or your car being keyed, did you?"

"No."

"Never filed a police report? Did you take pictures of it?"

"What? No."

"Did you tell anyone else about it? Annabelle? A friend?"

"No. I didn't want to make a big deal of it. I felt bad for hurting Farrah. She was in law school. I knew she'd eventually have to pass a character and fitness background check. I didn't want her getting arrested or anything."

"How thoughtful."

"Ms. Leary?" Judge McGee said before Bailey could voice his objection.

"Mr. Sommerville," I said. "You don't know who sent those texts to you, do you?"

"What?"

"The texts you claim were from Farrah between April and July four years ago. You don't know for sure who sent them, do you?"

"They're from Farrah's phone. Who else would have sent them?"

"You were living in Evanston at the time, isn't that right?"

"Yes."

"And Farrah was in Ann Arbor?"

"As far as I know, yes."

"You didn't see her send those texts, did you?"

"No."

"When was the last time you tried to call Farrah Sibley?"

"I don't know. It's been years. I went no contact after those crazy texts came through."

"So you don't have any idea whether Farrah Sibley kept the same cell phone, do you?"

"No."

"And the phone number you're talking about for Farrah. Do you know whether it was registered to her?"

"I don't know. It was the phone she had when we were in college. She was on her dad's plan."

"Her father. Victor Sibley. How well do you know him?"

"Not well. We didn't get along."

"Why is that?"

"He's kind of old school. Religious. Judgmental. He didn't like me, um ... fornicating with Farrah."

"Fornicating. Mr. Sommerville, can you reread the text you received from Farrah's phone on March 8th?"

"Uh ... sure. She said You're a sinner. God says Thou Shall Not Commit Adultery. Hell is waiting for you."

"Farrah herself never quoted scripture to you, did she?"

"Not that I recall, no."

"Her father did though, didn't he?"

"Oh yeah. All the time. Like I said, we didn't get along."

"In what way?"

"He just never liked me. I'd come over to pick Farrah up and he wouldn't invite me in. He'd barely speak to me. One time I just waited in my car for Farrah to come out and he walked up to me. He didn't say anything but he pointed to his eyes then back to me. You know, to let me know he was watching me. He was creepy. I stopped going to her house not long after that. Who needs that crap?"

"Would it surprise you to know that Farrah Sibley hasn't used the cell phone number associated with those texts in over four years?"

"I wouldn't know. Like I said, I blocked that number from my phone."

"But you knew that number was from a phone on Farrah's father's cell phone plan."

"I knew that. Yes. She had it in college."

"Her father could have sent those texts, couldn't he?"

"Objection." Bailey said. "Calls for speculation."

"Cass, don't!" I turned, shocked that the protest came from Farrah herself. Jeanie leaned over and whispered in Farrah's ear. Farrah pleaded at me with her eyes. Why was she protecting her father?

Judge McGee banged her gavel.

"Sustained," McGee said. "Stick to observable facts, Ms. Leary."

"Mr. Sommerville, it's possible someone else could have sent those texts because you didn't see Farrah send them, correct?"

"I didn't see her send them. I just received them."

"And you blocked her number so you have no idea whether that phone number remained in use after that."

"I don't know. That's correct."

"And you never saw fit to tell the police, specifically Detective Eklund, if you had any knowledge that might help his investigation, did you?"

"I didn't tell him about them then, no."

"Thank you," I said. "I have no other questions."

"Redirect, Mr. Bailey?"

"Just one question, Your Honor," Bailey said. He passed me on his way to the lectern.

"Mr. Sommerville, to clarify, why didn't you tell Detective Eklund about the texts and voicemails?"

"I didn't want to reopen old wounds with Annabelle. Farrah is a sore point between us, as you can imagine. Annabelle has had two miscarriages during our marriage. I didn't see the need to upset her. I hate that this is upsetting her now. It's been really hard. She's hurt. She's angry. I wanted to stay out of this. And nobody asked me about them. But now? I just ... I couldn't sit by and not say something. It could have been me. What happened to this Dowd guy? It could have been me."

"Thank you, Mr. Sommerville. No further questions."

"All right," Judge McGee said. "You may step down. Mr. Bailey, you may call your next witness."

"Your Honor, at this time, the prosecution rests."

Kurt Sommerville walked past our table. Jeanie had a hand on Farrah's arm. Her face changed, becoming a mask of hatred. I stood up, trying to shield her from the jury. I couldn't tell if any of them saw. But she had murder in her eyes as Kurt got within a foot of her.

Chapter 22

"You wanna tell me what that was all about?" I asked.

Farrah sat with her back against the wall in the courthouse conference room. I wouldn't see her again until Tuesday morning when court reconvened and I started my case in chief. At that moment, I wanted to wring her neck.

"Kurt's a liar. And going up there, throwing his happy life and happy wife in my face. It's a lie, Cass. All of it. Annabelle made him miserable when we were together. He's with her because of the kids. And I've heard things. Their son may not even be Kurt's."

"Are you still in love with that guy?"

"No! God, no. I just don't like liars."

"I told you. Your one job in that courtroom is to keep your composure. The second that jury thinks you have a temper, we're sunk. Do you get that?"

"It's not your life in the balance. It's not easy."

"I know. But this is going to get harder before it gets better. You understand what I was trying to do out there?"

Farrah pursed her lips so hard they turned white. She stared at me. "Please don't."

"Don't what?"

"Don't do this. Don't drag my dad into this."

"I don't have a choice. You've sworn up and down you didn't send Kurt those texts. But they came from a phone registered to you. If you didn't send them, then someone who had access to your phone did. As far as I can figure, there's only one person who falls under that category."

"Please. Don't."

"Do you have that old phone in your possession?"

"No."

"I thought as much. You left it at your father's house when you moved out, didn't you?"

She looked down. Her answer came out as little more than a whisper. "Yes."

"All right then. And the substance of those texts doesn't sound like you, does it? Filled with references to scripture. That's something your father would do, isn't it?"

She pressed a thumb to her eye. "He's not part of this."

"How do you know that? I'm serious. Terrence Dowd is dead. Shot with a gun like the one you had stored at your father's house. Kurt Sommerville just testified under oath that your father basically threatened him in the past. You never told me that. I threw a Hail Mary pass out there and got lucky."

"My dad didn't kill Terry. He couldn't have. He wouldn't."

"Are you sure?" I said. I got close to her, forcing her to meet my eyes. "Are you willing to bet the rest of your life on that?"

"I don't know. God. I don't know. But he's my dad, Cass. It's ... it's just complicated. You wanna tell me your relationship with your father isn't just as complicated?"

"My relationship with my father isn't the issue."

"Isn't it?"

"Stop. Just. Stop."

"I don't want this. You work for me, remember? I don't want you dragging my father through the mud. I don't approve of it."

Rage bubbled up inside of me. She was the most difficult client I'd ever worked for. And she was making her own defense impossible.

"Either you let me do my job, or find another lawyer."

The color drained from Farrah's face. "You can't do that. You can't quit. I don't even think the judge would let you at this point."

"You wanna put that to the test? You're a lawyer. You can represent yourself from here on out. What I'm giving you is the best shot you have of walking out of this a free woman. Take it or leave it."

She sat in silence for a moment. Finally, she rose to her feet. "Fine," she said.

"Fine what? Fine, you'll let me do my job?"

"Yes. But be very careful. He's my father. And I know he didn't do this. I know it as much as I know I didn't do it. I don't want to trade my freedom for his."

"It won't come to that." What I wanted to say is it probably wouldn't come to that. But in all honesty, I wasn't sure. I just needed her to believe it. For now.

"Trust me," I said. "That's all I'm asking. I know what I'm doing."

"I hope so," she said. And so did I.

An hour later, I was back in my office in Delphi. Jeanie, Eric, and Tori had assembled in the upstairs conference room. Eric was pacing in front of the bookshelves.

"Great work today," Jeanie said. "I was just telling Eric. You've planted a hell of a seed."

"I just spent a half hour getting chewed out by my client for trying to keep her out of prison."

Eric stopped pacing. "She's mad at you?"

"What was that today?" Jeanie asked. "Her outburst. I had to practically sit on Farrah to keep her quiet."

"Thanks for doing that. She's inexplicably trying to protect her father. I came this close to quitting over it. Eric, what did you mean with that note? What do you have?"

Eric grabbed a brown accordion file off the table.

"I spent all day yesterday in Mount Pleasant. I talked to Victor Sibley's neighbors. A couple of people in town who know him.

Who knew Mrs. Sibley. A pretty disturbing picture started to emerge. I think you can use it."

"Show me," I said, taking a seat at the table. Eric pulled out a photocopy of a court pleading file stamped three years ago in the Isabella County Circuit Court.

"This is a petition for a personal protection order," I said. My heart stopped as I read the names of the petitioner and respondent.

"Farrah's mother got a PPO against her father? As recently as three years ago?"

"Not exactly," Eric said. "The order was never entered. Leighann Sibley withdrew the petition before it went to a hearing."

I flipped through the pages. There was no attorney of record. It was something she filed on her own. The affidavit in support was handwritten, presumably by Leighann Sibley. The facts were chilling.

"She was living in Grand Rapids at the time," Eric narrated as I quickly scanned the rest of the documents.

"She started dating a dentist. It got serious. Somehow, Victor found out where she was. Found out about her new man. Then he started getting nasty. Showed up at the bar where she worked. Threatened her. She got fired over it."

"She left the home when Farrah was just a kid. This affidavit was filed over a decade after they split up."

"They never formally divorced," Eric said. "It seems to be a pattern with Leighann. She filed for divorce but never followed through with it. Same thing with this PPO. I talked to the prosecutor up there. He remembers interviewing her. She was terrified of Victor. But he couldn't go forward when she decided to withdraw her petition. He lost track of her after that."

"She's still scared of him," Jeanie said. "We've all seen this kind of thing a thousand times."

"Farrah's terrified of Victor as well," I said. "I think that's the real reason she doesn't like the idea of me throwing suspicion his way."

"I just don't get it," Tori said. "Why would Victor kill Terrence Dowd, if that's where you're headed with this? I understand his jealousy of his wife's new boyfriends. But his daughter's?"

"The tone of those text messages on Kurt Sommerville's phone," I said. "The ones Farrah insists she didn't send. They're all fire and brimstone. Victor Sibley is an Old Testament kind of guy. If he thought his daughter's immortal soul was in danger for fornicating with Sommerville. Or later, getting involved with a thrice-divorced man."

"This feels like real right hand of God stuff," Eric said. "It's twisted. But it's a motive."

"I don't know how you're going to get it in," Jeanie said. "Victor Sibley's not the one on trial. You know Bailey's going to hammer that home."

"I still think Judge McGee made an appealable mistake when she allowed those texts in from Sommerville's phone. On paper anyway. But maybe she did me a favor. Maybe that ruling is the thing that'll help me deliver a Trojan horse of sorts. The jury heard the texts. Bailey's going to argue they show a pattern on Farrah's part. McGee has to let me rebut that. She has to let me bring evidence that Farrah didn't send them. And that Lars Eklund never bothered to pursue any of this."

"Do you think he did it though?" Tori asked. "Do we have any evidence that Victor Sibley was in Ann Arbor the day Terrence Dowd was shot?"

"Not so far," Eric said. "There's no footage of his car coming or going from the Belz Building parking structure. I took down his plates when we went out there. The neighbors confirm Sibley's been driving the same red Chevy pickup for the last fifteen years. I'm checking surveillance cameras from the buildings across and next to the Belz Building. Trying to see if he could have parked on the street. It's a long shot but ..."

"It's good, Eric. Really good. Keep at it."

"There's something else," he said, pulling another sheet of paper out of the accordion file. It was a printout of a social media profile of a Dr. Randall Baumgartner, DDS.

"This was Farrah's mom's boyfriend?" I asked, picking up the pages. "The one Victor got bent out of shape about?"

"One and the same," Eric said. "I tracked him down at work yesterday. It took some doing, but I got him to talk to me. He confirmed what Leighann wrote in her PPO affidavit. Sibley came after him, too. Quoting all kinds of fire and brimstone scripture."

"Just like the texts on Kurt Sommerville's phone," Tori said.

"Exactly," Eric agreed. "Baumgartner said Leighann was terrified of him. That she broke off their relationship because of it. Baumgartner offered to send a cop friend of his over to Sibley's to try and scare him off but Leighann wouldn't hear of it. She ghosted him not long after that. Me showing up was the first time he'd heard anything about her in three years."

"This is his pattern," I said. "He's been running off anyone Leighann got close to. And he started doing it with Terrence Dowd."

"We don't have proof of that," Tori said. "Do we? There's no indication that Victor Sibley ever contacted Terrence Dowd. We've been through his phone records. Nobody at Harriman Dowd has said Sibley ever showed up there."

"That's for Bailey to argue," I said. "We just need to give the jury a plausible alternative suspect. And I argue that Eklund never pursued it. Eric, this is great work."

"Something else is bothering me," Jeanie said. "Looking at Bailey's witness list. Why hasn't he called Shondra Dowd? She gave a statement to Eklund, saying roughly the same thing Lionel Harriman did. That Dowd told her he was afraid of Farrah."

"I don't know," I said. "Maybe he doesn't want to give me the chance to cross-examine her."

"You did damage when Lydia Whitford was on the stand, showing she's biased against Farrah because of her friendship with Shondra," Tori said. "My guess is Bailey doesn't want to give you another crack at that. So, should *you* call her instead?"

"I don't know," I said. "I'll think about it. For now, I'll just take it as another unintended gift from Bailey."

"I've got one more thing," Eric said. He produced three pieces of paper from the file. A smile spread across my face. Subpoenas for Randall Baumgartner, Victor Sibley, and Leighann Sibley to appear in court first thing Tuesday morning.

"These just need your signature," Eric said. "I'll serve them all today. But for this one it's just a formality. Baumgartner volunteered to come to court before I even asked him. He *really* doesn't like Victor Sibley."

"How did you find Leighann?" I asked.

"It wasn't that hard. Baumgartner heard from a friend of a friend she was working at a bar inside Detroit Metro. I called and found out she's working this afternoon."

I reached across the table and grabbed hold of Eric's collar. I pulled him to me and planted a big, sloppy kiss on his lips.

"You're brilliant," I said. "I love you! Eric, I think we've got it. I think we have reasonable doubt."

He kissed me back. For the first time since I heard Farrah Sibley's name, I was starting to believe I could save her.

Chapter 23

RANDALL BAUMGARTNER WOULD BE TRICKY. I knew he had plenty to say about Victor Sibley. But any of their dealings were riddled with hearsay that I had no clear path to getting in. Still, the jury had to hear his story.

Farrah bristled beside me as I called Dr. Baumgartner to the stand.

He seemed calm, confident, and at ease in the witness box. Eric learned Baumgartner had extensive experience testifying as an expert witness in dental malpractice cases, mostly for the insurance companies.

"Dr. Baumgartner," I started. "Will you please explain how you came to know the defendant in this case?"

"I know of her more than I know her. Three years ago, I was engaged to her mother Leighann Sibley."

"How long had you been dating Leighann?"

"We met online. I want to say five years ago. We communicated that way for several months before finally meeting in person. We hit it off and things got serious from there."

"I see. But you're no longer in a relationship with Leighann?"

"Regrettably, no."

"Can you tell me what happened?"

"It was a number of things. Some practical, some less so. As I said, we were engaged to be married. But the wedding couldn't take place until Leighann formally divorced her first husband, Victor Sibley. We ran into some issues regarding that. Things unraveled from there."

"What type of issues?"

"Leighann was reluctant to proceed with the divorce."

"Do you know why?"

"She was afraid of him. We spoke to a lawyer and came to understand that in order to get a divorce judgment from a Michigan court, Victor would have to be personally served. Leighann would have to communicate with him, at least through her lawyer. She didn't want to do that. And we were told she'd possibly have to disclose her current address. That was a deal-breaker for Leighann."

"Why is that, if you know?"

"Leighann was afraid for her physical safety where Sibley was concerned. She didn't want him in her life in any way. I pressed the issue. I felt her remaining married to this man was untenable. It was my understanding they'd been separated for over a decade at that point."

"Did you ever have contact with Victor Sibley during the time you dated Leighann?"

"Yes."

"What were the circumstances of that?"

"At my urging. At my insistence, actually, Leighann did file for divorce and have Victor served. Things went kind of how Leighann said they would. Victor started harassing her. Showing up at the bar where she worked. Threatening her."

"Objection," Bailey said. "Lack of foundation. It's unclear whether this witness has personal knowledge of the events he's describing. If it's something that was told to him, then it's improper hearsay."

"Ms. Leary," Judge McGee said. "He has a point."

"I think I can help clear that up, Your Honor."

"Please do."

"Mr. Baumgartner, do you have personal, firsthand knowledge of the harassment you just described?"

"Yes, ma'am. Leighann worked at Tipple and Toast in Grand Rapids. That bar is about a half a mile from my dental office. When we dated, I would frequently come in for lunch or hang out at the bar after I got done for the day. One of the times I was in for lunch, Victor Sibley came in. He made a scene, calling Leighann a whore. An adulterer. Quoting biblical verses. The bar manager had him thrown out."

"What did you do?"

"I confronted him. At one point, Victor reached across the bar and grabbed Leighann by the wrist. I pulled him off of her. He took a swing at me. We tussled a bit. That's when the manager stepped in."

"Were the police called? Did anyone make a report?"

"No. Leighann didn't want that. She wanted to handle it quietly. She was afraid the more we engaged with Victor the more dangerous he might become."

"Was that the only contact you had with Mr. Sibley?"

"No, ma'am. We went through a period of weeks where he would call her constantly. No idea where he got Leighann's cell phone number. That alone terrified her. And he started calling me at my office. Or leaving messages. Crazy stuff. All about fire and damnation and how we were sinners."

"Did he ever threaten you personally?"

"You mean that he was going to hurt me?"

"Sure. Or in any other way."

"It was mostly religious ramblings. Quoting scripture. But yes. That day at the bar when I pulled him off Leighann, he made a gesture with his hand. Like a gun. He pointed it at my chest, you know. Pantomiming like he was going to shoot me. I don't know what he specifically said to Leighann though. I just know that she was pretty scared. Like it triggered things for her. I got the impression that Victor had done a number on her."

"What do you mean?"

"Just ... it seemed obvious that this man had victimized her in her past. She would shake uncontrollably if he called or left a message. Run around cleaning the house or scrubbing the floors at all hours of the night after a text came through. I couldn't talk to her. It was disturbing. I begged her to get help. I begged her to call the police and get a restraining order."

"Did she?"

"Finally, yes. I picked up the paperwork to file a personal protection order. Leighann had to fill out this form where she had to describe in detail the types of things Victor was doing and why she felt he might harm her. I helped her fill that out. She could barely think straight. Then I took her down to the courthouse to file it. I thought things would change for the better after that."

"Did they?"

"No. They got worse. At least as far as our relationship."

"What do you mean?"

"I mean ... a few days after we filed the paperwork, Leighann came to my office and broke things off. That was it. She blocked my calls. Wouldn't talk to me again after that. I found out later that she'd dropped the petition to get a protection order."

"Did you talk to her again after that?"

"No, ma'am. As I said, Leighann blocked my calls. I went to try to see her at Tipple and Toast. I was told she no longer worked there. That was the end of it. I felt terrible, but Leighann clearly didn't want me in her life at that point so I respected her wishes."

"Did you hear from Victor Sibley after that?"

"The text messaging stopped pretty close to that time. I don't know if Leighann was in communication with him. I don't know if she got back together with him. I prayed that wasn't the case. But the messages stopped. So I assumed either Leighann had gotten back with him or that he knew we were no longer together and didn't have a reason to harass me anymore."

"Dr. Baumgartner, just to be clear, you're saying the messages you got from Victor Sibley were religious in nature?"

"Yes, ma'am. Quotes from scripture. He liked Corinthians 6:13 a lot. I think I had maybe four separate messages quoting that one."

"Do you recall what Corinthians 6:13 says?"

"I do indeed. My grandfather was a Baptist preacher. He drilled that one into my head pretty regularly. The body is not meant for sexual immorality but for the Lord and the Lord for the body."

I paused and got a quick look at the jury. Dr. Baumgartner had their rapt attention.

"Thank you," I said. "I have no further questions."

Bailey waited a moment, then rose. He made a show of shaking his head and holding his palms up as if he were at a real loss for words.

"Dr. Baumgartner, I don't even know where to start. How about this? You said you know who the defendant Farrah Sibley is. But have you met her?"

"No, sir."

"Have you ever laid eyes on her before today?"

"No, sir. I have not. She looks exactly like her mother though. It's uncanny."

Bailey's shoulders dropped. The comparison helped me more than it did him and he knew it.

"And you've never met Terrence Dowd, have you?"

"No, sir."

"Never even heard of him until you stepped into this courtroom, have you?"

"Well, that's not technically true, sir. But I think I understand your point. It's true I never heard of Terrence Dowd until I was informed about this case."

"Who was it who informed you?"

"A man working for Ms. Leary. Her investigator."

"I see. So this investigator told you all about the case, did he?"

"I wouldn't say all about it, no. Just that Leighann's daughter was on trial for killing an ex-boyfriend. And he asked me if I could tell him about my relationship with Leighann. I told him basically what I just testified to in court today. And he asked me if I'd come to court. Of course I said yes."

"Of course? Why of course?"

"Because I saw no harm in it. It's the truth. If it helps one way or another, that's not up to me. That's up to all of you."

"But you don't know anything about Farrah Sibley, do you? Other than the fact she's Leighann's daughter."

"I don't know her personally, no."

"So you have absolutely no knowledge of the facts of this case, do you?"

"Not really. No. Only what's been reported in the local media. Though I don't hold much store in that."

"And by your own admission, it's been years since you had any communication with Leighann or Victor Sibley."

"That's true, yes."

"And you never knew Farrah Sibley?"

"No, sir, I didn't. I don't believe Leighann was in contact with her at the time we dated."

"You really don't know anything at all about the people or facts of this case then, do you?"

"Objection," I said. "Mr. Bailey has asked a variation of this question multiple times. He's gotten an answer, multiple times."

"Sustained. Do you have any new ground to cover, Mr. Bailey?"

Bailey had a smug smile on his face. "No, Your Honor, I guess I don't. Thank you for your time, Dr. Baumgartner."

"You may step down," Judge McGee said. "Your next witness, Ms. Leary?"

I rose. I waited for Randy Baumgartner to clear the courtroom. "Your Honor, the defense calls Victor Sibley."

There were audible rumblings from the jury. Farrah dropped her chin to her chest. I turned. Eric was at the back of the courtroom. He gave me a quick thumbs up. Then both courtroom doors opened and Victor strode in holding his own Bible.

Chapter 24

Before I could ask my first question, Bailey had us at a sidebar.

"Your Honor, this has gone on long enough. Defense counsel is flinging wild, irrelevant theories. She's calling witnesses that were never disclosed. There's no proof this witness has any firsthand knowledge of the events of this case."

"Once again," I said. "The prosecution opened the door when they suggested my client sent texts to an ex-boyfriend they can't prove she sent. Mr. Bailey wants to try showing a pattern of behavior on my client's part? Fine. It's proper and relevant to allow me to bring witnesses that can cast doubt on that."

Judge McGee chewed on the end of her pen. "I'm inclined to agree with Ms. Leary on this one," she said.

"And you can't say Victor Sibley wasn't disclosed," I said. "He's the defendant's father. It's not my fault or responsibility that your detective failed to run down other leads."

"All right," Judge McGee said. "Now's not the time to rehash that. Save it for your closing argument. I'll allow this witness to testify. But I expect you to confine your questioning to events and facts that have something to do with this case. No fishing expeditions from the witness box."

"Yes, Your Honor," I said. "Thank you."

Bailey walked back to his table in a huff. Victor Sibley seemed nonplussed by the whole affair, clutching his red Bible like a talisman in front of him.

"Mr. Sibley," I said. "Thank you for being here. I need to ask you a few questions that might seem obvious, but that nice lady over there is making a transcript of everything we say. And it's my job to make a record."

"I understand," he said.

"All right. Would you mind telling the jury how you're related to the defendant, Farrah Sibley?"

"She's my only child," he said. "My daughter."

I didn't dare look back at Farrah. It was Jeanie's job to keep her under control. I didn't like her color right after Victor waltzed into the courtroom.

"Prior to her arrest, how frequently did you speak to your daughter?"

"We've grown apart," he said. "It's not my wish. But Farrah wanted to follow her own path. She's made choices I don't necessarily approve of, but that's what happens with children when they become adults."

"What choices don't you approve of?"

"I would have preferred had she stayed closer to home."

"Mount Pleasant?"

"That's correct. I own a farm … well … I don't actually farm it myself. But I live alone in the big house she grew up in. The one that's been in my family for two generations before me. I'm not getting younger or more mobile. I would have preferred my daughter was around to help me. The way I did for my parents and they did for theirs."

"I see. So is it just that she's moved to Ann Arbor that you disapprove of?"

"Farrah has always been strong-willed. Independent. She's made choices I wouldn't have made for her."

"Like what?"

"I would have preferred she pursued a more noble profession. Teaching. Or her own ministry. Or if she'd settled down with someone and kept a home."

"You don't like that she went to law school?"

"I said it wasn't my choice for her, no."

"You don't regard the legal profession as particularly noble, then, do you? Is that what you're saying?"

"It's not exactly the Lord's work, in my opinion. Woe to you lawyers also. For you load men with burdens that are difficult to carry and you yourselves won't even lift one finger to help. Luke 11:45. He who justifies the wicked and condemns the righteous are both alike, an abomination to the Lord. Proverbs 17:15."

"You like to quote scripture?"

"I follow the Lord's path," he said. "That is all I wish for my daughter."

"Did you ever express that opinion to Farrah?"

"She knows how I feel. She knows my expectations."

"Have you argued with her about those expectations?"

"She's always been willful. She knows how I feel. But she also knows my door is always open to her to come home. I'd hoped someday she would. Now?"

"Now what?"

"Now, I'm afraid she may be too far gone."

"Too far gone from what? Godliness?"

"Yes."

"But it's not your place to judge that, is it? It's God's place, isn't it?"

"It's my job to help steer Farrah to a righteous path. That's every parent's job. My biggest regret is that I've failed in that. Farrah has fallen from grace. She lives in a state of sin. But she's not beyond redemption. No one is."

"A state of sin. Mr. Sibley, what sin are you referring to?"

"That's between Farrah and the Lord."

"Is it? Because you're the one proclaiming it here today. What exactly is it that you think Farrah has done?"

"The sexually immoral person sins against his own body," he said.

"That would be Corinthians again? Fornication," I said. "It upsets you that your daughter has had relations with men she wasn't married to. Is that her sin in your eyes?"

"Not my eyes. She has sinned before God."

"But she's not alone in her sin, is she? Fornication, as you call it, takes two people, doesn't it?"

"That's a ridiculous question."

"All right, then let me ask another one. You've been vocal about your opinion of your daughter's so-called sins, haven't you?"

"She knows my opinion, yes. And she knows what the Bible says about it. There are no shortcomings in her religious education."

"She's a disappointment to you, isn't she?"

I heard a choked sound behind me. Farrah was crying but trying to hold it in.

"I'm not her final judge. But she will be judged. She knows that."

"By God."

"Of course. As will you, Ms. Leary."

"Thanks for the reminder. Mr. Sibley, you've made a habit of sending messages to your daughter quoting scripture to her, haven't you?"

"Sometimes."

"You send them to your ex-wife on occasion too, don't you?"

"If you mean Leighann, there's nothing ex about her. We are legally married and spiritually married for eternity."

"You're not too happy with the state of Leighann's immortal soul either, are you?"

"Objection," Bailey said. "Your Honor, we've gone beyond relevance here."

"I agree. Stick to the issues at hand, Ms. Leary."

I was close. Very close. I could smell blood in the water. If I could push the man just a little more, pop the seal, if you will. But I also knew Judge McGee had granted me about as much leeway as I was likely to get.

"Mr. Sibley," I said, abruptly changing tactics. "When did you first allow Farrah to have a cell phone?"

His face changed to confusion. Good. I wanted him off guard as much as possible.

"When she was sixteen. When she got her driver's license and started working outside the home, I felt it was a safety measure. But I had very strict rules about how much screen time she was allowed. And what she was permitted to use her phone for."

"Naturally. But you paid for the phone, correct?"

"Yes."

"It was part of your cell phone plan, wasn't it?"

"It was. Yes."

"Do you recall how long you paid for that phone? How long she remained on your plan?"

"I believe when she graduated from college, from Central Michigan, she finally purchased her own phone and her own plan."

"You cut her off, essentially, didn't you? When she left for Ann Arbor to go to law school."

"I stopped financially supporting her, that's true."

"You threw her out of the house, didn't you?"

"I wouldn't say that. But I told her if she insisted on pursuing that profession, she would do so without my financial backing."

"I see. And that included everything. Rent. Tuition. Her car insurance. Her cell phone. Everything, right?"

"That's correct, yes."

"What happened to the cell phone when she left for Ann Arbor? The one you'd been paying for?"

"I don't recall."

"Did she take it with her?"

"Most certainly not. I told her I wouldn't be funding her anymore."

"So she left that phone at home?"

"I believe so."

"Did you keep it on your plan? Did you keep it active?"

"I might have, yes. For a time."

"Was it password locked, if you recall?"

"Farrah's phone? While I was paying for it? Most certainly not. I told her I'd take it away from her the second I couldn't get into it."

"Thank you. Have you ever looked through it?"

"Her phone? When she was younger? Of course. Any good parent should."

"You read her texts?"

"Yes."

"She texted boys sometimes, didn't she?"

Sibley frowned. "I don't know why you keep insisting on bringing this up. I told you. I didn't approve of some of the choices my daughter made."

"You didn't approve of Kurt Sommerville?"

"I didn't approve of his intentions."

"His intentions. He was having sex with your daughter, and that upset you."

"Are you determined to embarrass me, Ms. Sibley?"

"You didn't approve of any of Farrah's boyfriends, did you?"

"They weren't boyfriends. They weren't honorable men. My daughter chooses to live in a state of sin. It is the great shame of my life."

"In a state of sin. You mean fornicating. That's what you believe?"

"Objection, Your Honor ..."

"Ms. Leary, I think ..."

"How dare you!" Victor Sibley boomed. He rose from his seat. He waved his Bible above his head. "They rely on empty pleas. They speak lies. They conceive mischief and give birth to iniquity. Isaiah 59:4. You want to embarrass me. You want to parade my daughter's sins in front of the whole world to shame me more. There is only one lawgiver and judge, He who is able to save and destroy! You mock me. You think this is some joke. That I'm some scapegoat for the horrible deeds my daughter has perpetrated. Well, I won't have it. I won't stand for it!"

Judge McGee banged her gavel. "Enough. Mr. Sibley, sit down. Ms. Leary? Mr. Bailey. Please approach the bench."

McGee was fuming by the time I got there. She clamped her hand over her microphone.

"That's enough, Ms. Leary," she said. "Other than Mr. Sibley's cell phone testimony, is there any other ground you need to cover with him?"

"No, Your Honor," I said. "I was just about to finish my direct."

"Good."

"You Honor ..." Bailey started.

"I'm going to ask that his last outburst be stricken from the record. Okay?"

Bailey glared at me. "It's a start."

"Let's get this over with," McGee said. We went back to our neutral corners.

"Mr. Sibley," I said. Then I paused. The man had turned beet red. Sweat poured down his cheeks. I turned and looked at Farrah. Her face was covered in blotches. She trembled beside Jeanie. I watched her mouth "I'm sorry, Dad" to her father.

"Mr. Sibley, were you ever questioned by the police in connection with Farrah's arrest?"

"No."

"You never received a phone call from Detective Lars Eklund?"

"No."

"He never came to your home or asked to search it?"

"Absolutely not!"

"Thank you. I have no further questions."

Bailey practically sputtered when he got to his feet.

"Mr. Sibley," he started. "Have you ever known your daughter to be violent?"

"What do you mean?"

"Well, isn't it true that you were called to her school on numerous occasions due to fights she got into with other girls?"

"She was a troubled child. Her mother wasn't the best influence on her, no. She was too lenient."

"Was that a yes or a no?"

"Yes. Farrah had some difficulties in high school. I homeschooled her in her senior year because of it."

"Because of fighting."

"Yes."

"Have you ever visited your daughter at work?"

"What?"

"Since she began her employment at Harriman Dowd. Did you ever visit her?"

"No. I wouldn't."

The Client List

"Because you don't approve of her chosen profession."

"That and because she never invited me."

"So you never met Terrence Dowd, Farrah's former boss?"

"No."

"You've never even been to Farrah's apartment in Ann Arbor, have you?"

"No."

"Ms. Leary has implied a few things in her direct examination. So I'm going to ask you directly. Did you ever text Kurt Sommerville using Farrah's old phone?"

"I most certainly did not. That's a ridiculous accusation. If I had something to say to that boy, I said it to his face. You can ask him."

"You're aware Farrah purchased a handgun. A Glock 19?"

"I'm aware of that. Yes. I encouraged it. Everyone should know how to use a gun."

"You taught her how to shoot?"

"Yes. I took her deer hunting with me when she was a child. Farrah was always a fantastic shot."

"Fantastic," Bailey repeated. "Thank you, Mr. Sibley. I have no further questions."

"Ms. Leary?"

"Nothing more from me," I said.

Victor seemed to tower over Farrah as he passed by our table.

"I can't breathe," she whispered to me. "I can't stay here. Cass …"

"Are you ready to call your next witness?" Judge McGee said.

"Yes, Your Honor," I answered. I just wasn't sure my client would be ready for it.

Chapter 25

I TURNED BACK TO ERIC. He gave me the subtlest nod as he walked back out into the hallway to retrieve my next witness. He'd kept her sequestered in an empty conference room with a deputy watching the door.

"Cass," Farrah whispered to me. "I've changed my mind. I don't want you to do this."

"Ms. Leary?" Judge McGee asked.

"You have to trust me," I whispered back to Farrah. "We have to see this through now if I'm to have any hope of raising reasonable doubt for you."

She kept her head down, but didn't protest anymore.

"Your Honor," I said. "The defense calls Leighann Sibley to the stand."

"I'd like to renew my objection as to the relevance of this witness's testimony," Bailey said.

"Do you have anything to add to your objection?"

"I do," Bailey said.

"All right," McGee said. "Let's have the jury take a fifteen-minute recess. We'll start lunch a little later today."

The jury rose and the bailiff ushered them out. I waited at my table until every last juror and their alternates cleared the courtroom.

"Cass," Jeanie whispered beside me. "Eric hasn't come back yet."

I turned and looked at the double doors to the hallway. Eric should be back in the gallery by now. He should have Leighann Sibley with him.

"Your Honor," Bailey started. "The court has been more than lenient with Ms. Leary's last couple of witnesses. But she's attempting to put Victor Sibley on trial. She's called witnesses who have no personal knowledge of the facts of this case. Now she's attempting to drag the defendant's estranged mother to the stand. Her own witness, Mr. Baumgartner, testified that Farrah and Leighann Sibley haven't had any sort of relationship in over a decade. There can be no probative value to Mrs. Sibley's testimony. It's a wild goose chase. It's irrelevant at best and highly prejudicial at worst."

"Ms. Leary?"

"Again, Mr. Bailey raised questions during his case in chief regarding my client's alleged behavior with previous boyfriends. Over my objections, I might add. I have every right to rebut that evidence with these witnesses. Additionally, the conduct of the investigators of this case is always at issue. Mr. Sibley admitted that he was never even interviewed by Detective Eklund. It is absolutely relevant and appropriate for me to explore that further."

"And how is Leighann Sibley going to help you do that?" Judge McGee asked.

"By showing the jury that there are alternate suspects and theories of the case that were never explored. Leighann Sibley has unique insight into how Victor Sibley operates. She can establish a pattern of conduct that will refute Mr. Bailey's patently false implication that Farrah Sibley was in the habit of stalking and threatening her boyfriends."

"It wasn't an implication," Bailey said. "My witness has proof of it."

"Your interpretation," I said. "Not proof. You never even bothered to find out who else might have had access to that cell phone."

"All right, enough," Judge McGee said. "Ms. Leary, are you suggesting that Leighann Sibley has personal knowledge of her husband texting from a phone belonging to their daughter or impersonating her?"

"No," I said. "But ..."

Judge McGee put a hand up to silence me. "Was Mrs. Sibley in contact with her daughter during the timeframe she dated Kurt Sommerville?"

"I don't believe so," I said. "But once again, this is a pattern of behavior we're talking about."

"Your Honor," Bailey interjected. "Not only was Mrs. Sibley not in contact with her daughter during the Sommerville relationship. It's my understanding she wasn't in contact with her during her relationship with the victim in this case, either."

"Ms. Leary, I'm sorry. I'm inclined to agree with Mr. Bailey here. You've failed to convince me that Leighann Sibley will have anything relevant to say."

"With all due respect, Your Honor, it's for the finder of fact ... the jury to determine whether her testimony is credible."

"I'm not talking about credibility. I'm talking about relevancy and that's a matter of law, not fact."

The courtroom doors banged shut behind me. I turned my head. Eric had just walked back in. Alone. He made a chopping gesture across his neck. Jeanie had her head turned as well. She whispered something to Eric. He charged forward and leaned down to whisper something back to her in her ear.

Something was wrong. Farrah's mouth dropped as she heard whatever it was Eric had to say.

"Ms. Leary?" Judge McGee asked. "Is there something wrong?"

"I'm ... I'm not sure, Your Honor. Could I have a moment to confer with my co-counsel?"

"You may, but I'm ready to render my ruling here."

"One moment," I said. I walked back to the table.

Eric straightened. I didn't like the expression on his face.

"What's going on?" I whispered.

"She's gone," Eric said.

I turned back to the judge. The scowl on her face didn't instill any confidence in me.

"What do you mean, gone?" I asked.

"Leighann Sibley's AWOL," he said.

"Cass," Farrah said. "If she saw my dad ..."

"She didn't," Eric said. "I made sure of it. She was one floor below and out of sight. There's no way he knew how to find her."

Farrah buried her face in her hands.

"Ms. Leary?" Judge McGee said. "Your moment is up."

"Your Honor," I said. "If I could just have a brief recess. I need to ..."

"No," she said. "We need to move on. I'm going to sustain Mr. Bailey's objection. Unless you can provide some offer of proof that Leighann Sibley has personal knowledge of the events of this case, the bulk of her testimony will likely fall under MRE 403. The probative value is outweighed by undue prejudice. Not to mention, she wasn't on your witness list to begin with. I have to strike a balance here. I believe I've struck that by allowing the testimony of Victor Sibley. But ..."

"Your Honor," I said, letting my temper get the better of me. "My client is on trial for her freedom. For the rest of her life. She is accused of murdering a man. You cannot deny her the ability to call witnesses in her own defense. The prosecution will have the opportunity to cross-examine Mrs. Sibley. He will be free to argue as to the weight he feels the jury should afford her testimony. But to deny me the ability to put her on the stand at all? That is a denial of Farrah Sibley's basic right to a fair trial."

I'd gone too far, perhaps. For a moment, I expected flames to shoot out of Judge McGee's eyes by the way she glared at me.

"Ms. Leary, this is my courtroom. You're not in Woodbridge County today. I'm not sure how it works there, but here? When I'm speaking, you don't. Got it?"

"My apologies, Your Honor. I'm just ..."

"Just going to speak whenever you feel like it. This is my ruling. I will not prevent you from calling Mrs. Sibley. But if she can't establish that she has personal knowledge of the events of this case, I'm going to sustain Mr. Bailey's objections on those grounds. Are we clear?"

"Yes, Your Honor," I said.

"Are you ready to proceed?"

Lord. The thin ice I stood on started to crack. "If I could just have another fifteen minutes," I said.

"You have the five minutes we have left on the original fifteen-minute recess I granted the jury."

She banged her gavel. I got the impression she would have preferred lobbing it at my head.

"Stay with Farrah," I said to Jeanie. Then I rushed out of the courtroom with Eric in tow.

"We're screwed," I said. "Where the hell is she, Eric?"

We raced down one flight of stairs and made our way to the first-floor empty jury room. The door stood ajar. The room was empty.

"Let me go talk to the deputies at the front entrance," he said. "There's only one way in or out of here to the general public.

They were supposed to make sure nobody went back there. They were supposed to tell me if she tried to goddamn leave!"

"Where's Victor? Did anyone see him leave?"

Two deputies were busy ushering three people through the metal detectors. One of the deputies looked well past retirement age. Eric started his cop-to-cop smooth talk. I hung back, knowing he'd likely get better results if I stayed out of it. I couldn't hear what they were saying, but a frown settled on Eric's face. He ran a hand through his hair in a gesture of frustration. Then he walked back to me.

"She left with him," he said.

"With Victor?"

"Ten minutes ago," he said. "Somebody from the bar association offices went into the empty jury room and brought her out. Another lawyer wanted the room to talk to a client between hearings."

"He saw her. Victor saw her."

"Deputy Smitty over there says she didn't seem upset or in any kind of distress. He said they were arm in arm when they walked out the front door. Sibley was parked across the street and she got into his car."

I pulled my phone out and dialed the number Leighann Sibley reluctantly gave Eric. It went straight to voicemail.

"Can you stall for more time with the judge?"

"Not likely," I said. "She's about to rip me a new one as it is."

"How bad do you need her? I mean, really. Bailey's got at least half a point, hasn't he? Victor's the scary one."

I hit redial. Again, my call went straight to Leighann Sibley's voicemail. I wanted to throw the damn phone through the wall.

"She's under subpoena," I said. "I can ask for a bench warrant."

"If we can find her again. Dammit, Cass, I should have sat on her."

"It's not your fault," I said.

A text came through from Jeanie.

"Judge McGee's about to start without you. Better get up here."

"I'm out of time," I said.

I took the stairs two at a time to the second floor with Eric right beside me. My heart raced. My head pounded.

"Are you ready to proceed, Ms. Leary?" Judge McGee asked, though it felt like a rhetorical question.

"Yes," I said. The jury filed in. Beside me, Farrah looked like she was about to be sick. "Call your next witness," McGee said. I clenched my fists. There was only one thing I could do.

"Your Honor. At this time, the defense rests."

Judge McGee's head snapped up. She gave me a puzzled look. Then turned to Jason Bailey. He had a smug smile on his face. I wanted to knock off.

"Do you wish to call your first rebuttal witness, Mr. Bailey?"

"No, Your Honor," Bailey said in a clear, assured voice. "The prosecution is ready to proceed to closing arguments after lunch."

"All right," she said. "Then that's what we'll do."

Farrah Sibley let out a sob. All twelve members of the jury fixed their stares at her. As I stood there, I couldn't tell whether their collective expression signaled sympathy or hatred.

Chapter 26

When Farrah Sibley fell apart, she did so loudly, epically, and for five whole minutes I couldn't get a word in edgewise.

"You have to find him! I have to talk to him!" Her skin had turned an awful shade of purple. For long pauses, she flat out forgot to breathe.

"Farrah, there's nothing we can do right now. In five minutes, Bailey will deliver his closing argument. As hard as this is, you have to stay calm. You can't let the jury see these big swings of emotion from you. It's what Bailey wants."

"He's not part of this. My father can't be part of this. He just can't be."

Eric was still out there, trying to find out what happened to Leighann Sibley. Jeanie went to get a bottle of water for Farrah.

I got in Farrah's face. If she raised her voice again, two deputies would likely burst in to interrupt us. This was my last chance to get through to her.

"It's almost over."

"You don't understand my dad. He's going to think this was all my idea, you putting him on the stand. Accusing him of ..."

"I didn't accuse him of anything. He had his opportunity to tell his side of it. But what I argued to the judge is the truth. You and I both know it was your dad who sent those awful messages to Kurt Sommerville. That had to come out. Now stay with me. Keep it together for just a little while longer. We'll have a chance to talk again after closing arguments are over and jury instructions are given."

Jeanie walked back in with the water bottle. Farrah's hand shook so badly she couldn't unscrew the top. I did it for her. She downed more than half the bottle's contents in one giant chug. Immediately after, her color returned to normal.

"I just need a Xanax. Do you have one?" she asked.

"No. Afraid not. But you're doing fine without it." It was a complete lie, but one I needed her to believe.

The door cracked open again. One of the deputies poked her head in. "Judge is ready for you. Time to go, Sibley."

Farrah rose almost on autopilot. It was okay that she was scared. She was human. But she could *not* make another outburst during closing. Jeanie gave me a dubious glance behind Farrah's back. Then the three of us headed into the courtroom together.

Jason Bailey was already at the lectern as the jury filed in. Farrah's whole posture had changed. She looked small, almost childlike. She twisted her body as far away from the jury as she could. I think if she could have crawled into Jeanie's lap, she might have.

"Ladies and gentlemen," Bailey started. "I commend you. You've been patient. You've been asked to put up with a lot. To witness a lot. The attention you've paid to this case has impressed me. You've hung in there with me for almost two weeks of difficult, sometimes gruesome testimony. I know you're anxious to do what you were selected to do. So I'll try not to waste any more of your time telling you things you already know. Things that have been right in front of your face this whole time, in spite of the outlandish theories Ms. Leary has tried to throw out there."

Here we go.

"In some ways," Bailey continued. "This is one of the easiest closing arguments I've ever had to give. The facts are simple. Straightforward. Largely undisputed. But none of that can lessen the tragedy of what happened.

"Terrence Dowd was murdered by Farrah Sibley for one of the simplest, oldest, most common motives there is. She loved him. He didn't love her back in the way she wanted him to. He tried to end it. Tried to ignore her. Tried to undo what he knew was a mistake. Because that's the awful truth. To Terrence Dowd, Farrah was a mistake he knew he shouldn't have made.

"In a sense, through Farrah's text messages and voicemails, you got to eyewitness the unraveling of this relationship. I'll admit, those things were hard for me to hear as well. You could see what was coming. You want to reach through time and warn Terrence Dowd. This woman is going to hurt you. Don't be alone with her. Watch your back.

"Let's look at the facts. On July 17th, Terrence Dowd went to work. He thought he was taking his life back. He'd gone to Lionel Harriman and confessed his great sin. He went about his day. He treated Farrah Sibley like a professional. He thought he was doing the right thing. What made Farrah snap that day? At that moment, we don't know. But we know she had become unglued throughout the weekend. You heard it in her voice. She told Terrence she would make him deal with her. She went to his home. Stalked him. And he ignored her. He didn't play into her breakdown. He went to work.

"We know he left the office just before 8:00 p.m. and headed to his car. We know Farrah was the only other person in the building. The defense wants to sell you some fantasy story that some phantom past employee swooped in, used Farrah's copy code, then what, levitated out without being caught on any security camera?

"Just like the defense wants you to believe someone else posed as Farrah when she sent her threatening texts? It's ridiculous. You know it's ridiculous. It's an insult to your intelligence really. And none of it's true. Farrah Sibley knew exactly how to get down to that garage without being seen. You saw her leave through the elevator to the parking structure every day. Every time. In full view of the cameras in the weeks leading up to the murder. I didn't have to prove that to you. You witnessed it on that footage. Except this day. She didn't want to be seen. So she took the stairs. So she could sneak up on Terrence Dowd unseen by any cameras.

"She confronted him using the Glock 19 registered to her. That her father taught her how to shoot. We don't know what Terrence said to her. If he pleaded with his life. But Farrah Sibley shot him through the chest. The coroner said he was dead in seconds. Losing almost his entire blood volume in a matter of minutes.

"And you saw Farrah Sibley and only Farrah Sibley emerge from that parking structure at 9:33 p.m. Nobody else went in. Nobody else came out. Only Farrah. The one person with the purest motive to do Terrence Dowd harm.

"Second degree murder only requires that we prove an unplanned but intentional killing. A crime of passion. Farrah Sibley loved Terrence Dowd. She wanted to own him. Control him. Possess him. And when she didn't get what she wanted, she ended his life. She made him pay. Just like she swore to him she would.

"This case is simple. Tragic. And it didn't have to happen. We can't warn Terrence Dowd. We can't help him. But we can bring him justice. I know you'll do that. Thank you."

I straightened my suit jacket and walked to the lectern. Farrah had changed. Gone robot. I wasn't sure if that was better or worse as far as the jury's impression. But I couldn't control it now.

I surveyed the panel. I had all of their eyes. Serious. Dedicated people. I thanked them for it.

"Mr. Bailey tells a good story. But as I said to you at the beginning of last week, that's all he's got. All he's been able to do is tell you a story about a woman with character flaws. Who made some bad decisions. But he hasn't proven murder. He's proven circumstances at best.

"Farrah Sibley was the easy mark in this case. The low-hanging fruit. The jilted soon-to-be ex-girlfriend. So let's look at his evidence piece by piece. Imagine, if you will, a movie playing in your mind. The scene of the crime. We'll play it backwards from the moment Terrence Dowd was shot.

"Mr. Bailey has put forth that the bullet that killed Terrence Bailey came from a Glock 19. That's it. A Glock 19. One of the most common handguns in circulation in this country. He thinks, aha! Farrah Sibley bought a Glock 19 several years ago. So did thousands of people in this state alone. He can't prove that the bullet that killed Terrence Dowd came from Farrah's gun. That's more than reasonable doubt. That's complete doubt.

"But let's step back and widen the shot. He says Farrah Sibley must be guilty because it appears she took a different route to the parking garage than she normally takes. The stairs.

"First of all, that's conjecture. There's no proof that she took the stairs. There's no proof when she entered the parking structure. All we have is footage of her leaving the parking garage well after Mr. Dowd entered it. Their cars weren't parked on the same floor. They were in different parts of the structure. There's no proof of anything other than what time Farrah Sibley left for home. Mr. Bailey wants you to think that's something more than what it is. She worked in the Belz Building. She had a reason for being there. There's nothing nefarious in that.

"Mr. Dowd suffered a mortal wound. He was shot through the heart. There was blood spatter on his car door. On his pant legs. His windshield. And yet there was no physical evidence tying Farrah Sibley to this case. They found no blood on her clothing. Clothing that was found in her laundry hamper and tested. There was no gun residue on her hands. No evidence that she fired a gun or was anywhere near Mr. Dowd when he was shot.

"Now let's widen the lens even further. Farrah Sibley was in the office, working late like Mr. Dowd. If we take Mr. Bailey's argument at face value, he claims the use of a copy code proves she was working in the office after hours with Mr. Dowd. Aha! he thinks. Except ... if the rest of his theory is true, that she tried to hide her movements by using the stairs instead of the elevator, why would she use the print code that she knew could be used to track her movements? It doesn't make sense. Why would she bring her cell phone with her? It makes no sense, this theory that she was trying to hide her presence there in the office after hours. He can't have it both ways. Either she's this cold, calculating manipulator, or she's not.

"The voicemails. They're awful. I can't deny that. She said things in the heat of the moment that put her in the worst light. Psycho girlfriend. That's the picture Mr. Bailey wants to paint. Only Mr. Bailey's own witnesses, Lionel Harriman and Lydia Whitford, testified that things seemed normal, cordial, even affectionate between them the day Terrence Dowd died. It was a normal day. No one sensed any tension. Terrence Dowd and Farrah Sibley fought. But then they made up.

"Lionel Harriman claims Terrence Dowd joked about something happening to him. Joked. Harriman admitted that's how he took it. He admitted that he was so nonplussed by Dowd's statements, he got on a plane and went to Aruba right afterward. Never checked in with Dowd. Never felt the need to see if the man he supposedly loved like a brother was doing okay after this so-called dangerous revelation.

"On the day of Dowd's death, Lydia Whitford admitted she observed nothing unusual about Dowd and Farrah Sibley's interactions that day. These arguments she claimed she overheard ... from her office clear on the other side of the building from Dowd and Farrah Sibley's, I might add, took place weeks earlier. She never bothered to ask Terrence Dowd about them. Or Farrah Sibley. She never brought it to Harriman's attention or HR or anyone else. Despite what she's claiming now, these incidents never rose to a level that she felt she should do anything at all.

"And let's go back even further, as the prosecution wants you to do. They paraded Kurt Sommerville in here to claim Farrah Sibley threatened him once, too. Aha! Only there's no real proof that the texts Sommerville says he received came from Farrah at all. They were sent from a phone she was no longer using. That she was no longer in possession of. They were filled with quotes from scripture. In all these other texts Farrah allegedly made to Dowd, she didn't quote scripture. No. Her father did that. Her father was in the business of threatening the men in his daughter's and estranged wife's lives. Her father had access to that phone. That's not just reasonable doubt, folks. That's absolute doubt.

"The prosecution has told you a story. That's all. They've proven none of the elements of their case. They've raised questions that should have been answered by the lead investigator in this case, Detective Eklund. But he didn't answer those questions. He never even asked them. He never interviewed Victor Sibley. Never interviewed Randall Baumgartner, the one man who got the same treatment from Victor Sibley that Terrence Dowd might have gotten. Eklund never looked into it. He made assumptions. Just like Jason Bailey has. Just like he wants you to do. But you can't. Your duty prevents it.

"The prosecution's case should leave you with far more questions than answers. You should be frustrated by it. Angry even. I am. Mr. Bailey and Detective Eklund have left gaping holes in this investigation. Ones that lead not to just reasonable doubt, but absolute doubt. As such, your duty demands that you find Farrah Sibley not guilty. There is no other just outcome.

There is no other choice. Thank you. I trust you'll do the right thing, the only thing you can, and deliver a verdict of not guilty."

I had five minutes at best with Farrah. Eric walked back in the courtroom grim-faced. I looked back at the jury one last time and prayed I'd done enough.

Chapter 27

It was a long, silent drive back to Delphi. We could have gone home. None of us would get any work done for the rest of the day. But home didn't suit me or any of us. One by one, we filed into the office conference room. Jeanie either called ahead or Miranda, being Miranda, sensed what we all would need. She had a full spread of comfort food waiting for us. Donuts, bagels from the good place, fresh coffee. Jeanie grabbed a bottle of Bailey's from her secret stash and made the coffee Irish.

"You did good, kid," Jeanie said as she took her first sip. She'd foregone the coffee and drank her Bailey's over ice.

"I don't feel good about this one," I said. "Too many loose ends. I should have asked for more time. Should have demanded it."

"Would it have really made a difference?" Tori asked. "The evidence was the evidence. I mean, unless you found a literal smoking gun to exonerate Farrah ..."

"Hush," Jeanie said. "You're making it sound like this ship's already sunk. It's not. I'm telling you. You gave that jury a lot to think about. That's all you had to do and you did it great."

I reached for the bottle of Bailey's and added a generous amount to my coffee. "It would have been better if I could have gotten Leighann on the stand."

"What happened with that?" Tori asked. "She was all lined up. I confirmed with her just this morning."

"Victor Sibley happened," I answered. "That man is evil. I'm telling you. He got into Leighann's head somehow. Called her. Saw her. Something. If we could just have kept those two apart."

"You can't control the universe, Cass," Miranda said. "I'm sure you're being too hard on yourself. I'm sure your closing was brilliant."

While I appreciated the support, I didn't feel brilliant. I felt like I was chasing my tail. I'd felt that way for weeks.

"You did far better than Anderson Rix could have done," Jeanie said. "He'd be proud of you."

"On that," Miranda said. "Glenda Rix called twice asking for a status report. She was planning on being in the courtroom today, but chickened out. She told me she was afraid it would remind her too much of her husband."

"I owe her a visit," I said. "Later. After the jury comes back. When I have something to tell her. Assuming I haven't just crapped all over his legacy."

"Stop," Jeanie said. "This case isn't Rix's legacy. And it's not yours either. You started this thing with nothing. Less than nothing. All you had was a client who swore she was innocent and Rix's wishful thinking that she was telling the truth."

"Wishful thinking? I think the Irish cream is making its way to your brain. Tell me how you really feel, Jeanie?"

"I feel like you've had a problematic client from the beginning. You knew that. Rix knew that. And I'm not naïve enough not to realize every client who claims they're innocent is, but Farrah strikes me as someone who's smart enough just to not say anything if she was guilty. Like she did with the cops. So ... heart of hearts ... I want to believe she's been telling us the truth. But if I'm on the outside looking in? I don't know. Maybe I wouldn't buy it. And that's not because you didn't do your job selling it. There's a difference."

"Thanks," I said, and I meant it.

"What's next if the verdict doesn't go your way?" Tori asked. "Will you stick with her through an appeal?"

I wanted something stronger than Bailey's. "I don't know. I can't think that far ahead. I told Farrah not to think that far ahead."

"Won't be an issue," Jeanie said. "I'm telling you. I don't think the jury liked Farrah all that much. But they didn't like Bailey either. They *really* didn't like Victor Sibley. Or Lionel Harriman and Lydia Whitford, for that matter. The younger members of the jury saw right through Lydia, I think. Judgmental old bat. And you scored real hits with the office geography. I'm telling you. They don't believe good old Liddy heard all the things she claims to have heard. And if she did, she's lying about how she heard them. She was eavesdropping. Like glass-to-the-wall eavesdropping. She wasn't credible. And Harriman jetting off to Aruba hours after he claims Dowd told him he was scared for his life or whatever? Uh uh. No way. The jury saw through that too. They're gonna come back for us. You watch."

Downstairs, we heard the front door open and shut.

"Who the hell's that?" Jeanie asked. "Miranda, didn't you lock it?"

"I did," she said.

Heavy footsteps took the stairs two at a time. I knew instantly who it was.

"Eric?" I said as he opened the conference room door.

His hair was disheveled, like he'd been running. "Good," he said. "You're all here. I've brought you a visitor."

"I'm not up for it," I said.

"Leighann Sibley's downstairs," he said. "I set her up in Jeanie's office."

A wave of anger went through me. "Now? She's ready to talk now?"

"She called me from a truck stop off 94. Begged me to bring her here so she could apologize."

"She's okay?" Jeanie asked. "Sibley didn't try to hurt her?"

"I'll let her tell you all of that," Eric said. Judging by his tone, he was as irritated as I was. I took another swig of Bailey's, then collected myself to go downstairs.

Chapter 28

If it were possible, Leighann Sibley looked like she'd shrunk since the last time I saw her. She stood at the mantle in Jeanie's office, watching her anniversary clock. The chrome balls danced in their rhythmic circle.

"My grandma had one of these," she said. "It used to mesmerize me. Calm me down when I was upset. She'd have me watch it."

"Mrs. Sibley," I said. "What happened to you today? You were under a court order to testify."

"I'm sorry," she said. "But I did you a favor. I did my daughter a favor. Nothing I could have said would have helped her. I don't know anything."

"That's not what you told me a few weeks ago. You understand we believe your husband was responsible for making threats to one of Farrah's ex-boyfriends? In the same way, he ran off Randall Baumgartner. You could have confirmed that. Explained his pattern of conduct. It might have helped."

"Victor's not who you think he is," she said.

"He threatened Randall Baumgartner," I said. "Made a gesture like he was going to shoot him in the chest. You saw him do it. He did something similar to Kurt Sommerville, Farrah's last boyfriend. How many other men did he terrorize to keep them away from you, Leighann?"

She turned back to the clock. "I didn't want to be a part of this. I never should have reached out to you."

"Yes. You should have. If you know something. If you're protecting Victor at Farrah's expense, it's not too late to do the right thing."

"Farrah can take care of herself. She always could."

The room started to spin. I realized I'd been holding my breath, trying to hold back my anger.

"Do you know something?" I asked. "Did Victor threaten you again today? We know you saw him. We know you left with him. You have to tell me what you know, for your daughter's sake."

"I don't want this," she said. "I don't want to be back here. It's taken me so long to get out from under all of this. You know the sick part? I still love him. When I'm around him ... when I saw him today, it took me right back to when I was sixteen years old. He's so confident. Strong. Self-assured. All the things I wasn't. I grew up around so much chaos. You don't know what it was like. And Victor? He just ... he just handled things. Made things easy. Took me in hand, you know?"

"You left him because he was abusive," I said. "You've spent the last decade hiding from him. You tried to get a restraining order against him when he caught up with you. What do you think would have happened if you hadn't left Randall? If you'd have gone through with the divorce and married Randall?"

She shook her head. "I can't be here. Mr. Wray, could you call that Uber you promised me?"

"What would have happened?" I pressed her.

"I don't know. It doesn't matter now."

"It very much matters now. Because I think Victor would have made good on his threats. He would have tried to put a bullet in Randall Baumgartner. You knew it. You took off again because you didn't want to find out. You were protecting Randall in your own way, weren't you?"

"It just ... it just wasn't going to work out. Randy and I wanted different things."

"Then why are you here?" I said. "Why call Eric and ask him to bring you here? What is it you wanted to tell me?"

"Just that I'm sorry. I shouldn't have given you a false impression that I know more than I do. I was just ... I wanted to know about Farrah. Wanted to make sure she was doing okay."

"She's not," I snapped. "She's facing a life prison term. The rest of her life, Leighann. Farrah is twenty-eight years old ..."

"I know how old she is!" Leighann shouted.

"It'll kill her," I said. "Women like Farrah don't do well in prison. It will break her down, hollow her out until there's nothing left. And it's already started."

"The jury will do the right thing," she whispered. "It's all going to be okay. You'll see."

A car pulled up in front of the office. Leighann saw it through the window.

"Is that my ride?" she asked.

"I think so," Eric said. "I'll find out."

"Please," I said. "Victor killed Terrence Dowd, didn't he? To keep him away from Farrah. To punish him for having relations with her. The same way he wanted to punish Randall."

"I have nothing more I can do for her," she said.

"You can tell the truth."

"I don't know anything. I swear."

"What did he say to you today that made you leave the courthouse? Skip out on a subpoena."

"Nothing. Just nothing. We talked. That's all. Now I really have to go. Tell Farrah I love her. I'm praying for her."

"Tell her yourself," I said.

"I can't. I just can't. I have to go."

"Just like you always do," I said. I couldn't keep my anger at bay any longer. "You're gonna run out of here and disappear. Abandon your daughter just like you did when she was a little kid!"

"Cass!" Jeanie said. "That's not helping."

She was right. I knew it. And yet I couldn't help but think about Farrah sitting alone in her jail cell with no family support. She just had me.

Eric walked back in. Leighann rushed past him.

"I'm sorry," she cried. "I really am sorry. Tell Farrah that for me, please?"

Then she ran out the door and slammed it behind her.

"She was like that the whole ride over," he said. "I didn't have any luck laying guilt on her, either. She won't budge. She's still too terrified of Sibley. He did a number on her today."

I sank into one of the chairs.

"I shouldn't have yelled at her," I said. "I'm a jerk."

"You're frustrated," Miranda said. "And you're trying to advocate for her daughter in a way she doesn't seem capable of. I know she's a victim too, but I want to wring that woman's neck."

"Eric," I said. "We have to dig deeper. Are you sure nothing came up when you looked into Sibley? We have to find out where he was when Terrence Dowd was shot. We have to do the things Lars Eklund refused to do."

"You really think he killed Dowd?" Miranda asked.

"If Farrah didn't," I said. "He's the only other person with a motive. Eric, are you sure you can't get a hold of his cell phone records?"

"You don't have grounds for a court order," he said.

"What about without one?"

Eric frowned. I knew what I was asking him.

"You sure you wanna go down that road?"

The office phone rang. Miranda left to go answer it.

"What choice do we have?" I said to Eric.

"Why don't we just wait and see what the jury decides before we cross over to the dark side?"

"Eric's right," Jeanie said. "For the time being, you've done all you can do. If Farrah gets convicted and you still want to fight for her, we'll dig deep. Just trust that you did a good enough job, Cass. I do."

Miranda came back. "That was Judge McGee's clerk. The jury came back with questions. They're asking to see the transcript of those text messages Kurt Sommerville says were from Farrah. And they're asking to review a portion of Victor Sibley's testimony."

"Cass!" Jeanie said. "They're taking the bait. They're questioning what you wanted them to question. This is good news."

I rubbed my temples. The only good news I wanted to hear was a not guilty verdict. Only then would I declare victory.

Chapter 29

After their second full day of deliberations, the jury still hadn't reached a verdict. Bending to the pressure of Jeanie, Miranda, and Tori, I did something I rarely do. I took half a day off.

My niece Emma met me for lunch at the Sand Bar, a popular local restaurant on the north end of Finn Lake. She'd worked there part time since she was fifteen years old. Now, they'd made her assistant manager. She got us a high top out on the patio where we could watch the boats going by.

"You look good," I told her. And she did. She would graduate from college at the end of the year with a degree in psychology. Emma looked so much like my mother, it took my breath away at times. Long blonde hair and bright green eyes that pierced right through you. She smiled a lot. That was the main difference between her and Mom. My mother had been frequently sad. My father being the main cause.

"I'm glad you came," Emma said. "I miss hanging out with you."

"How's school?"

"That's what I wanted to talk to you about, actually."

"Oh?"

"Well, not so much school as what comes after."

"Is this you or your dad talking?" I knew my brother Joe had issues with Emma's chosen major. I could hear his voice in my head. *What the heck do you do with a psychology degree if you're not going to grad school?*

"I was thinking maybe you'd let me shadow you at the office the rest of this summer. A day or two a week at least. I won't get in the way. And I'll do whatever you tell me."

The question caught me off guard. "I didn't realize you had any interest in the law."

"I do. Or at least, I think I might. I took the LSAT this spring."

Emma pulled her phone out and pulled an image up from her camera roll. She handed it to me.

It took me a second to realize what I was reading. "Your scores?" I said. "You're in the 95th percentile. Emma, that's amazing. Are you thinking about law school? Really?"

I didn't know how to feel about it. Emma was smart enough, that was for sure. But she tended to flit from one thing to the next. She'd gone through something like five different majors before settling on psychology. It's what put her behind and had taken her five years to graduate.

"I'm just thinking about it. That's all. That's why I thought hanging out with you this summer might help me make that decision."

"Have you talked to your dad about all this?"

The Client List

She rolled her eyes. "I can't talk to him about anything lately. That's the problem. He's angry all the time. He's negative about everything. It's just ..."

"A lot," I answered for her. "I know. I've been worried about him. He's taking this divorce harder than we all thought."

"I've been trying to get him to go out. To date. I set up an online dating profile for him. I mean, it's not the greatest. Online dating. But he's got to get out there and meet people. He just sits around brooding. I can't stand it."

I had similar concerns, but didn't know how to help him either. He pushed me away every time I tried.

"He just needs more time," I said. "It's still so new."

"He needs to find a new place to live. Sorry. I don't mean there's anything wrong with your place. It makes me happy that you're there keeping an eye on him. And I know he stays busy with the boats and all. It's just that he's stuck in time, you know. Not moving forward. He just gets grumpier and grumpier."

"I know," I said. "But you shouldn't worry about him. Joe will figure himself out in his own time."

The moment I said it, I knew I needed to take my own advice. The look on Emma's face told me she was thinking the same thing.

"But law school," I said, bringing the focus back to Emma.

"It would be a while," she said. "I don't graduate until December. So I wouldn't be eligible to enroll until a year from this fall. I've got time to decide. They're going to move me to full-time hours here after graduation. It's not huge money, but enough I can afford my rent and stuff. Affording law school will be something else but I'll worry about that later. I'm not even sure I can get accepted anywhere."

"If you want it bad enough, you'll figure it out."

"But you'll help? I mean ... you'll support me?"

"Of course. You don't even have to ask. And yes, I'd love to have you around the office a couple of days a week if you can swing it with your schedule here."

"I might hate it. I just want to see if it's something that would be a good fit."

"There are all different kinds of lawyers," I said. "Do you have any idea what type of law interests you?"

"Maybe family law. I'd like to help kids like Jeanie does."

"Well, she'd be thrilled to have you around as well. She'll talk your ear off, that's for sure."

"She already has." Emma laughed, then her face got serious.

"You've already talked to her?"

"A little. But only because she was bugging me about what my post grad plans are. I don't want you to think we were going behind your back or anything."

"Don't worry. It's fine. I've been a little busy these last few weeks. Jeanie's as much your family as I am, really."

Emma beamed. There was something else I wanted to tell her. If she was serious, I would help her with more than just job shadowing. After selling off my real estate up north, I'd started an education fund for all of them. Emma, Jessa, and baby Sean.

"You're the best, Aunt Cass," she said. "It's going to be fun. And I promise. Like I said, I'll do whatever you ask me to. I can even ..."

"Hello!" A bright voice drew our attention away. Emma and I looked up at the same time. For half a second, I didn't register who I was looking at. The voice didn't match the face.

Katie, my newly former sister-in-law, stood at our table, beaming. She'd had something done. Botox. Fillers. Something. It changed the shape of her lips.

"Katie," I said, rising. Tension poured off Emma in waves. Before I could react, Katie came to me, throwing her arms wide. She pulled me into an embrace. Every muscle in my body went rigid. I pulled away. I didn't want to make a scene, but Katie and me? We weren't in a hugging place, to say the least. "What are you doing here?" Emma said through gritted teeth.

"We came for lunch," Katie said, breathless. "We?" Emma and I said it together. I scanned the dining room. Sure enough, there sat Tom Loomis, Action Sports in a corner booth next to the bar. He at least had the decency to pretend he didn't see us.

"You look terrific, Cass," Katie said. An odd thing. I looked the same. Dressed down if anything, changing out of my work clothes into a pair of gym shorts and a tank top. This was the Sand Bar, after all, and it was summertime.

Emma vaulted to her feet. "What are you doing here? There are a dozen other places where you could eat lunch. You know I work here."

Katie's face fell. "Oh honey. I was hoping I'd see you." Katie reached for Emma's elbow. She jerked it away before Katie could make contact.

"Don't be that way. Honey, I love you. At some point, you're going to have to talk to me again."

"Tell me why again?" Emma said.

"Because I'm your ..."

"Your what? My mother? Is that what you're going to say? You're not. You're just the asshole who cheated on my dad. I don't want to talk to you. I don't want to see you or your fake face."

"Emma," I said softly. "Not here." Emma might look like her grandmother, but she had her grandfather's temper.

"Exactly," she said. "Not here. You knew you were going to run into me. In your stupid brain, you thought that would be a good idea. So let me be clear. Stay away from me. Stay away from my dad. You're not one of us anymore. You mess with one of us, you're dead to all of us."

Katie blinked rapidly, stung by Emma's words. At the same time, they couldn't have been a surprise to her. Emma was right. You screw one of us, you screw the entire Leary clan.

"I can see this was a mistake. I thought you were an adult, Emma."

"Knock it off," I said, my own temper rising. "Emma's entitled to feel how she feels. I don't know why you thought she wouldn't protect Joe. Or why you thought she'd want to celebrate you marrying whatshisname."

"I invited her to my wedding reception as a gesture of reconciliation. Tom's not the enemy here. Neither am I."

Emma threw her napkin down. She had that look on her face I'd seen on too many hot-blooded Learys. In another second, she was liable to throw hands. I grabbed Katie by the arm and led her away from the table and out of Emma's earshot.

"Get your hands off me!" Katie seethed. She ripped her arm out of my grasp.

"It's too soon, okay? Emma doesn't want a relationship with you right now. If she ever does, that's up to her. She'll reach out. If she doesn't, that's your cue to back off."

"Joe's not perfect," she hissed. "He's not some saint that I wronged, Cass."

"He's my brother. Right now, that's all you need to know. And don't come in here. Emma's right about that, too. She's allowed to set a boundary. You might try respecting it if you're serious about wanting to have a relationship with her again down the road. That's my advice."

"I wasn't asking for it."

"Maybe that's one of your problems, Katie. This thing isn't about you anymore. Go live your life. Be happy."

"But go away? Is that it? I live in this town too, Cass. I'm not the bad guy you think I am."

"I don't think you're a bad guy. But you're not family anymore, okay? And we're not friends."

She lost a bit of color in her cheeks. I suppose if I were a bigger person, I could feel compassion. I didn't hate her. But I felt like I was still in the middle of cleaning up the mess she made. It wasn't my job to try to make her feel better about that.

"Fine. I'll go. This time. But Emma's going to have to deal with me sooner or later."

"She's an adult. She can decide for herself. If I hear you've been harassing her or getting in her face when she doesn't want it, we're going to have a problem, you and me. Are we clear?"

Katie looked at me with uncharacteristic hatred. I *did* feel bad for her. Something was going on with this woman I felt certain went deeper than just what happened with Joe. She turned on her heel and stomped off. She collected a miserable-looking Tom Loomis, Action Sports and left the restaurant.

"Thanks for that," Emma said, joining me again.

"It's nothing," I said. "I don't think she'll be back. Just let it roll off your back, kiddo. Now I'm hungry. What's good on the menu today?"

We walked back to our table. Emma ordered clam chowder and turkey Reubens for both of us. It was all delicious. I had just taken my last bite when a text from Miranda came through.

"They need you back in Ann Arbor," she wrote. "Judge wants to talk to both lawyers. I told them you'd be there in ninety minutes or less."

Emma read the text upside down. She met my eyes. "Bad news?" she asked.

"Can't be good," I answered. "Why don't you tag along? Consider your summer internship starting now."

Chapter 30

Judge Claudia McGee met us in chambers. It was the first time I'd actually seen her without her robes. She wore a sharp red suit with matching heels. The gold bangles on her wrist dangled as she adjusted her desk chair and motioned for us to take the two seats in front of her.

"Here's the situation," she started. Jason Bailey had been pulled off the golf course for this meeting. He sported a navy-blue windbreaker and tanned face.

"The foreman reached out to me claiming the jury is deadlocked. They've got two holdouts. I don't know what way and wouldn't disclose it if I did. I've given the foreman my best pep talk and instructed them to go back at it and work this out. About twenty minutes later, they came back asking for a portion of Lydia Whitford's testimony to be read back to them."

"Which portion?" Bailey asked.

"They're reviewing her testimony regarding the office bookkeeping. The Lexis/Nexis logs."

Of all the things they could have asked for, I wasn't expecting that. But juries are fickle beasts. You never know what they'll fixate on. I knew it would do me no good to try to guess.

"So that's where we're at," McGee said. "We're heading into their third full day of deliberations here. Are plea negotiations ongoing?"

"No, Your Honor," I said. "This isn't a civil suit. We're talking about the rest of my client's life."

McGee waved me off. "Save the lecture. I get it. And you're right. It's the rest of your client's life. You sure she understands that?"

"She understands," I said.

"All right then. Stay close. If they come back with more questions, I'll let you know. That's all I've got for now."

"Thank you, Your Honor," Bailey said, rising. He gave me a smug glance as we walked out of McGee's chambers together.

"There won't be any further plea offers," Bailey said as he shut the door behind us.

"I wasn't asking if there were," I said.

"Well, no matter what happens, I've enjoyed trying this case with you. I hope to see you back in Washtenaw County again."

He caught me off guard a bit. The sentiment seemed genuine.

"I don't have anything on the horizon," I said. "This was a one-off."

"Really? I would think Woodbridge County gets a little boring for someone with your background."

"It's more interesting than you might think."

"Anyway, I've got to get back to the office. Have a safe drive back."

Bailey shook my hand. Emma came around the corner carrying two water bottles from the second-floor vending machine. She gave Bailey a polite smile as he passed her on the way to the stairwell.

"Anything interesting?" she asked.

I filled her in on what the judge had to say.

"Two holdouts," Emma repeated. "But they keep asking to review evidence that was favorable to the defense, right?"

"So far."

"Then I'd guess your holdouts are on the prosecution's side. I bet anything the other ten want to acquit. They're trying to make the two look at the exculpatory evidence closer."

"It's a good guess," I said. "But impossible to know."

"I wouldn't mind sitting in on the next case you try, Aunt Cass. Would you mind if I were in the courtroom?"

"No," I said. "If you can work it out between school and your job."

We headed for the stairs. On the way down, I saw a familiar face I wasn't expecting. Detective Lars Eklund stood at the security station chatting up one of the deputies. He caught my eye and gave me a friendly nod.

"Emma," I said. "Would you mind hanging out for a little bit yet? There's a civil trial in Courtroom 3. You can go sit and watch if that sounds interesting to you."

"Sure thing," Emma said, but she looked puzzled as Eklund walked toward me.

"Ms. Leary," Eklund said. "Heard your jury's got more questions."

"Do you have a minute?" I knew what I was about to ask him would probably make him mad. He was more likely to tell me where to stick it than entertain my request. But something Eric said kept nagging at me.

"Sure," Eklund said, the confusion on his face growing. As Emma headed back upstairs, Eklund and I went to the open conference room next to the bar association offices.

"Why didn't you look harder at Victor Sibley?" I said, deciding on the direct approach.

"Oh, come on," Eklund said. "You can't really be asking me that."

"I can. I know you're up to speed on how he testified. Bailey filled you in, didn't he? And you sat there during closing arguments. You're a good detective. You know I raised valid questions."

"You're a defense lawyer. You do what defense lawyers do. Maybe it'll work. Maybe it won't. But my job is done on this case. I'm confident in my investigation."

"He had a motive. You never even interviewed him."

"You got to say all that crap during trial. I didn't take it personally. But now I'm beginning to."

"I'm sorry," I started, then changed my mind. "No. I'm not. I think you took an instant dislike to Farrah Sibley and that was the end of it as far as you having an open mind."

"What's your purpose in this? You want to lecture me about how to do my job? Well, here's a piece of advice for how you should have done yours. Farrah Sibley should have taken a plea deal when it was offered. If you counseled her otherwise, you're the one who screwed up. Not me. She's guilty. Nobody else. Not her dad. Just Farrah Sibley. She pulled the trigger and killed that man in cold blood. If you ask me, I think Bailey was weak not going for premeditation. She brought that gun to work with her."

"There's no proof of that."

"The proof is she shot him with it."

"She didn't. I'm sure of it."

He smiled. "You're sure of it? Well, as long as you're sure of it. You're right. I give up. I'll tell Bailey we have to be wrong because Cass Leary says so."

"I just want to know why," I said.

"Why what?"

"Why didn't you look at Victor Sibley? Pull his cell phone records. It would have been easy."

"There's a little thing called probable cause. Maybe you've heard of it."

"If that jury comes back with the right verdict, what are you going to do?"

"What?"

"Terrence Dowd's killer is still out there."

"My job ended the day I delivered this case to the prosecutor. I don't have to explain myself to you. You know? The only reason

I've been polite to you today is because I've known Eric Wray a long time. He was a good cop. I gotta admit, I was surprised he agreed to cross over to the dark side and start working for defense lawyers. But out of professional courtesy to him, I'm having this conversation with you. That courtesy is over."

"Eric believes Farrah's innocent, too."

He had one hand on the doorknob and turned back to me. "You sure about that?"

"What?"

"Are you really sure Wray believes Farrah's innocent? Because I doubt that. Have you ever asked him? Point blank?"

"Of course I have," I said. Though I tried to keep my face neutral, Eklund acted like he saw something in it. Just the slightest upturn to the corner of his mouth.

"Right," he said. "That's what I thought. Have a nice day, Ms. Leary. You've been hanging on too tight to this one. It happens to all of us. Anderson Rix was a good guy. Even I knew that. You don't want to let him down. Maybe you didn't. Who knows? Juries surprise you sometimes."

With that, Eklund walked out, leaving me alone in the room. He passed by Emma, seated on a bench in the hallway.

"Dammit," I muttered under my breath. That meeting hadn't gone how I expected. Hell, I didn't know what I expected. I just wanted him to hear me. I wanted him to open his mind to the possibility he might have been wrong. As I took a step toward Emma, a voice popped into my head.

Maybe he wanted the same thing. Maybe I was the one who needed to open my mind to the possibility that I was wrong.

"You really pissed him off, huh?" Emma said.

"Probably."

"You want him to reopen his investigation? Can he even do that?"

"If there's new evidence, sure. If Farrah's acquitted."

"She will be," Emma said. "I mean ... right?"

"Come on. I've had enough of this courthouse for a while. Did you see anything interesting upstairs?"

"They're in the middle of some kind of evidentiary hearing," she said. "It's an auto-neg case, I think. Have you handled any of those?"

"No. We don't really do much personal injury. Jeanie handles the family law stuff. Tori was doing probate and estates before her accident."

"Is there a lot of money in it? Personal injury?"

"There certainly can be. That's how Professor Rix made his fortune. It's what Farrah Sibley was working on, too. Workers' comp."

"Hmm."

"Why hmm?"

"Well, I was just thinking. If that's something I'm interested in doing, would there be room for me at your firm?"

I smiled. "The short answer is yes. The long answer is let's not get ahead of ourselves. See if you actually like life in a law practice first. It's not for everyone."

"I think I'd like that though. Advocating for the downtrodden. Sticking it to the insurance companies. It sounds kind of fun."

"It can be entirely boring," I said. "You'll spend your life in discovery more than in the courtroom. It's not like TV."

"Oh, I know. I'm just saying. It's something to think about."

We were about to go back through security when a female voice shouted my name.

"Ms. Leary! Wait!"

I turned. Judge McGee's clerk had rushed down the stairs. Her heels clacked on the tiles as she reached me.

"Don't leave," she said. "I was hoping I could catch you. I've got to find Mr. Bailey next. Judge McGee just got word. They're back. The jury reached a verdict. Judge has already had me call over to the jail. They're bringing your client over in the next fifteen minutes. Judge wants to be back on the record in thirty."

"They're back?" I said, incredulous. It had been less than an hour since Judge McGee sent the foreman back with instructions to keep at this.

Two holdouts. Guilty or Not Guilty?

"Thank you," I said. I reached into my bag and pulled out the bag of quarters I kept there. "Emma, put another buck or two in the meter. I'll wait for Farrah."

"Should we call Jeanie?" Emma asked, breathless. "Shouldn't she be here for this, too?"

"She won't make it in time," I said. "She's in court in Delphi."

My knees felt weak. The usual adrenaline rush I got during times like these hadn't kicked in yet. I tried not to take that as any kind of sign.

Emma ran outside to deal with the parking meter. I hustled upstairs. Jason Bailey's paralegal was already in the courtroom looking as bewildered as I felt. I took my place at the defense table.

A moment later, Emma came back in. I had her sit on the bench behind me. There was nothing we could do but watch the seconds tick by.

Twenty minutes later, I stood beside Farrah Sibley in the courtroom. She'd barely spoken since they brought her up. I tried to reassure her. To prop her up as she faced that jury as they filed in one by one.

Two holdouts.

None of them would look our way as they took their seats in the jury box. Each of them stared straight ahead, waiting for the judge's instructions.

Jason Bailey rushed in. He'd hastily changed from his golf attire. His tie was still loose and crooked. He fumbled with it as Judge McGee took the bench.

"All right. Madam foreperson, I understand you've reached a verdict in this matter?"

The foreperson was Juror Number Eleven. A retired school teacher from Ann Arbor Skyline. A good choice, I thought. She'd been attentive during the entire proceeding, taking copious notes. Jeanie said the younger women on the jury definitely seemed to defer to her.

"Will the defendant please rise," Judge McGee said.

"I can't do this," Farrah whispered.

I put an arm around her and helped her to her feet. She sank against me.

The clerk took a small piece of paper from Juror Number Eleven and walked it up to the judge. McGee read it with the poker face required of the job. She folded it and handed it back to the clerk. Juror Number Eleven stood straighter as the clerk gave her the verdict form and the judge instructed her to read it into the record.

"In the matter of the People of the State of Michigan versus Farrah Sibley, on Count One of the complaint pursuant to MCR 750.317. We, the jury, find the defendant guilty."

She folded the verdict form and handed it back to the clerk.

"Is this your unanimous verdict?" Judge McGee said.

"It is, Your Honor," the foreman answered.

I heard myself asking for the jury to be polled. Beside me, Farrah had registered no reaction. She stared straight ahead. I wasn't sure if she'd taken a breath.

Twelve times, the individual jurors read out their vote. Guilty. Their voices echoed through the courtroom like gunshots. On the last one, Juror Number Four, a young electrician who sat in the back, Farrah Sibley finally reacted. She quietly whispered the word no, then crumpled to the floor in a dead faint.

Chapter 31

GUILTY. Guilty. Guilty.

The word echoed through me. For hours. All night. I'd heard it before. This wasn't the first case I'd ever tried. The first verdict that hadn't gone my way. But those five minutes after the jury came back replayed in my mind on a continuous loop.

It had been Emma who'd rushed forward and got to Farrah first. The deputies quickly surrounded her. By the time I bent down, Farrah had already opened her eyes. She pleaded with me. Couldn't believe it. Over and over, she screamed that she hadn't killed Terrence. That it was all a lie. A nightmare.

And there was nothing I could do to help her at that moment.

I sat in my office now, well after dark. We held a sort of Irish wake, all of us. Jeanie. Miranda. Tori. Eric. Emma. I stayed long after most of them went home. Eric drove Emma. I wanted the quiet solitude for just a little longer.

I sat at the conference room table with my trial notes spread out over every surface. They'd commingled with Anderson Rix's now.

I missed something. Somewhere. A witness I should have called. A question I should have asked that I'd let slip.

"You okay?"

I looked up. Jeanie stood in the doorway.

"I thought you'd left?"

"I was about to. So should you. You're not doing yourself any good brooding over those files."

"There's got to be something here." I had copies of evidence and Bailey's discovery materials everywhere. The phone logs. Printouts of text messages. Copies of Dowd's calendar. Of Farrah's. Names, dates, places, it all just swam in front of me.

"I just wish ..."

"Stop. You're hanging on too tight to this one. You have been for a while."

"I don't like losing."

Jeanie sighed and came further into the room. "You didn't lose, okay? You did your job. You put on the best defense anyone could have. Better than Anderson Rix could have. I think if he were here he'd be the first to say that."

"You should have seen her, Jeanie. Farrah's broken. I'm worried about her. I'm thinking about talking to the jail about having her put on suicide watch."

"It's that bad?"

"I just don't want to take any chances with her."

"You gonna help her appeal?"

I steepled my fingers under my chin. The mound of paperwork I had in front of me felt like it could actually bury me.

"I don't know. I'm not sure I'm the best person for that. My strength is in front of a jury. Well ... usually."

"Come on. Put this away for now. You're no good to anybody if you exhaust yourself."

"He counted on me," I said. It was the first time I'd really given voice to it. As soon as I said it, something crystallized in my mind. I was heartbroken for Farrah. But I couldn't shake the specter of Anderson Rix tonight.

"Jeanie, I owed Rix this. I wanted to deliver a win for him. For his legacy. God. Glenda. I still have to face her."

Jeanie pulled up a chair. "Bullshit."

"What?"

"You heard me. Bullshit. You don't owe Rix a thing. You seem to be forgetting that the man treated you like dirt at the end."

"He was just worried about me. And it's not like his fears about what would happen if I went to work for the Thorne Law Group didn't come true. I almost died over it. I almost lost everything. He told me money wasn't everything and at the time I couldn't see it."

"Cass, you were a grown woman. And you had responsibilities and life experiences that were different than that old privileged white man's were. He was wrong."

"What? You were just as pissed at me for taking that job."

"I wasn't pissed. I was just worried. And I didn't cut you out of my life over it like he did."

I reached for her. She clasped my hand.

"Listen," she said. "All I'm saying is it's time for you to stop putting the likes of Anderson Rix on a pedestal. He was a good mentor to you at a time when you needed one. He helped you realize your potential. But you don't owe him anything. And if Rix were here, he'd tell you the same thing. And if he didn't, then he's an ass."

I laughed. Jeanie had a way of putting things succinctly if not crudely. And it was exactly what I needed to hear.

"I'm beat," she said, slapping the armrests. "I'm heading home. You okay to drive?"

"I'm fine. Eric's gonna swing by after he drops off Emma."

"It was good she was here today. I miss seeing her."

"Oh. On that. You might be seeing more of her in the future. I hear you've heard she's thinking about law school."

"It's not too late to talk her out of it."

"Oh, I've got a better idea. I've agreed to let her shadow us this summer. She's particularly interested in what you do."

"Well then, maybe there's hope for her yet. All right. I'm outta here. Get some sleep tonight, kiddo. This was a tough one. But you left it all in the courtroom. Remember that."

She gave me a wink, then headed back downstairs. Rix's paperwork and mine could wait until tomorrow. I had a message from Glenda that could keep as well. I knew by the time I hit the pillow, I might sleep all the way through tomorrow. At the moment, that sounded like heaven.

I pulled Terrence Dowd's picture off the whiteboard and gently placed it in the nearest box. His professional smile felt a little judgmental. But maybe that was my own misplaced guilt. His murder wasn't mine to solve. At least, it shouldn't be.

I packed up a few files after all, not wanting to deal with the bulk of it later. I turned the light off in the conference room and headed downstairs. We'd left a bit of a mess in reception. That's where the wake had started. I gathered our solo cups and empty bottles and tossed them in the trash. The lights were still on in Jeanie's office. I turned those off too.

I was just about to head back up to do a last check of lights when the front door opened.

"You forget something?" I called out. Jeanie usually came through the back. It was odd nobody had thought to lock the front door.

I came back out of the kitchen. It wasn't Jeanie.

Victor Sibley stood in the foyer, his face drawn into a scowl.

"Mr. Sibley?" I froze.

"I know what you did," he said. "You think I don't know what you did?"

"I'm sorry?"

Jeanie was gone. There was nobody else here. But he didn't have to know that.

Sibley took a step toward me. Could I turn and run back through the kitchen if I needed to? My mind immediately went to possible weapons. So far, he hadn't done anything. He'd just shown up. He hadn't broken in. But the menace in his eyes couldn't be denied.

"This isn't a good time," I said. "If you'd like to make an appointment, I'll be back in the office next week."

He moved so fast, charging me. I took a step backward but he grabbed my arm.

"You think you can just try to trash my reputation? Spread rumors and lies and think there won't be consequences?"

I thought of the photograph I'd just boxed of Terrence Dowd. Was this the last face he saw as well? Was he shocked? Or did he know Victor Sibley by sight?

"Mr. Sibley," I said, jerking my arm away from him. "This is inappropriate. I think you better leave."

"Not until I've had my say. And you're going to listen. You asked all your questions. I answered them. I heard what you tried to tell that jury. You wanted me to pay for somebody else's sins. You're just as damned as Farrah is. All you lawyers are."

"I'm sorry if you feel that way. I was doing my job. I didn't spread lies or rumors. I was ..."

"Shut up!" his voice boomed. "Shut your lying mouth. That's all it ever is with your kind. If your lips are moving, lies are coming out. A snake. Like Eve in the Garden of Eden. Lies. Temptation. Damnation. You. Leighann. Farrah. You're all the same. I thought there was hope for Farrah. I tried hard enough with her. She could never keep her legs closed and look where it got her. She's going straight to hell. You punched her ticket."

"You need to leave." I reached for the phone on Miranda's desk. Sibley pounced, ripping it out of my hand. He backed me against the wall.

"It's your turn to listen. Now sit down."

He grabbed my shoulders and pushed me hard. Forcing me into the chair in front of Miranda's desk.

Sibley looked around desperately. "I should tie you up. Duct tape your mouth shut so you can't tell any more lies."

Should I fight? Run? Try to reason with him?

"I try and I try and I try," he said, talking to the air more than to me. "I pray and I pray. It does no good. They're damned. They're all damned. But I will not let you damn me. You hear me? I will wipe their sins from the earth."

"Like you wiped Terrence Dowd from the earth?" I said. It just came out. But my own anger started to rise.

Sibley whirled around. "The hell you say?"

"You know what I said."

"Oh, I heard you. They all heard you. You wanna make them think I'm some kind of monster. I knew it the day you showed up. Telling me you're fighting for Farrah. That you're on her side. She didn't want this. She knows the truth. She knows it was her actions that brought that man's ruin. Not mine."

"No," I said. "You were just the instrument, weren't you?"

"Shut your filthy mouth!"

I wanted to kick out. To smack him before he knew to expect it. I'd faced up to far worse than Victor Sibley and I wasn't about to sit here and have him lecture me to death.

"You wanted Dowd dead because he wouldn't stay away from your daughter, is that it? Because he lured her into working for him. In a profession you think is evil."

"It is evil. Look at what you did. You couldn't prove your case so you tried to make them all think I'm the villain. I'm a good man. God fearing. I've tried to force the evil out of that girl. Tried to undo all the terrible things her mother taught her. The things that were bred into her. But I can't. I'm only one man. But I'm no killer. I'm a just man."

Was that an admission? If this lunatic truly believed killing Dowd was just, did he not view it as murder?

"We're done talking," I said, rising from the chair. Sibley might be used to women cowering in front of him. He'd victimized Leighann and Farrah for years. I wouldn't allow him to do it to me.

"Get out," I said. "You tripped a silent alarm when you barged through that door after hours. The sheriff's deputies will be here in minutes. There's a security camera pointed at the front door. You might have gotten sneaky at the Belz Building with Terrence Dowd, but you're caught here, Mr. Sibley. The best thing you can do for yourself now is to turn around and leave. Maybe I won't press charges."

"Charges? For what? This is a public building, isn't it? The door wasn't locked. I've broken no laws."

"You put your hands on me," I said. "That's enough to ..."

He turned toward me. Fire lit his eyes. He wore a coat even though it was late June and almost eighty degrees outside. Slowly, he slipped his hand inside the coat and began to draw it out.

I was an idiot. So stupid. I should have run when I had the chance. The gun. Farrah's gun. Of course, we couldn't find it where she said it was. Of course, Victor Sibley used it on Terrence Dowd. And now he was about to use it on me.

I whirled around, looking for anything I could throw at him. Then I froze.

It wasn't a gun he pulled out of his coat. Instead, he held a thick pack of folded papers. He slapped them on Miranda's desk.

"Here!" he shouted. "That's what you wanted. I don't owe you any of it, but here."

"What is ..." I picked up the stack of papers.

"I wasn't there!" he shouted. "You never bothered to ask me. You just assumed. You didn't care. You wanted a scapegoat. You didn't care what people thought or how it might ruin me."

I flipped through the papers. Cell phone records. Credit card bills.

"What is this?" I asked.

"July 17th. I wasn't anywhere near Ann Arbor. I was at the farm all day. Then I went to a livestock show in Gaylord. I didn't get home until late the next day."

My hand shook as I skimmed through some of the data. He bought gas. Dinner at Culver's. All Gaylord, Michigan addresses. All on July 17th.

"Your alibi?" I said. "You came here to bully me and give me your alibi?"

"I didn't kill that man!" he shouted. "And you should be ashamed of—"

A shadow moved behind him. No. Not a shadow. I never heard the back door open. Eric came down on Victor Sibley with the force of a tsunami. He tackled him and drove him down to the floor.

"Eric!" I shouted. But he was gone. Rage colored his face. He cocked an arm back, ready to drive a fist straight into Victor Sibley's nose.

"Stop!" I shouted. I lunged forward and grabbed Eric's arm.

"Did he lay a hand on you?" Eric asked.

"Well, he ... but ..."

"Sinners," Sibley hissed, bracing for the blow he knew would come.

"Eric, stop!" I shouted again. "Let him up. Only so you can throw him out."

Something changed in Eric's face. I got through to him. He shifted his weight, grabbed Sibley by the lapels and hauled him to his feet.

"You're not welcome here," he said, shoving Sibley on the word welcome. "Get out. Get in your car. Keep driving. I so much as see you crossing the county line again I'll end you. You don't come near her? You understand?"

Sibley straightened his coat. Hatred filled his face, but he didn't protest. He scowled at me for good measure, then showed himself out the front door.

I moved in front of Eric and locked the door behind Sibley.

"Are you all right?" he asked. "I saw that truck. I heard the tone of his voice. Cass, there's only one reason he waited to catch you all alone."

"No," I said, my mind still reeling. I was wrong. How could I have been so wrong? I picked up the papers Sibley left and handed them to Eric.

"What is this?" he asked, leafing quickly through it. Before I could answer, Eric's eyes went wide as he registered what he was reading.

"July 17th," he asked.

"Can you verify it? He brought those. I don't want to believe it. But ..."

Eric's nostrils flared. He set the papers down. "Christ," he muttered.

"Exactly," I agreed. Then Eric pulled me to him. Suddenly, my knees turned to water. I was glad for Eric's quiet strength holding me up. Otherwise, I would have hit the floor.

Chapter 32

Three days later, I sat in the passenger seat of Eric's truck, staring at the Dogwood tree in full bloom in Anderson Rix's front yard. Beside me, Eric seemed equally mesmerized by it. The branches swayed in the gentle breeze making the white blossoms seem like they were waving just to us.

The tree, however, was the only part of the landscaping that seemed happy to see us. When we first pulled up, we both double checked the street numbers on the mailbox. Because the house and yard itself seemed to have undergone a metamorphosis in the four months since we'd last been here. Gone were Rix's meticulously manicured shrubs. Instead, they had overgrown into uneven, bulbous shapes, one of them nearly blocking the front doorway. The normally cheery pink and white impatiens in the window boxes had long since died. Their browned carcasses drooped over the boxes as if they had expired while trying to jump for their lives.

Delivery boxes piled up on the corner of the porch. Weeds sprouted through the cracks in the sidewalk and paving stones leading up to the house.

"She knows we're coming?" Eric said. "You talked to her?"

"Just this morning," I said. "She sounded so excited to see us."

"It looks like she maybe hasn't left the house in weeks."

"If this is what the outside looks like, I'm afraid to see the inside."

A knock on my window made me jump. An older couple dressed in matching tracksuits waved and gave us a bright smile. They were walking two identical Yorkshire Terriers, one with a pink harness, the other blue.

I shot a look at Eric, then opened my car door and climbed out.

"Hello!" the man said. He had roughly four strands of white hair hanging on for dear life and combed over the top of his head. The woman, I assumed his wife, had a full head of blonde hair sprayed into a stiff helmet.

"Are you here to call on Glenda?" she asked.

"We are," Eric answered. He'd come around the back of the truck and took sentry at my side.

"Well, thank heavens," the woman said. She extended her hand. "We're the Oglethorpes. Marv and Karen."

I shook her hand. As I moved toward her, the dog in the pink harness began to yap uncontrollably until its voice went suddenly hoarse.

"That's just Bonnie," Marv said. "And her brother Clyde."

"Nice to meet you," I said to the dogs, but didn't bend down to pet either of them. They didn't seem in the mood.

The Client List

"We've been pretty worried about Glenda," Karen whispered. "We've tried to call on her a few times ourselves but she won't open the door. She just calls out from the upstairs window saying she's not feeling well or up to visitors. It's been like that for months. And you can see what we're dealing with out front."

Karen gestured toward the wilting flowers and overgrown yard. Glenda's house stuck out like a sore thumb compared to the scrupulous landscaping of her neighbors.

"We're not judging," Marv said in a tone that sounded pretty judgmental. "We know Glenda's been through hell over this last year. Anderson was her world. And he did everything around the house for her. We've all offered to pitch in but she won't hear of it. She said she was going to hire a lawn care firm but she hasn't so far. She keeps saying none of them can take care of things to Anderson's standards."

"At this point, we'd be happy if she could just handle the bare minimum," Karen chimed in.

"Well," I said. "We'll look in on her and see what's what if we can."

"We've given her grace," Karen continued. "But there's the Homeowner's Association to think of. We answer to the whole community, you understand."

"Of course," I answered. "Has anyone else been by to see her?"

"Not that we know of. She's all by herself," Marv said. "No kids. Both she and Anderson were only children, so there are no nieces or nephews. Anderson's kids were his students. They're the only ones who seemed to care. Now that he's gone, there's not even that anymore. Glenda's just all alone in there."

"Thanks for the information," Eric said. "As Cass said, we'll do what we can."

Both Bonnie and Clyde started yipping again, loud enough that further conversation became impossible. We waved our goodbyes and headed up the walk.

The closer we got, the more alarming the state of the Rixes' yard became. I could see around to the side garden. It was a wasteland of dead leaves and rotting tomatoes.

I rang the doorbell. "Mrs. Rix!" I called out. We heard a thump then just as the Oglethorpes warned, a second-floor window swung open and Glenda shouted down.

"Can you come around the back? The front door's been stuck for a while. I've got someone coming out to take a look but he won't be here until next week."

"I'll be glad to take a look, Mrs. Rix," Eric shouted up. She slammed the window shut. Eric met my eyes. All I could do was shrug back as the two of us rounded the sidewalk and found the back door leading into the kitchen.

It was open. Eric knocked softly, then pushed it open. The state of the kitchen was worse than the front yard. She had dirty dishes stacked up in the sink. A sour smell emanated from the garbage can next to the stairs.

"Come on in!" Glenda shouted. We heard her thumping her way down the stairs. We walked through the kitchen and met her in the living room. She had newspapers stacked against one wall, every surface was covered with dust, but it seemed this was the tidiest room in the house.

The Client List

"I'm so glad you came," Glenda gushed. She rushed forward and hugged me. She felt like skin and bones in my arms. I shot a look of alarm over her head to Eric.

"Let's have a seat," she said. "Can I get either of you anything?"

"No!" Eric and I spoke in unison, perhaps too forcefully. But Glenda didn't seem to pick up on it. She sat in the oversized yellow velvet wing-backed chair in the corner. Eric and I took the couch opposite her.

"How's Farrah?" Glenda asked, her voice breaking.

"She's bearing up," I said. "Trying to adjust. But she still has hope. She wants to pursue an appeal."

"Will you help her with that?"

"I'm not sure. I mean, of course I'll help her find an appellate attorney. And I'll be available for anything they need. But I think she might be best served having someone who specializes in criminal appeals if that's the route she wants to take."

Glenda looked crestfallen. "Oh," she said. "I suppose you know best. It's just ... it gave me peace of mind knowing one of Anderson's protégés was taking care of her."

"I'm sorry the verdict didn't go as we hoped," I said. "But it really was an uphill battle from the start."

"He was so sure," Glenda said. "He knew she didn't do this, Cass. There's a part of me that's glad Anderson didn't make it to see what's happened. If he wasn't gone already, that verdict would have killed him."

Guilt washed over me. Maybe she saw something on my face. Glenda quickly covered.

"Oh! Oh no. I didn't mean you didn't do your best. Of course you did. And I don't think anyone other than Anderson could have done any better."

If it was her attempt at making me feel better, it failed. I felt Eric stiffen beside me. I put a hand on his knee to settle him.

"I'd like to see her," Glenda said. "Do you think they'd allow that at the jail?"

"She'd probably like that," I said. "And yes. You just call to schedule a visit. If you want, I can have someone from my office take care of that if you let me know when you'd like to go."

"Soon, I suppose," she said.

"Mrs. Rix," Eric said. "Is there anything we can do to help you? I can have a look at that stuck door while I'm here."

"I saw you out there talking to Marv and Karen," she said, her tone taking on an edge of anger. "A couple of nosey Nellies, those two. I suppose they mean well. Anderson never liked Marv. He's been on a power trip ever since they elected him head of the HOA. Anderson used to do it. Did you know that?"

"No," I said. "I didn't. And honestly, I just got the sense the Oglethorpes are worried about you. They said you're missed around the neighborhood." A small fib, but a kindness, I hoped.

If she registered my words, she didn't show it. Instead, she abruptly changed topics.

"Have you gotten anywhere looking into that awful father of Farrah's? Victor? Maybe if you can find the evidence the police missed..."

"Victor Sibley is innocent," Eric said. "At least of killing Terrence Dowd. We had a ... uh ... run-in of sorts with him the other day. As much as I'd love to pin this on him, his alibi checked out. He wasn't anywhere near Ann Arbor the day Terrence Dowd was killed."

Glenda went a bit pale. Her shoulders sank. "You're sure? There's no room for error there? I thought for sure you were on to something with him. It would make perfect sense. If he felt his daughter was being corrupted by the likes of Terrence Dowd …"

"There's no mistake," I said. "Believe me. I wish there was. I wish there was an easy answer or a smoking gun. I was wrong about Victor Sibley being involved in Terrence's murder."

Glenda went silent for a moment. She almost seemed in a trance. Then she snapped out of it and met my eyes. "Do you think … was he wrong? Was Anderson wrong about Farrah? Did she really do this? Did she kill that man?"

"We might not ever know for sure," Eric said. "But sometimes the simplest solution to a problem is the right one."

"The law of parsimony," she said. "Occam's Razor. That's something Anderson would have said. His last case … I just hoped …"

"We all hoped," I said. "And Victor Sibley *is* guilty of being a lousy father and a horrible husband. He terrorized his ex-wife and Farrah too. But he's not a murderer."

She slapped her hands on her knees as if that would help her accept what we told her. "All right then," she said. "All right."

"Mrs. Rix," I said. "I don't mean to be blunt. But we're worried about you."

"Me? I'm fine. I feel terribly for Farrah. And I do want to go see her if you think that will bring her some measure of comfort. But I've been a trial lawyer's wife for a very long time. I know how these things go."

"I don't mean about the trial," I said. "I mean about you. I'm worried you may need help you're not asking for. You're all alone here. I'm sorry I couldn't deliver the verdict you and Anderson hoped for, but maybe I can do something else that would mean even more to Anderson. I can help you get things sorted."

She closed her eyes. When she opened them, they were filled with tears.

"You're so sweet. I know why Anderson loved you so much. But I don't even know where to start. I thought I was fine. Anderson did such a good job of taking care of things. He made it look so easy. Now, I just don't know what to do. Sometimes I don't know how I'm going to even get out of bed in the morning. Everyone tells me I need to move on. This house? Everything here holds some essence of Anderson. At first, it brought me comfort. Now ... my goodness ... this is going to make me sound so awful. But now I feel like I'm drowning in it. It's choking me. Am I horrible for saying that?"

"No," I said. I went to my knees in front of her. "Not at all. It's healthy for you to want to move on a little. To let go."

"I don't ... I don't want to live here anymore. And I can't believe I'm even saying that."

"You don't have to," Eric said. "You can do whatever you like. Whatever feels best for you. This was your home with Anderson. There's nothing wrong with you wanting something that suits your needs better. This is a lot of house. A lot of grounds to maintain."

"You'll help me?" she asked. "You'll both help me?"

"Of course," I said. "And it doesn't have to be all at once. You can take all the time you need. Baby steps."

She cupped my face in her hands. "You're such a dear. Oh honey. I know one thing. The thing that's been the hardest for me every single day. There's nothing wrong with the front door. It's just ... I have to walk by Anderson's office to get to it and every time I do, it reminds me of too much. His things. I keep looking in there and expecting to see him at his desk like always. And when he's not and it's so empty. It breaks my heart all over again. But I don't know what to do with it."

"I do," I said. "So let me work on that one thing today. Eric and I can pack up the rest of his files and put them in the truck. What can be burned I'll burn. What needs to be archived, my office can handle."

"Oh, thank you!" Her whole body lifted. Hope filled her eyes.

"I'll pull the truck up," Eric said.

Glenda hugged me so tightly with strength I didn't know she had.

I gave Eric a quick wink and mouthed a thank you. But I knew he was happy to help, too.

It was one thing. A small thing. But it seemed to mean the world to Glenda.

Chapter 33

I spent the next couple of hours in Anderson's office, making two piles. By state law, attorneys were required to keep old client files for at least five years. Anderson had dozens upon dozens of folders that could safely be destroyed. He had far fewer files that would need to be stored for another couple of years. It would make a perfect summer project for Emma to work on digitizing them so the physical files could be shredded.

Some of the names on these files were part of Michigan's legal history. I found the very first asbestos client Rix agreed to represent. The case made it all the way to the Supreme Court. It was still taught in first-year tort classes all over the country. Though the paperwork could safely be destroyed now, I wouldn't dream of it. I put it in the pile for archiving.

The whole process took longer than it should have, as waves of nostalgia washed over me. I understood why this room caused Glenda so much pain. Anderson Rix's life work had been reduced to paperwork and bankers boxes. But he was still present here. His scrawling notes. The drafts of legal briefs he wrote longhand until the day he died.

Over the course of the Sibley trial, I'd gotten good at reading his shorthand. I could hear his voice through them. His cadence of speech.

You're asking the wrong questions, Leary. Marry the facts to the rule. Law is math. Law is logic.

Even his law books. Glenda planned to donate Rix's casebooks to the local community theatre, but they hadn't picked them up yet. As I opened random volumes, each one had copious notes in the margins and heavy highlighting.

These were gold, I thought. In Rix's notes, you could see his thought process. The way he analyzed cases. I wondered if they might be valuable. Maybe the law school would rather have them to put on display or make available for scholars. It seemed almost criminal to destroy any of this. And yet, I knew Glenda felt like she was drowning in the specter of the great Anderson Rix.

I sat at his desk, running my hands over the leather ink blotter. "I'm sorry," I found myself whispering to a ghost. "I wish I could have got an acquittal for you."

Me. Of all the students Rix had taught. Of all the other lawyers he must have known. It was me he chose as the steward of all his files. His legacy. I only hoped I was worthy.

I managed to get the few more recent files organized into one box. These were clients whose cases had settled but Rix was still doing minor work here and there. He helped open an estate on one. Handled real estate closings for a few others. There wouldn't be much for me to do for any of them, but you never knew. Someone might call with a question or two.

His last big asbestos settlements were outside the record retention rule. I counted five cases, each with files big enough for their own box. With two of those the settlements were paid out in annuities. I put notes on those so Emma would know not to destroy them.

I could hear Eric outside, running a lawn mower. Glenda had gone out with him, watching the progress he made, calling out answers to questions he had as he went along.

I was almost done here. I picked up another file, one of the last large settlements Rix had handled. Susan McCord. I don't know why the name gave me pause, but there was something familiar about it I couldn't place. Had I worked on this one with him?

No. The dates didn't line up. It was another asbestos litigant, but the complaint was filed long after I'd fallen out of Professor Rix's good graces and gone to Chicago.

Susan McCord.

I said the name out loud. My blood chilled.

Susan McCord. McCord. McCord. McCord.

"You about ready, boss?" Eric said. He was sweating. He'd taken off his dress shirt and wore just the white tee shirt he had on underneath. I had him haul boxes out to the truck for the last hour. Before that, he'd taken it upon himself to get Glenda's kitchen back in order. Before *that,* he'd gone out to assess the damage to Glenda's gardens. Mowing was the last thing he wanted to do before we left today.

I didn't answer him. I kept staring at that name.

"Cass?"

"What?"

"I don't know what kind of luck you had in here, but she's got a real mess out there. This isn't something she's gonna be able to pay some teenager a few hundred bucks to fix. She's looking at several thousand dollars' worth of landscaping. There's more crabgrass than actual grass. She's got weeds choking the flower beds. A lot of it's going to have to be dug up and started over from scratch. But I talked to the Oglethorpes again. They just *happened* to be walking by. I think I've bought her some time. They might be busybodies, but I think they've got good hearts."

"Eric ..." I said. Susan McCord. I needed to get back to the office. I needed to check my notes and make sure I wasn't just losing my mind and seeing things that weren't there. Only I knew I wasn't. I *knew* it.

"I'm worried about Rix's Beamer sitting in the garage too," he said. "Glenda says she hasn't driven it since Rix passed away. I'm sure the battery's dead by now. Next time we come out, I'll see if I can't get that figured out for her. She's agreed to sell it. It's a beautiful car."

"Eric?" I asked. "This file. This name."

I handed him the McCord file. Puzzled, he took it.

"What am I looking for?" he asked.

"I don't know. But that name. Susan McCord. I've seen it before."

His face fell. He remembered at the same time I did. We'd both memorized Terrence Dowd's appointment calendar for the weeks before his murder.

"Susan McCord," he repeated.

"Yes."

He snapped the file shut.

"You two are angels," Glenda sang. She walked into Rix's office, probably for the first time in weeks.

"We're all set here for today," I said. "I've just got this one box left to take out. But we'll be back next week."

She came to me and hugged me for the third time. Then she went to Eric and hugged him, too.

"We'll talk soon," I said. "And I can make those arrangements for you to visit Farrah Sibley if you want."

It would be easy, I thought. But I planned to pay my own visit to her first thing tomorrow morning with Susan McCord's file in tow.

Chapter 34

It's a strange thing meeting with a newly convicted client. In a healthy brain, they will go through stages of grief, moving often between bargaining and denial. Or sometimes they may become stuck in anger. In someone like Farrah, I knew acceptance would come the hardest. If she truly hadn't killed Terrence Dowd.

She looked thinner since I saw her in court a week ago. Her jumpsuit hung off her. Her hair, normally straight and lustrous, hung in strings. We wouldn't have much time. I had to walk a tightrope. She was the only person who could tell me what I needed to know. But the last thing I wanted to do was give her false hope.

"My father came to see me," she said.

"He came to see me, too."

"He told me. Cass, you have to stop harassing him. He didn't kill Terry."

"I know that. We came to … an understanding."

She nodded. I bit my tongue past the urge to ask her how she was holding up. I could see it with my own eyes. The answer was not well.

"You have to take care of yourself now," I said. "I'm doing what I can for you out here. But for the foreseeable future, this is your life now."

"I know. They want me to see a shrink. Maybe put me on antidepressants."

"That might be helpful."

"I'm glad you came. I know you did the best you could."

"Farrah, I came because I wanted to see how you were doing. But I also came because there's something I have to ask you. About Terry."

Her expression didn't change. It almost seemed like she was already doped up. I pulled out a one-page printout from Terrence Dowd's calendar. His appointment with Susan McCord was listed for 10:00 a.m. on the morning of April 28th. I'd highlighted it in pink. I slid the paper across the table to her.

"Do you know what this appointment was about? I know Lydia kept the sheets on his schedule. But you were involved with all of his clients, right?"

She furrowed her brow as she read the name.

"I didn't meet with this one. I don't know who that is."

"Can you tell anything from the notations in the calendar? We reviewed this in discovery. She was listed as a potential new client. But there was no reason to follow up on it."

"It's listed as IC," she said.

"Right. Initial consultation. And I don't see any further entries after it. It doesn't look like he met with her again."

"Yeah. I don't know. We went over all these names before. And I did it with Anderson too before you came on board. It's weird though."

"In what way?"

"Terry didn't often take initial consultations. He generally left that to me or to one of the paralegals."

"And can you tell from this whether a file was ever opened on Susan McCord?"

"I can't tell from this, but I know one wasn't. I never worked on anything for whoever Susan McCord is."

"And he never discussed her with you?"

"No. Cass, what's this about? You're showing me a meaningless calendar entry from almost three months before Terry was killed. And like I said, we went over all this before. You, me, me, Anderson."

I debated what to tell her. It would be cruel to get her hopes up until I knew more. It could be a coincidence. The name wasn't so unusual that it might not even be the same woman in Anderson Rix's former client list.

"The truth?" I said. "I'm not sure. Not yet. But I'm trying to run something down. Assume that it's going to be nothing until I tell you otherwise."

"But you're still working on it," she said. "You're still working on my case?"

"Of course." I could hear Jeanie and Eric in my brain. They would have warned me not to say anything of the kind. To help her find a good appellate lawyer, then wash my hands of it.

"Thank you. I know I can't pay you anymore. I don't even know how I'm going to afford my appeals. Because I have to appeal. I know now it might not matter to the courts, but I'm innocent, Cass. The truth has to be out there somewhere. Do you think it's to do with this woman?"

"I don't know, Farrah. Right now, I'm chasing wild gooses, you know?"

"But this is a lead? This Susan McCord?"

"She might be. But she probably isn't. That's the real truth. You have to take care of yourself. Keep your head down. Follow the rules."

"I told you everything. Every client Terry was working with during those months. Nobody threatened him. This wasn't a client. I'm sure of it. I wish it were. I wish I could tell you why somebody would have wanted him dead. But I can't."

"Farrah, you can't worry about that part of this right now. Your job is to keep your head. Get through this hour by hour if you have to."

"I don't know where I'll end up. Everyone says probably Huron Valley."

"We'll know soon enough. I'll stay in touch with you. You know you can call me anytime. Your sentencing is in three weeks. I'm working hard on that too. I can still argue mitigating circumstances."

"Judge McGee is going to give me life. I know it. Maybe I was stupid. Maybe I should have taken Jason Bailey's plea deal. Maybe I ..."

"Stop. No second guessing. You knew that meant you'd have to admit to killing Terry."

"What does it matter anymore? Everyone believes I did it. Even if this lead of yours pans out. Or somebody finally does the right thing and steps forward. I'm the better story. The crazy stalker girlfriend."

"Okay. Enough. I'm not going to tell you everything's going to be all right. But I'm going to tell you I *am* out here working for you still. And when I have some news, I'll be back."

"Okay," she said. "Okay. You're right. Okay."

"Good. I'll come back in a couple of days."

Farrah thanked me. She rose and let the guard take her back to her cell. More than anything, I wanted to be able to give her good news.

By the time I made it to my car, I had the first glimmer of hope. It came as it often did, in the form of Miranda Sulier.

"Hey, kiddo," she opened as she often did. "I found her."

"Susan McCord?"

"Yep. Tracked her down to a new address right outside of New Buffalo. It's a bit of a hike, but she agreed to meet with you at her daughter's house. I'll text you the address. Nine o'clock tomorrow morning."

A rush of heat went through me. "Did you tell her what it was about?"

"Not exactly. I told her you were working on a case with Terrence Dowd. I'm pretty sure she doesn't know he's dead, Cass. I decided not to break the news. But the second I said his name, she perked right up. Can't wait to meet you."

"Thank you, Miranda. You're the absolute best. You're never allowed to retire."

She let out a haughty laugh. It was something we all told her. I'd actually pulled her out of retirement to come and work for me years ago.

"Just drive safe. I told Jeanie and Tori you wouldn't be coming into the office tomorrow. Tori's elbow deep in those Rix files of yours. She's showing Emma the ropes. Good news is we haven't scared the poor kid off yet. Bad news is it's only a matter of time."

"Thanks, Miranda," I said. "For all of it."

I clicked off and looked back toward the entrance to the jail. If my hunch was right, I might have a way to get Farrah out of there. But the price would be steep.

Chapter 35

Susan McCord's daughter lived in a lakefront condo on the shores of Lake Michigan. She met me in her driveway before I even got out of my car. I found her polite, but direct. A protective daughter looking out for her elderly mother. She introduced herself as Kim McCord. Brunette. Pretty with carefully applied makeup and a smooth forehead only Botox could produce.

"She barely slept last night," Kim said. "She's been so agitated about this meeting."

"I'm not here to cause her any stress, I promise."

"She doesn't trust lawyers. Especially now. Don't be surprised if she tries to throw you out of the house. She's doing this for me. She needs closure."

I smiled, not wanting to let on yet that I had no idea what Kim was talking about. It became abundantly clear my purpose for this meeting wasn't what Kim and her mother thought it was. Which only made me more eager to get started.

Kim led me into her immaculate home. Coved ceilings, terrazzo floors in the foyer, gleaming stainless steel appliances. And everything in the place was a shade of white. The carpet, the walls, the furniture. Susan McCord sat in the living room looking out at the water. She herself was dressed in all white. A linen pants suit and white espadrilles. She'd adorned her wrists with chunky white costume jewelry and wore a long, triple strand of pearls.

"Good morning," she said, turning to look me up and down.

"I'm Cass Leary," I said, extending a hand. She shook it, but didn't rise from the couch. She gestured to the chair opposite her. Kim excused herself to go bring us all coffee.

"Thank you for meeting me. I know you probably have a lot of questions about why I've come all this way to meet with you."

"You work with Mr. Dowd?"

"Not exactly," I said. "But I understand you met with him last year. I don't want to waste your time. I'm hoping you can tell me what you talked to him about."

"He didn't tell you?"

Kim came back in. She set a tray of coffee cups out along with a fresh pot. She poured me a cup. I thanked her and added my own cream.

"I know you were a former client of Anderson Rix's. That he secured a settlement for you regarding your husband's mesothelioma claim."

Her face darkened. Kim put a comforting hand on her mother's shoulder, then took the seat beside her.

"My father died of the disease," Kim said. "It's been twenty years now this past March. He suffered a great deal."

"I'm so sorry."

"He was the best," Susan said. I thought she meant her late husband. Then she met my eyes. "Anderson Rix was who you went to if you had an asbestos claim. Everyone knew that. My Ernie idolized him. Thought he walked on water. And everything he promised us, he delivered."

"That's what's been so hard about all of this," Kim said. "Why my mom was reluctant to ask any questions. Everything we have now is in part because of the work Mr. Rix did. We weren't supposed to discuss the terms of the settlement, but I can tell you it was in the millions."

"I'd give back every penny if I could just have my Ernie back again. Healthy and whole."

"Of course. Professor Rix was a mentor of mine. In law school. Did he refer you to Mr. Dowd? I understand there were a few clients he sent there some years ago when he retired from practicing law. But I didn't realize he was still actively referring."

Susan and Kim exchanged a look. "I'm sorry," Kim said. "My mother didn't go to see Mr. Dowd about her own case. She went on behalf of a friend."

"A friend?"

Susan McCord's hands started to tremble. Her coffee cup rattled on the saucer. She put them both down.

"Perhaps we should start from the beginning," I said. "The reason I'm here … Terrence Dowd passed away last year."

I let my words settle. I wouldn't say murder. Not yet. Susan looked like she was about to faint as it was.

She put a hand on her daughter's sleeve. "Kimmie, I'm going to go get those papers."

"Are you sure, Mom? I can get them for you."

"I need a moment. I need some air," she said. "You two keep chatting. Tell her whatever you need to tell her. I'll be right back."

Susan stood. She grabbed a white pearled cane and leaned on it as she walked down the hall and out of sight.

"Kim," I started. She held up a hand to stop me.

"You have to understand. My mother has become somewhat of an icon among the families who lost people to asbestos-related cancers. She started an online forum in the mid-nineties. Back when it was just chat rooms. At the time, it helped her cope. Gave her a purpose. But over the years, she just started to drown from all the horrible stories. Then when my father finally passed ... well, it was touch and go there for a few years. I thought I'd lose her too."

"You've been through so much. She's very strong."

"She wants you to know about Greta Goranski. That's what she's going to bring you papers about."

"Greta Goranski?" I'd seen the name on another of Anderson Rix's client files I now had at my office.

"She met her on the forum a long time ago. Greta was in the same boat. Her husband had end-stage lung cancer. Mom was her rock. And she brought her to see Anderson Rix. It was one of the last cases he took on before he retired."

The Client List

"Was he able to get the Goranskis a similar settlement?"

Though I'd seen the Goranski file, I hadn't looked through it. It went on the pile to be digitized and stored.

"We thought so," she said. "Two million dollars. Only … Greta saw only a fraction of that. Just a few thousand over the years."

Susan returned from one of the back rooms. She had a stack of stapled papers in her hand. She put them on the table in front of me.

"May I?" I asked.

She gestured for me to pick them up. I recognized the letterhead on the top paper right away. The Law Firm of Anderson Rix. These were billing statements. Status letters.

"He lied to her," Susan said.

"I'm sorry?"

"Anderson Rix lied to her. He stole over a million dollars from Ms. Goranski's settlement money."

My head spun. I flipped through the pages. It was hard to make sense of them all on the spot. But certain things jumped out at me right away. Several of the invoices had duplicate entries. It was subtle. If you didn't know what you were looking for, maybe you'd miss it. But over two quarters, I counted almost fifty thousand dollars in double billings. I flipped through more pages. Susan had entries dating back almost ten years.

"Greta and I didn't want to believe it at first. We thought maybe we'd gotten things wrong. Mr. Rix was such a godsend to my family," Susan said. "A hero, really. But there were other rumors that started to surface from a couple of the other families I knew he represented. It was small. Here and there. But I believe Mr.

Rix embezzled large sums of money from some of his last clients, Ms. Leary."

"You took this to Terrence Dowd?" I said. Now it was my hand starting to tremble. "That's the meeting you had with him in April of last year?"

"Yes," Kim answered for her mother. "And he told Mom he was going to look into it, but we never heard back from him."

"I should have known he'd cover for Mr. Rix," Susan said. "I should have known all the lawyers would stick together."

"Then why did you agree to meet with me?"

"I thought maybe a woman would have a more sympathetic ear," Susan said. "And I looked you up. You're a criminal lawyer. So I thought maybe finally someone was looking into this crime."

"Mrs. McCord, you're aware Anderson Rix passed away early this year?"

"I read something about that, yes. It made its way to the community. I know many of his former clients went to his funeral. I couldn't bring myself to do it."

"I can see why you'd feel that way," I said.

"And now I know why Mr. Dowd never followed up with me. I'm sorry. I assumed the worst. I didn't know the man died. He said he would look into things and get back to me. When he didn't, I just assumed he wasn't interested in helping."

I felt light-headed. A few weeks before he died, Terrence Dowd was given evidence of a potential embezzlement case against Anderson Rix. My God. I came here hoping for answers. Now I only had more questions.

The Client List

"Do you think Greta Goranski would meet with me? I can't promise you anything but this. I *am* interested in getting to the bottom of this. What you've shown me so far does raise some serious questions."

"I mean there's an estate, right? Anderson Rix?" Kim asked. "A claim could be filed."

"Possibly," I said. "And I'm not the lawyer who would help her do that. But I can help her find one who might."

Susan shook her head. "Then you'd better hurry. Greta's got cancer herself now. Ovarian. She's in hospice care, Ms. Leary. That's the other reason I agreed to meet with you. Poor Greta's time is running out now, too."

"I'll do what I can," I said. "Do you mind if I take these?"

"Go ahead," Susan said. "They're copies. Greta still has the originals. I left a copy with Mr. Dowd, too."

Heart racing, I rose to my feet. We said our goodbyes and Kim walked me back to my car.

"You believe her, right?" she asked. "I don't know you, Ms. Leary, but I think I can see it on your face."

"Yes," I said. "I believe her. And I meant what I said. I'll do whatever I can to help."

I had wanted to be wrong. I still did. But I knew what I held in my hand was a motive for murder.

Chapter 36

By the time I got back to the office three hours later, Tori and Emma had converted the conference room. They had Rix's files spread out all over the table. Emma hand wrote a chart on the whiteboard with monetary totals.

"They've been like this all day," Miranda said, sipping from her insulated tumbler. She leaned against the doorframe. "There's no talking to either one of them. I can't even get them to stop for lunch."

"Thanks for trying," I said. I wanted their answers to be anything other than what I knew they would be.

"It's concentrated to these five files, Cass," Tori said. She sat cross-legged on the floor in the center of a semicircle of papers.

"Goranski, Spitzer, Wallingford, Geary, and Sesnick. These are the last five litigants Rix took on," she continued.

"It's little stuff at first," Emma said, her words rapid-fire with excitement. "Like this, he's charging court costs in two different invoices. Then multiple duplicate entries for copy charges. But where it gets really nefarious is here. See this?"

She handed me the invoice for Adam Sesnick, a line worker in a Detroit area cement factory. Rix secured a million-dollar settlement for him in 2010. The invoice showed a ten-thousand-dollar charge for an expert witness fee to a Dr. Coleman Price.

I took a seat at the table. "Okay," I said. "That's high. What's Price testifying about?"

"That's the thing," Tori said. It took her a moment to get herself up off the floor. She waved Miranda off when she tried to help her. Tori took the chair beside me.

"He's got him listed as an industrial hygienist. And Price's name shows up on all five of these cases. He charges five grand in the Geary case. Ten grand on Goranski. Ten grand on Wallingford. But there's no corresponding ledger entry from accounts payable. No check was ever written to Dr. Price. But there's a withdrawal from Rix's IOLTA account that corresponds to these expert witness fees. It's transferred directly into Rix's business checking account, but then stays there."

"So he stiffed Dr. Price. Wouldn't Price send it to collections after a while?" I asked. Eric walked in. From the look on his face, Tori and Emma had kept him apprised of their findings.

"He doesn't exist," Eric said. "There is no Dr. Coleman Price. Rix made him up."

"And he's not the only one," Tori said. "There are tens of thousands of dollars in fees going to another expert named George Hewitt. An economic damage expert. But the same thing. No checks written to him from accounts payable. Only the transfer from Rix's lawyer's trust account to himself."

"There's no George Hewitt either," Eric said. "Not one that serves as an expert witness in asbestos litigation."

I looked back up at the whiteboard. Emma had written in red ink, circled a staggering figure. $512,000.00.

"Half a million dollars?" I said. "Rix embezzled half a million dollars from these five clients?"

"That's what it looks like," Eric said. "You'll need a forensic accountant to take a hard look at his business records. But I suspect this was the tip of the iceberg."

"I just don't understand it," I said. "Rix took these cases on contingency for the most part. He made millions from these settlements the legitimate way. Where did all the money go?"

"We have to talk to Glenda," Eric said. "But you know what that house looks like. Maybe the reason she's not dealing with the landscaping is because she can't afford to pay the crew. I want to take a look at their personal bank records if she'll let us. But to blow through this kind of money? You're looking at either drugs or gambling most likely."

"Susan McCord knew it," I said. "She figured it out with regard to Greta Goranski. She took Greta's billings to Dowd three months before Dowd ended up murdered. Dowd knew something. Rix found out."

Eric had his laptop tucked under his arm. He took the chair on the other side of me and flipped it open.

"I wanted to wait until you got back. I wanted to be sure I was seeing what I think I'm seeing. But I am now."

His tone had darkened. I felt sick.

"What is it?" I asked.

"Remember when I asked to look at the surveillance cameras from the surrounding businesses to the Belz Building on the night of the murder? The street views?"

"Yes," I said.

"I was looking for Victor Sibley's pickup truck. I didn't pay much attention to the other vehicles. I was the one with tunnel vision, Cass. Not Eklund."

"What are you saying?"

He pulled up a grainy photograph showing the street view facing the side entrance to the Belz Building parking lot. He pressed play.

The counter in the lower left recorded the date and time. July 17th, 7:41 p.m. A silver sedan pulled up. This was a time lapse video. The camera took still photos every five seconds. As such, the camera skipped over the driver exiting the vehicle. But the next photo showed a male figure walking toward the entrance to the parking structure. I could only see him from the back. He had the same build as Rix. He wore a blue baseball cap. There would be no way to make a positive ID from this photo. But the car. The license plate could be enhanced. We would be able to find out for sure. Eric hit pause.

I stared at the vehicle for a moment. My brain seemed to lag behind my eyes. Or maybe it was that I didn't really want to believe what he was showing me. Some last shred of hope that what I knew to be true was wrong, somehow.

"Rix's Beamer," I said. It was unmistakable. I could see it clearly even in the low definition of the photo.

"Eric," I said. "My God."

"We have Dowd on surveillance leaving his office and heading into the parking structure at 7:46," Eric said.

"He knew," I said. "Rix doesn't just coincidentally pull up right when Dowd is leaving. He called him."

"But there was nothing on Dowd's cell phone?" Jeanie walked in. "I've been looking at the transcripts. There are no incoming or outgoing calls after 7:30 that night. It was just that text to Lydia Whitford just after seven o'clock."

"They could have pre-arranged to meet earlier in the day," Eric said. "There's no way to tell."

"Rix's phone," I said. "Eric, we have to see Rix's cell phone records. They were communicating in those last few weeks. They had to be. They met. Dowd let him know what he knew. Could he have blackmailed him?"

"It wouldn't have had to be as nefarious as that. Dowd might have just been giving Rix a chance to make this right. What matters is we can assume Dowd knew Rix was cooking his own books and stealing money from these clients. Keeping him quiet about it was a motive for murder."

"None of this proves murder. Yet."

"He had a gun, Cass," Eric said.

"How do you know?"

"I did some digging once I saw the surveillance footage. Rix bought a Glock 19 ten years ago. Probably for home protection. But he owned the same kind of gun that was used to kill Terrence Dowd."

"We have to talk to Glenda," I said. "Get those cell phone records if she'll turn them over willingly. His car ... Eric, if Rix shot Dowd then drove off in that car, there could be physical evidence, couldn't there?"

"Maybe. The shooting happened in July. Rix didn't die until February. That's seven long months where he could have disposed of evidence."

"And how well does that work?" I said. "How many cases have you solved with microscopic forensic evidence? Carpet fibers. Specks of blood. You said Glenda said she hasn't driven the car since Anderson died. It's just sitting there in his garage. Nobody's that good at cleaning up after themselves."

"No," Eric said. "They aren't."

"We have to go to Glenda."

"No," Eric said, his voice booming.

"What?"

"We have to go to Lars Eklund."

"No. No way. Eklund won't take any of this seriously. He refuses to believe anyone other than Farrah Sibley committed this crime. I don't trust him."

"I do."

"Eric? No. Eklund's part of the problem. It's his shoddy detective work that got us into this mess."

I could see Eric's anger rise from the set of his jaw.

"Come on, ladies," Jeanie said to the others. "Let's take a breather and get some lunch."

This time, no one argued. They cleared the room, leaving Eric and me alone.

"Eric," I said. "I mean it. I don't trust Eklund. He's had it in for Farrah from the beginning. And I haven't earned brownie points with him either during the trial."

"Eklund's a good cop. He knows how the system works. I promise you he didn't take your cross-examination personally. And we're going to do this the right way. That surveillance footage alone puts Rix at the crime scene during the critical window. He'll have probable cause to search the vehicle and take a look at those cell phone records. I'll talk to him. Cop to cop."

"He doesn't see you as a cop anymore. He sees you as a traitor. He told me as much. Said you've made a deal with the devil by coming to work for me."

Eric smiled. "That's probably exactly what I would have said if the roles were reversed."

"I want to have our own people search that car, Eric."

"Cass," he said. "We go through Eklund or I'm out."

"What?"

"I mean it. If I'm gonna work with you, we deal with law enforcement the way I say we do. If Anderson Rix is guilty of this crime, I am damn sure gonna see to it that the evidence is handled properly. I trust Eklund to do that."

"He's been wrong about everything. About Farrah."

"He put together the best case he could with the evidence he had. Anderson Rix is the bad guy here, not Lars Eklund. Eklund didn't hang Farrah out to dry, Rix did. I am not going to make the same mistakes again."

His voice dropped. And suddenly, this wasn't just about Farrah Sibley and Anderson Rix. A long time ago, Eric nearly let someone else take the fall for a crime he committed. He had just reasons for doing it. But it seemed he might forever serve penance for that one terrible choice. A choice I was glad he made. A choice I was the only other living soul who knew he made.

"All right," I said. "If you trust Eklund …"

"I do. I've already called him. He's gonna meet me at his office in an hour. I'll take my surveillance footage. And I'll get him up to speed on Rix's cooked books."

"Glenda," I said. "You have to let me talk to her. We can't just let Eklund ambush her with this."

"We have no idea how Glenda's going to react to any of this. We don't even know for sure if she was kept in the dark, Cass. What if she knows what Rix did? His car is still in her possession. The gun could be too for all we know. I know you feel you owe her something. But she's a material witness in a murder case now."

"She doesn't know," I said. "Eric, she invited us into her home. Rix's files have just been sitting there in his home office for months. If Glenda was in on it, she could have destroyed all of this. She alone had the power to protect him after the fact. She didn't. Because she didn't know. I'm sure of it."

"I can probably get Eklund to agree to let us be there when he serves his warrants. But that's it. You need to stay away from Glenda. You can't be seen as coaching her or influencing this in any way."

"What are you worried about?" I said. "Anderson Rix will never stand trial for this. He's dead. There won't be another defense attorney out there trying to suppress evidence on this one, Eric. It's just us. It's just Glenda."

"Still," he said. "We're playing this the way I would want if I were in Eklund's position."

He was right. I knew it. And yet I wished I could trust Lars Eklund as much as Eric did. Farrah's future depended on it.

Chapter 37

Three days later, Eric was proven right. Eklund immediately secured search warrants for Anderson Rix's home, cell phone, and computer. When he brought Glenda Rix in for questioning, he let me sit right beside her. Though she was understandably shocked and confused, somehow she didn't seem surprised. She clutched my hand beneath the table the entire time.

"I didn't know how bad it got," she said, her voice barely more than a whisper. "You have to understand. Anderson took care of everything. He was old-fashioned that way. When we got married, he didn't want me to work. He wanted me to stay home and take care of the house. I was happy to do it. I loved cooking for him. He worked such long hours. In those early years, we barely saw each other. He was at the office twenty hours a day sometimes."

"Mrs. Rix," Eklund said. "I know how hard this must be for you. I can't imagine what you must be thinking. Losing your husband was enough of a blow. But to find out he might have had something to do with Terrence Dowd's death must be devastating. I appreciate your willingness to cooperate. Were you aware of any financial difficulties your husband was having?"

"No," she said. "Like I've been telling you. He took care of all the bills. When he started winding the practice down, he let go of all his support staff. He was doing his own billings and everything. I begged him to keep at least a bookkeeper on but he wouldn't hear of it. And everything was just taken care of. If I needed something for myself, Anderson just had me put it on the credit card. We took trips. Not as many as I would have liked, but Anderson made sure I wanted for nothing."

"Did you ever observe him spending large sums of money on anything?" Eklund asked.

"He liked to gamble," she said. "When we'd go on cruises, he'd always take out fifty thousand dollars to play with at the casinos. He liked going to the casinos in Detroit, too. He'd take trips with friends. I didn't care for that scene. But he'd go at least three times a year. Maybe more."

It would be easy enough to check into, but I knew Eric's instincts were right. If Rix was in financial trouble, gambling losses made sense.

"After he died," she said, "I thought it would be taken care of too. He promised me it would be. That I'd never have to worry about anything. But when I called our insurance agent, he told me Anderson cashed in a life insurance policy two years before he died. Then all the auto payments for some of our bills bounced. The bank started calling. I couldn't understand it. Where did all that money go? It just didn't make sense. Anderson promised me."

She dabbed at her eyes with a tissue. I squeezed her hands.

"I wish you'd have told me," I said.

"Oh honey, you and Eric have been so sweet. I was embarrassed. I knew Anderson would have been embarrassed to have you know he left such a mess of things. That he left me poor after all of this."

He left her more than poor. When the families of his clients found out what he'd done, they'd come after his estate for restitution. She'd lose the house and almost everything in it. Terrence Dowd ended up with a bullet through the chest, but Glenda Rix was just as much one of her husband's victims.

"I'm so sorry for all those people," she said. "I didn't know he was taking their money. I swear it. I never would have let him do that if I'd known. We could have lived in a trailer. I wouldn't have cared. I would have helped him. We could have figured out what to do together."

"I appreciate you bringing in Anderson's cell phone," Eklund said. It sat on the table between us. At Eklund's urging, Glenda unlocked it. She still knew Anderson's pass code.

Eklund scrolled through it, his scowl deepening. He shot me a look, then slid the phone to me.

There were a series of calls to one number. Then a few returned from the same number. The caller ID read Harriman Dowd.

"Dowd's law firm," I said. The calls started in early May. I counted twenty-three of them over a ten-week period. The last one was the day before Dowd's murder. Then they stopped. After July 17th, there were no more incoming or outgoing calls from Dowd's firm to Rix. I passed the phone back to Eklund.

"You can have anything you want," Glenda said. "Whatever you think you need. I want to help. If Anderson took money from all those people, I want to try to make it right. I don't know how I can. But I want to try."

She didn't know about Terrence Dowd. Everything was right in front of her, but Glenda Rix seemed to keep an invisible membrane of denial around her. She could start to process the fact Rix was a thief. She wasn't ready to admit he was a murderer. There was a knock on the interview room door. Eklund excused himself for a moment.

"Did I do all right?" Glenda asked me. "I don't want to be in trouble. Oh, I'm so sorry. And I'm so angry with Anderson. How could he do all of those things? What must you think of him now?"

"It doesn't matter what I think," I said. "What matters is you're here. And none of this was your fault. I'll help you in whatever way I can going forward. But you have to be prepared. This might get a lot worse before it gets better."

She dropped her chin and met my eyes. "Cass," she said. "No one is saying it. Not even you. But I'm not a fool. I know what this is. I know what you think. Did he ... did he kill that man? Did Anderson shoot Terrence Dowd?"

I looked back at the door Eklund had just exited. I wasn't sure if it was my place to tell her. Then I decided I didn't care. She clung to me. She trusted me. And nothing I said now would change a thing.

"Yes," I said. "I think Anderson is the one who killed Terrence Dowd. I think Dowd knew what was going on with Rix's former clients."

"And Anderson panicked," she said. "He must have panicked. I can't believe he went to that office with the intent to kill him. I just can't. Something must have happened. I don't know. Oh God. I don't know anything anymore. This is a nightmare. I have to wake up at some point, don't I?"

Before I could answer, Eklund poked his head back in. I could see Eric in the hallway behind him.

"Cass," he said. "You got a second?"

I patted Glenda on the back, then excused myself. Eric looked grim. He took my hand and followed behind Eklund as we walked back to his office. He motioned for us to take the chairs in front of his desk then sat behind it.

"Just got word from the crime scene techs out at Rix's place," he said. "I'm letting you know what I know out of professional courtesy. It'll all be in my report later anyway. Wray, you were right about the car. Techs found stains on the steering wheel and center console that look like blood. Obviously, we won't know until the labs come back, but ..."

"Transfer," Eric said. "Rix shoots Dowd at point blank range. Blood spatter on Rix's hands or his sleeve or something. He gets in his car, every surface he touches gets Dowd's blood on it."

"We don't know if it was Dowd's blood yet," Eklund said. "But that's a pretty safe bet. But there's something else. We dug up the garden like you suggested."

"The garden?" I asked.

Eric turned to me. "It was bothering me. I told you when I went out there, there was one area where the earth was all turned over. I asked Glenda about it. She said late last summer Rix got a bug up his ass to transplant all the Hostas they had in front of their mailboxes. It made no sense. That's not the kind of thing you would do that late in the season."

Eklund pulled out his phone. He pulled up a picture text and showed it to us. It took me a second to understand what I was looking at. When I did, bile rose in my throat.

It was a close-up of a blue-gloved hand. One of the crime scene lab techs held a dirt-covered gun in a plastic evidence bag.

"They found it buried about two feet down," Eklund said. "It's a Glock 19."

"Same kind used to kill Terrence Dowd," I whispered.

Eklund and Eric were talking. Their words made no sense to me, as if I were hearing them underwater. What a waste. All this time. Over what? Money? His reputation? It felt so meaningless.

"Farrah Sibley," I said. "Eklund, you have to call Jason Bailey. You have to let him know. Farrah didn't do this. She was telling the truth. We have to start the process to get her out."

"We will," Eklund said. "But there *is* a process to this. I have to see the lab reports come back. That will take some time."

"I'm filing an emergency appeal," I said. "I want Farrah out pending all of that. Will you cooperate? Will you lean on Bailey to cooperate?"

Eklund looked at Eric. It infuriated me. "Don't look at him," I said. "Look at me. I'm asking you. Will you stand in my way if I ask to have Farrah released on bond pending your findings?"

Eric put a hand on my knee. I was about to explode.

"No," Eklund finally said. "I won't stand in your way. You may not want to believe this, but I don't want the wrong person in prison for this crime. I never wanted that. No good cop does. What you two have done in this case is remarkable. I'm grateful.

And when this all shakes out, I'll be the first in line to apologize to Farrah Sibley. You have my word on that."

"Thank you," I said. Slowly, I rose. Eric stood beside me.

"When can I take Glenda Rix home?"

"They're just finishing up at her house," he said. "Give me one hour. They did their best not to disturb too much, but there will be some clean-up. It was unavoidable."

"I understand," I said. "I'll help her handle it."

"So will I," Eric said.

We thanked Lars Eklund, then went back to Glenda Rix. She had done the right thing. But I knew in my heart there was no way we could ever help her put her life back together again.

Chapter 38

Eight days later, on the one-year anniversary of Terrence Dowd's murder, Farrah Sibley walked out of the Washtenaw County Jail a free woman.

Jeanie and I picked her up and brought her back to my office in Delphi. Her own apartment wasn't an option anymore. She'd sublet it during the court proceedings. I didn't think she wanted to spend another second in Ann Arbor anyway.

Tori and Emma arranged an impromptu welcome home party for Farrah, complete with a festive banner, balloons, and a cake. Farrah had tears of gratitude in her eyes as she took it all in. It was just us. Me, Jeanie, Miranda, Tori, and Emma. Neither of Farrah's parents were there for her. Though I imagined Eric would have had a thing or two to say if Victor Sibley ever tried to cross my threshold again. So would I.

"Thank you," Farrah said. "All of you. I'm not going to forget what you did for me."

"A toast!" Jeanie shouted. She produced a bottle of champagne. Miranda had a tray stacked with plastic champagne glasses left over from New Year's Eve.

Jeanie popped the cork and filled glasses for everyone. Farrah's hand shook as she took hers.

"Speech!" Tori yelled.

Farrah laughed. "I'm not good at speeches. I was never going to be a litigator like you, Cass. Or like Terry was. Give me books to read and I'm happier."

"Then I'll give one," I said. "Thanks for sticking with us, Farrah. You stayed strong. You did everything I asked of you even when I knew you weren't sure it was the right thing ..."

"That's not true," she protested. "I trusted you."

I put a finger to my lips. "Congratulations," I said. "Enjoy the day and the next ones to come."

"Hear, hear!" Jeanie said.

"Wait," Farrah said. "I do have a thing or two I'd like to say. I might get a little choked up here so there's your warning. I've been alone a lot in my life. Or at least I've felt that way. I'm used to people having preconceived notions about who I am. But everyone here in this room ... you didn't prejudge me. You gave me the benefit of the doubt. I know how rare that is. It made all the difference. So thank you. You've given me a gift. I promise not to waste it."

Jeanie, tough as she was, was always the first to break. She had a soft spot for orphans. Right now, Farrah might as well be one. Jeanie crossed the room and pulled her into a tight hug.

Miranda broke the tension. "I'm starving. Let's cut this cake!"

The Client List

Things were lighter then. We shared a few war stories from the trial. Somehow, we all ended up in Jeanie's office stuffing our bellies with vanilla buttercream cake from the local warehouse store. It was delicious.

Farrah seemed happy. I hadn't seen her smile much since the day I met her. She hadn't had a reason. Today, she did.

Finally, she grew serious. It was hard not to. The gravity of what Anderson Rix did to Terrence Dowd and what he almost did to Farrah settled in. It would take a long time for her to process it all. Hell, it would take me a long time to process it all.

"Cass," she said. "Are you sure it's over?"

"It's over," I said. "It'll take a few days for the paperwork to go through formally dropping the charges against you, but that's only a formality. I got a call from Detective Eklund just this morning. The labs came back. It was Dowd's blood in Rix's car. The ballistics on the gun they found in his garden matched the bullet taken out of his chest. There's no doubt. You're one hundred percent cleared, Farrah."

Jeanie poured Farrah another glass of champagne. She downed it.

"All this time," she said. "I spent hours with Professor Rix when he first agreed to take my case. He looked me right in the eye, Cass. He asked me if I did it. I just can't wrap my head around it. He asked me if I killed Terry."

"He was covering his own ass," Jeanie said.

"Farrah," Tori said. "Was it you who reached out to Rix first after you were arrested? Or was it the other way around?"

She wiped lipstick off the rim of her plastic glass. "He called me. He came to see me in jail a few days after I was arraigned. I couldn't find a lawyer. Like I told Cass at the beginning, the top defense lawyers in the county wouldn't touch me. They were too loyal to Terry. But Rix reached out to me. Came to visit me in jail. At first we didn't talk about him representing me. He just said he wanted me to know he was thinking of me. Then a couple of days after that, I called him. I wasn't happy with the public defender I met. I asked Rix if he would defend me. He was the only one I trusted."

"And he said yes," Emma whispered. "I just can't fathom it. Why did he do it? Do you think he was actively trying to tank the defense?"

"We'll never know for sure," I said. "Just like we'll never know for sure what happened in that parking garage other than the last few seconds."

"I don't think he went there to kill Terry," Farrah said, her voice taking on a wistful quality. "I'd like to believe he just got caught up in it all, you know? Like maybe he was just going to try to scare Terry and things got out of hand. And I know I'm the last person anyone would think could sit here and defend anything that he did. Everyone thinks I should be angry. I am. But more than anything, I'm just sad. I miss Terry. I miss who I thought Anderson Rix was."

That last bit hit me right in the chest. I missed that man, too. A man who maybe never really existed.

"Maybe he didn't mean to let things get so out of hand representing you either," Tori said. "Maybe he was going to do the right thing."

"The right thing would have been to confess the second he heard Farrah was arrested instead of him," I said.

"It killed him," Farrah said. She stared off. "Whether it was guilt. Or stress. This thing killed him, too."

"It's no good wondering about the what-ifs," Miranda said. "You have to live in the present, hard as that can be, honey."

"Speaking of that," I said. "Have you given any thought about what your next move is? I can help you find a place to stay if you need it. Until you get back on your feet."

The reality was, although she had her freedom, Farrah was out of a job, a place to live, and most of her savings. She only had the money from her parents to start over. So perhaps Leighann and Victor Sibley did one thing right for her in the end.

Farrah checked her phone. She set her empty glass on the coffee table in front of her.

"I'm okay, Cass. I've got a plan. I signed a contract with NewsNite, the cable news show? They want to pay me a pretty nice chunk of change for an exclusive first interview. They're flying me out to L.A. the day after tomorrow. They wanted to send a camera crew out today when I was released. I just wanted it to be us for now."

"Are you sure?" I asked. "Do you want me to look at the terms?"

"I'm still a lawyer in my own right, Cass. I'm okay. And it's a really generous offer. Enough to get me started somewhere new. I don't want to stay in Michigan. They're putting me up in a nice hotel for a few days. After that, who knows? Maybe I'll stay in California. I've always dreamt about that."

"What about tonight?" I said. "You can stay with me and I'll take you to the airport."

"It's okay," she said. "That's the other thing I wanted to tell you about. I have a new man in my life. His name is Bodie. We met online and started corresponding while I was in jail. He's actually going to be here any minute to pick me up."

Jeanie met my eyes across the room. Bodie? She'd been someone's prison girlfriend this whole time.

"He's coming out to L.A. with me," she said. "Turns out he's got a cousin who lives out there who runs his own pot-growing business. He wants to take Bodie on as a partner. It's pretty lucrative."

As she finished her sentence, we heard two sharp blasts of a car horn out front.

"Bodie, I presume?" Miranda said under her breath.

Farrah lit up. She bolted out of her chair and came to me. She gave me one last hug.

"Thank you," she said. "For everything. I owe you my life. I'll never forget that."

There were a thousand reasons I knew Farrah was likely walking into another disastrous relationship. But I knew my job was done. Whatever mistakes she made from now on would be her own.

"Good luck, Farrah," I said.

The gang of us walked her to the front door. Farrah swung them open. Bodie drove a black Chevy Camaro with orange flames painted on the sides. He rolled down his window and slid his shades to the end of his nose.

The Client List

A cute guy, for sure. But his vanity plate read TTZMAN. I turned my head sideways. It took me half a second to realize what it had to mean.

"Motherfu ..." Jeanie started as she figured it out, too. I gently poked her in the ribs.

"Thanks again, everybody," Farrah yelled back. She bounded down the steps and vaulted into the passenger seat of Bodie's car. She threw her arms around him and the pair started making out. Bodie rolled up his window. The glass was tinted so dark we couldn't see them anymore. That alone could get him pulled over before they crossed the state line.

Then Bodie revved his engine and honked his horn again. I raised my hand and waved as he started to pull out.

"Poor dumb bastard," Emma muttered. "He's got no idea what he's in for."

My smile froze. I stopped mid-wave. Jeanie and Miranda laughed first. Then the rest of us broke. I laughed until my sides hurt. Jeanie wrapped an arm around me and we all went back into the office and locked the doors behind us.

Chapter 39

Two weeks later, I sat stretched out on the long seat at the back of the pontoon. It was just Eric and me today. I took a rare day off in the middle of the week. Late July and a brilliant sun beat down on us. Eric sat on the end of the bench, my bare feet in his lap. He pulled the anchor, allowing us to float along the water. A weekday, early afternoon, and we had the whole lake to ourselves, save for a pair of young fishermen at the boat launch.

"A person could get used to this," Eric said, turning his face skyward. I could see myself reflected in the mirrors of his sunglasses. I had my hair pulled back. My own sunglasses sat perched on top of my head.

"Good thing your boss is so lenient," I said. "Letting you slack off in the middle of the week."

"My boss?" Eric laughed. He ran his thumb across the center of my foot, tickling me.

"We should do this more often," I said.

"I've been telling you that for years."

"I've been telling you that for years, Detective Wray." Up until last year when Eric finally agreed to retire from the police department and come to work with me, he never would have considered taking a random day off like this. I suppose he was right. It wasn't something I did very much, either.

"Looks like somebody else has the same idea," Eric said, jerking his chin back toward my house. I twisted in my seat. Shielding my eyes from the sun, I could see where he pointed.

My brother Joe had just walked out to the end of the dock to cast a pole in the water. "Good," I said. "He could use some time off. He's gone from job to job all year."

"He's trying to keep his mind busy. This thing with Katie busted him up inside, Cass."

"I know." We'd mostly avoided talking about Joe's multiple rants about the pitfalls of marriage. The Sibley trial provided a welcome off-ramp from a heart-to-heart.

"He does this," I said. "Joe copes by getting angry. I lost count of the amount of lamps he broke after our mom died. Then when he and Josie, Emma's biological mom, broke up, that was a pretty dark time too. Katie saved him. At least, that's what he told himself."

"He apologized to me," Eric said. "I don't think I told you that."

"Apologized? For what?"

"For basically trying to stick his nose where it doesn't belong about you and me."

"Hmm ... maybe my apology got lost in the mail."

Eric smiled. "Cut him a break. It was big of him to come to me. And it doesn't have much to do with me. It has to do with you. Joe's worried."

"Worried about me? What for?"

"He wants to make sure my intentions are honorable." A mischievous smile crept onto Eric's face. It sent a flash of heat through me. I changed positions until I straddled his lap. Taking Eric's face in my hands, I kissed him.

"I very much hope your intentions are less than honorable, Detective Wray."

He smiled up at me. The breeze picked up my hair, blowing it across my face. Eric smoothed it away.

"I love you, you know. And it seems to me there's a conversation we've avoided having for a pretty long time."

I looked at him. Really looked at him. He was handsome. Rakishly so. But his dark hair had turned pure silver at the temples. His eyes were deeply creased. We were neither of us getting any younger.

"Don't worry," he whispered. "It's not a conversation we need to have today. Or ever if you don't want to."

"Eric ..."

"I love you," he said. "And I'm not going anywhere."

I settled in the space beside him, laying my head against his chest. We left the conversation unfinished. Or maybe we didn't. Maybe that was all either of us needed to say.

"Thank you," I said.

"For what?"

"For what you did for Farrah Sibley. For having my back. And for not letting me do something that could have compromised the investigation when we started to suspect Rix. You were right about Lars Eklund."

"That's my job," he said. "We're partners, remember? I've got your back and you've got mine."

"I couldn't see clearly," I said. "All this time. I didn't realize how much of a hold Anderson Rix still had on me."

"What do you mean?"

"I mean ... Eric, you didn't know him. He was proud of me. And that kind of pride? Coming from someone who really saw who I was? My mother was gone. My father was ..."

"Your father," Eric said, an edge of anger in his voice.

"Yes. It mattered having someone like Rix believe in me when I was in law school. Then he didn't. He was so angry. So hurt when I decided to take the job with the Thorne Group. Morally questionable people. That's what he called them. And maybe I believed I was one of them after a while. I was wrong about Eklund. I wanted to believe the worst. And I was wrong about Rix. I wanted to believe the best. I held him up as this paragon of morality. And he wasn't. He was more corrupt than any of the Thornes, Eric."

"Maybe he wasn't always. Maybe it's okay for you to hold him in your memory the way he was when you knew him. Twenty years is a long time. We don't know...we'll never know what Rix's life was after you left school. People change. Bad things happen to them."

"You're right. And I want to believe he felt guilty about all of this. But what he did is unforgivable. I wish I'd known. I wish I could have seen him with clearer eyes."

"None of that is your fault."

"I know it's not my fault. I just ... I thought I was a better judge of character."

"You are. And none of what he did later changes what he did for you all those years ago. Sometimes you just have to take the good things people bring you and cut out the bad."

"He was my moral compass," I said. "I didn't even know it."

"He was a dick," Eric said.

I laughed. He and Jeanie had that way of cutting through stuff with a crude economy of words.

"Well, I'm still glad you were with me on this one. You kept me, I don't know, tethered. I could have gone somewhere dark, I think."

"Cass," he said, kissing the top of my head. "You've brought me back from dark places, too."

I let the sun shine fully on my face. Eric felt good, solid, strong as I leaned back and let him wrap his arms around me.

We weren't alone on the lake anymore. A pair of jet skiers whizzed by. Their wake made the pontoon boat rock and bump against the waves. But Eric kept his arms around me. A moment later, the water returned to calm.

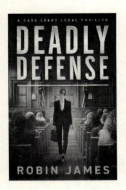

Up next...An unspeakably brutal killing. A shocking confession by an accused with no remorse. A case no other attorney would dare touch. But one look at the police report and Cass knows something doesn't add up. She's all in on a murder trial that threatens to ruin her career and cost her the one person she can't live without. Don't miss Deadly Defense, the next gripping novel in the Cass Leary Legal Thriller Series. https://www.robinjamesbooks.com/dd

A Note for Legal Thriller Fans!

HAVE YOU READ THEM ALL YET?

Get caught up with the Cass Leary Legal Thriller Series today!

What readers are saying...

"...like old school Grisham with a strong female lead..."

"Taut legal mystery that will keep you up at night turning the pages."

"Whatever Robin James writes, I'm going to read. These books are *that* good!"

A Note for Legal Thriller Fans!

Available for Kindle, Print, Hardcover and Audio!

DID YOU KNOW?

All of Robin's books are also available in Audiobook format. Click here to find your favorite! https://www.robinjamesbooks.com/foraudio

---

Want to know how to nab a FREE novella in the Cass Leary series and see what these characters really look like? Turn the page for more information.

Newsletter Sign Up

Sign up to get notified about Robin James's latest book releases, discounts, and author news. You'll also get *Crown of Thorne* an exclusive FREE bonus prologue to the Cass Leary Legal Thriller Series just for joining. Find out what really made Cass leave Killian Thorne and Chicago behind.

Click to Sign Up

http://www.robinjamesbooks.com/newsletter/

About the Author

Robin James is an attorney and former law professor. She's worked on a wide range of civil, criminal and family law cases in her twenty-five year legal career. She also spent over a decade as supervising attorney for a Michigan legal clinic assisting thousands of people who could not otherwise afford access to justice.

Robin now lives on a lake in southern Michigan with her husband, two children, and one lazy dog. Her favorite, pure Michigan writing spot is stretched out on the back of a pontoon watching the faster boats go by.

Sign up for Robin James's Legal Thriller Newsletter to get all the latest updates on her new releases and get a free bonus scene from Burden of Truth featuring Cass Leary's last day in Chicago. http://www.robinjamesbooks.com/newsletter/

Also By Robin James

Cass Leary Legal Thriller Series

Burden of Truth

Silent Witness

Devil's Bargain

Stolen Justice

Blood Evidence

Imminent Harm

First Degree

Mercy Kill

Guilty Acts

Cold Evidence

Dead Law

The Client List

Deadly Defense

Seasonable Doubt

With more to come...

Mara Brent Legal Thriller Series

Time of Justice

Price of Justice

Hand of Justice

Mark of Justice

Path of Justice

Vow of Justice

Web of Justice

Shadow of Justice

With more to come...

Audiobooks by Robin James

Cass Leary Series

Burden of Truth

Silent Witness

Devil's Bargain

Stolen Justice

Blood Evidence

Imminent Harm

First Degree

Mercy Kill

Guilty Acts

Cold Evidence

Dead Law

The Client List

Mara Brent Series

Time of Justice

Price of Justice

Hand of Justice

Mark of Justice

Path of Justice

Vow of Justice

Web of Justice

Made in United States
North Haven, CT
30 March 2024